PENGUIN BOOKS

ROOM 216

Mignon (Migs) Bravo Dutt is a writer and researcher who has published her works in several countries, regions, and cultures. She is the author of the contemporary novel *The Rosales House*. Migs has also published several essays, including one in *The Washington Post* about her pandemic experience in the USA. She has contributed prose and poetry to anthologies and journals and has been featured in literary interviews and programmes in Asia, Europe, and the USA. Her short fiction was selected for *22 New Asian Short Stories*, Kitaab's *The Best Asian Short Stories*, and *Growing Up Filipino 3*. Migs co-edited *Get Lucky: An Anthology of Philippine and Singapore Writings* in 2015 and its sequel, *Get Luckier: An Anthology of Philippine and Singapore Writings II*, in 2022.

Room 216

Mignon Bravo Dutt

PENGUIN BOOKS

An imprint of Penguin Random House

PENGUIN BOOKS

USA | Canada | UK | Ireland | Australia
New Zealand | India | South Africa | China | Southeast Asia

Penguin Books is part of the Penguin Random House group of companies
whose addresses can be found at global.penguinrandomhouse.com

Published by Penguin Random House SEA Pte Ltd
9, Changi South Street 3, Level 08-01,
Singapore 486361

First published in Penguin Books by Penguin Random House SEA 2023
Copyright © Mignon Bravo Dutt 2023

All rights reserved

10 9 8 7 6 5 4 3 2 1

ISBN 9789815144215

Typeset in Adobe Caslon Pro by MAP Systems, Bengaluru, India

www.penguin.sg

For my dearest Nenneng

Prologue

It was in their DNA. They were preordained to go as far as their wings could take them and find a home wherever they alight. Sandy and her roommates belonged to this flock, and today they were ready to leave their nest like birds poised for migration.

Sandy rushed past the administration building and the Oblation statue, the most enduring symbol of the University of the Philippines, on her way to meet the girls of the Hibiscus Residence Hall in Room 216. It had been three weeks since the last day of school and since they had bid Room 216 farewell for the last time. She glanced back at the amphitheatre, smiling to herself as she soaked in the scene: hundreds of graduates in their white outfits tossing confetti and releasing balloons, watching them rise and join in triumph in the air. Today, laughter and levity prevailed as these comrades-in-arms finally found freedom from the confines of the classroom walls. Sandy reluctantly tore her gaze away from the scene, turned left and walked briskly towards a decades-old acacia tree by the Academic Oval. Issa wasn't too far away, sauntering nonchalantly, even drinking a can of Coke on her way. Upon seeing Sandy, she waved excitedly and hastened her pace, stopping only briefly to throw her empty can in a nearby bin. 'I still can't believe this, Sands. Four looong years, I'd initially thought. And just like that, it's over,' Issa hugged her and attempted to twirl her around, though the gesture felt awkward and both of them almost lost their balance. 'Ooops! I forget you're stronger than me. But that might just work on Tintin or Serene,' Issa smiled.

Serene came in at her steady pace even as Sandy and Issa signalled for her to rush. 'Here comes the future Doctor Sy,' Sandy said, mindful not to crease the delicate material of Serene's elegant long dress as she gave her a hug.

'Phew. Now on to the next four or five years of blood, sweat and tears. And blood, my dear friends, is definitely on the table, literally and figuratively.' Serene said, still glowing from her acceptance into the university's highly selective medical programme.

'That sounds like some serious talk, ladies. Mind if I join you?' Tintin surprised the three from behind.

'Oh. My. God. You look flawless,' Serene couldn't help but gently touch Tintin's *barong* dress. 'Is this the one from *the* famous couturier?'

'Yep, it is. Mama insisted on getting my dress done by Mr P only. So here I am.' Tintin twirled around like a fashion model. 'Anyways, who's doing what?' she asked, looking even more petite than usual in her knee-length *Filipiniana* dress.

'You all know what's next for me.' Serene looked impeccable in her long blown-out hair and her professionally done make-up that made her lashes look thicker, longer and curlier. The most fashion-conscious of the four, Serene hardly gave the impression of being studious. But unknown to many outside of Room 216, she typically spent weeknights revising, sometimes to the point of over-preparing, applying the same meticulousness every time, whether preparing for a short quiz or the final examination. She would read and re-read her notes, and add even more neon highlights to the already colourful pages of her textbooks.

'I'm so proud of you,' Sandy said. 'As for me, I've accepted KPMG's offer. I'll be an economic analyst in two weeks.'

Part I

Tintin

Chapter 1

Atlanta, Winter 2014

Nothing could be more unsettling than waking up in the middle of the night and not remembering which season it was, or worse, where one was. Tintin was momentarily disoriented. She stared at the darkness of the ceiling for a few seconds before realizing that she was in her own bed, in her own room, in her own house. She blamed the pressure in her bladder for flinging her into this liminal stage between nightmare and wakefulness. She shouldn't have drunk too much water before bed. On her way back from the bathroom, she pulled up the window blinds and looked out into the backyard, out of habit. The two-door garage was bathed in light and the water from the fountain in the middle of the lawn flowed steadily. She had forgotten to switch them off. Patrick was travelling again this week, so she couldn't even ask him to do it. What a waste of electricity. But she was too exhausted and sleepy to go down now. Besides, the temperature outside had dropped to mid-thirties and she hated the hassle of putting on layers of clothing even to go outside only for a few minutes. Tintin pulled the blinds down and crawled back into bed, disappointed now that she remembered it was winter.

It seemed as if she had just fallen back to sleep when her morning alarm went off and sent her sitting upright. She had to make lunch for Jamie, who insisted on taking a lunchbox, even though his private school had a huge cafeteria with a wide selection of cuisines, because he didn't have the time to stand in the long queue at the cafeteria. Tintin descended to the kitchen and automatically switched on the coffee machine. Then she brought out meatballs, shredded cheese, marinara sauce and the other ingredients for Jamie's pasta, and placed them on the counter. She picked up her coffee and carried it to the breakfast table. On some days, she wouldn't even get this sliver of time, but today she deserved a proper start. Five minutes with her coffee wasn't much to ask for. Five minutes to 'live the dream', she remembered her sarcastic remark about their way of life in America. How she missed her mother's home back in the Philippines, where she didn't need to lift a finger. In contrast, her days here in America were easily filled with thankless chores: dishes, laundry, endless tidying up. Utter drudgery. American Dream, they said. 'Nightmare' was a more fitting description. She didn't even have a full-time job. She worked remotely as a communications consultant for a hotel chain and had more flexible working hours compared to their other employees.

Once the pasta was ready, Tintin rushed upstairs to wake Jamie up and ensure he got into the shower in time for the scramble to school. She had to drop him off and pick him up from school—another task that fell on her most days now, because Patrick had been travelling to other US cities for work practically every week this quarter.

When she didn't have to rush, the drive back after the school drop-off would be the highlight of Tintin's day. She would choose a scenic route that was lined with various genera of trees and was particularly lovely in spring or fall, when the trees and their foliage formed a veil-like canopy. Because of these canopies, birds were naturally a constant part of the landscape. Sometimes they would fly across Tintin's field of vision and swoop down in search of food or to join other birds perched on a lower branch. Tintin would slow down and grab her phone to take a photo of Georgian swallows with their striped black-and-yellow beaks or the Blue Jays with their perky crests and blue plumage. But alas, the birds, elusive creatures as they were, operated by optical flow. As though they had powerful peripheral visions, they would sense her presence and dart away before she could press the camera button.

On some days, the branches and leaves would sway in synchrony and tiny seeds and pollen would fall like yellow raindrops. Tintin would invariably roll down her window and listen to the rustling of leaves, which somehow reminded her of the roaring waves back home, ten thousand miles away, along the Gulf of Panay—a place that felt much more distant now, especially around Christmas; that time of the year when Filipino families tried to be together. Instead, here she was, on another cold and wintry day in America. The trees that were earlier vibrant with fall foliage, were now forlorn caricatures. Without any leaves to rustle, the wind simply passed through them silently. Tintin looked up and saw only an infinite canvas of greyness. On days like this, she yearned for the sun even more as she imagined how bright it could get in the tropics. And how she longed to be home, in her ancestral house, where she could live like a queen. But then she remembered that all was not well back home. And as with anything that didn't go well in her family, there was only one person to blame. Her older sister, Tonette.

Chapter 2

Atlanta and Iloilo, 2015

Hate is a muscle. Someone somewhere had said that before. And Tintin's hate for Tonette had only grown recently. Tonette had been pressuring their mother, Marina, to sell off the remaining real estate properties that they had inherited from their father, Roberto, former mayor of San Agustin, Iloilo. When Tintin had asked Marina about this, she had replied that she must settle unpaid debts in the aftermath of Roberto's death and that she had to continue paying the wages of the household staff— the cook, the driver and other helpers. Tintin understood this but she couldn't accept the lack of consultation prior to any sale. It had annoyed her extremely when she had learned about the most recent sale of their ten-hectare farm, which had held many childhood memories for her—it had now been acquired by an agrochemical company that would most likely turn it into another industrial farm.

Tintin rarely spoke with Tonette, but she immediately called her when she found out. 'You should at least have the decency to tell me before selling family property, even if it's in Mama's name,' Tintin screamed on the phone.

'Tintin, don't be greedy. You have much more than you'll ever need. You also have the trust fund that Papa set up for you,' Tonette said.

'So does Mama. And you.'

'I've got two kids. I don't have work. It isn't enough for my family. I can't even pay my mortgage now.'

Tintin scoffed. 'Can't your husband's illustrious family help?'

'You know yourself that they couldn't wait to get rid of Tom. Now he's become 100 per cent my liability.'

'Why don't you get rid of him if he's that much of a burden?'

'Why don't you tell Mama that? She thinks my kids need a father. She wants me to stick with playing the "good wife" even though we all know he's the biggest bum in San Agustin,' Tonette groaned.

'Whom you instantly assumed was a catch because he comes from a *buena familia*, huh?' Tintin couldn't help but sneer. Tom came from a prominent family, a 'buena familia', as some people would say, of former sugar barons in Western Visayas. While their fortunes had dwindled with the decline of the sugar industry, his family had remained influential and farmers who remembered the clan's heyday, still held them in high esteem.

'Please stop reminding me.' Tonette gritted her teeth in reply. 'I didn't want to get married then. Papa and Mama forced me into it—'

'And why was that? Who was it who got pregnant right after her high school graduation?'

'Maria Christina,' she stated Tintin's full name in exasperation. 'I've made mistakes in my life, I'm not denying that, but stop repeating them to me like a broken record.' Tonette paused before continuing more steadily, 'Look, I just want my kids to have proper education. Beyond that, I couldn't care less about family properties.'

'Mama, I didn't complain when you sold off the other properties because they didn't mean as much to me. But that farm, you know how much I loved that farm, why didn't you tell me about it?' Tintin called Marina immediately after her conversation with Tonette.

'We haven't been earning anything from that farm. Climate has changed so much, we have either had droughts or floods, in any given year. That farm is more of a burden, really,' Marina said. 'Besides, Tonette will run into issues if the banks repossess her house and her cars.'

'Don't blame climate change if you're selling it mainly for Tonette's sake. Can't her family move into a smaller house? One that they can afford?'

'But what will other people say? What will happen to the kids if they get evicted?'

'Can't Tom's family help them out for once? Why does it have to be you all the time?' Tintin knew the answer to this, yet she couldn't help but voice her thoughts.

'You know their family, *hija*. All they have now is an erstwhile illustrious name. I don't think they have anything left in the bank.'

'If Tom is squandering Tonette's inheritance, then that's more than enough ground for her to get rid of him,' Tintin ranted on.

'But your Papa didn't want any separation in the family. And a Catholic marriage can't be undone.'

'What about annulment?' Tintin didn't know where that came from. Sometimes, she would blurt out random things just to remind her mother about Tonette's ill choices in life, an old habit that she had yet to discard in her maturity.

'That's not for us to discuss. Nor decide. An annulment usually drags on for years, draining the bank in the process. It will gravely affect the kids.'

'How did that happen to Tonette? Why did she let her situation deteriorate just like that?'

'You should count your blessings, hija. You have a great education, a decent job and a dependable husband.'

'I had to work hard for each and every single thing. It's not as though they all conveniently fell into my lap,' Tintin said, reflexively lifting her chin. 'Obviously, I learned a lot from Tonette's experience. But then you should stop her from encroaching on your inheritance, whatever is left of it. And Tom, why can't he get some treatment?'

'Hija,' Marina closed her eyes in frustration, 'Tonette and I have tried convincing him so many times, even for just a six-month programme, but he said he'd rather die than go to rehab.'

'Aren't the kids worse off with someone like him around?'

'He isn't violent. He just stares into space and completely zones out. Tonette told the kids he has a medical condition.'

'Mama, there has to be a way out. I can contact someone from a regional centre to go and check on Tom. Maybe they can take him to rehab. Do you want me to do that?'

'If only it were that easy, hija.' Marina and Tonette had once managed to get Tom into the car, but when he had realized they were taking him to a rehabilitation centre, he had jumped out of the car and broken his knee in the process.

'But, Ma, you can't keep on selling our properties just to finance their vices,' Tintin said. 'Ma, are you there? What's going on?' Tintin asked when she heard Marina drawing a deep breath in.

'There are other reasons, hija. Just trust me on this. One day, I'll explain it all to you and you will understand.'

'Why can't you tell me now?' Tintin was suddenly alarmed.

'It's not something we can discuss on the phone, hija,' Marina exhaled. 'You have to be here.'

Chapter 3

Atlanta, 2015

When she and her family first arrived in Atlanta, a few years ago, Tintin had volunteered for a number of school activities at Gems Academy. She had prepared Thanksgiving food for the school feasts, chaperoned the kids to the theatre, and helped in managing booths during fairs. She had cut back on volunteering since she had started consulting for a hotel group. Work was partly to blame but she had also simply got bored of meeting the same group of moms every time, some of whom tended to gossip. But she couldn't really escape these moms as they were also in the two committees that Tintin retained. She remembered particularly one occasion last week with Jennifer, the current class parent in Jamie's section.

'Where are you from again, Tintin?' Jennifer had asked. She had chaired a charity auction committee this year.

'From the Philippines,' Tintin had said for the second time in the past thirty minutes.

'Is that a part of China?' Jennifer had flipped her long blonde hair and straightened out her light blue twinset.

'Nope, it's in Southeast Asia,' Tintin had said, pausing from wrapping another mug from the donation pile to deliberately enunciate the name of the region slowly. Some people didn't know their geography beyond the contiguous states of the USA. And sometimes, Tintin was tempted to tell them to get a passport and travel the world so that they would learn that the USA wasn't the world, and the world wasn't just the USA. And of course, that the Philippines wasn't part of China.

'But you speak very good English!' Jennifer's eyes had widened in disbelief.

'Have you been outside of America?' Tintin couldn't help but ask.

'Of course,' Jennifer had said, straightening her spine and flipping her hair yet again.

'Then you must know that English is spoken in other countries, too,' Tintin had plastered on a smile. 'And you, are you originally from America?' She had asked.

'Oh yeah, "born and bred in ATL", as they say. But my mom was from New England.'

'Boston?'

'Nope. Nashua.'

'Where is that?'

'New Hampshire,' Jennifer had replied, turning away from Tintin as she folded some wrapping papers. 'We're almost done for the day. We can do the rest of the pile next week. Wendy and her team will join us then.'

'Here you go. That's the nth mug I've wrapped today.'

'I've no idea why these parents keep on donating mugs, really. I'm sure all this will just end up in Goodwill again,' Jennifer had said, washing her hands in a corner sink. 'Would you like me to drop you off? I have time,' she had smiled almost patronizingly.

'No, thanks. I brought my car,' Tintin had said, picking up her purse and fishing out the key from its front pocket.

'I thought you didn't drive. Have a good one, y'all,' she had waved blankly at Tintin and the other volunteers at the far end of the room. She had flipped her hair once more as she had turned toward the door.

Over the years, Tintin had met many parents at Gems Academy, but she could count on her fingers those she had genuinely connected with. Caroline, a former class parent, was one of them. After a few meetings, they had gravitated toward each other and eventually become friends. Today, they had decided to meet at Phipps Plaza in the Buckhead district.

'What size do you need?' Caroline asked while browsing through the clothes racks in the women's section of Nordstrom.

'Small or Extra Small, depending on the design,' Tintin said.

'You probably need extra small. Small would be too large for you,' Caroline said, looking at the stack of XS blouses.

'That's the problem. This is the smallest size they have,' Tintin pointed at the S size tag.

'What a wonderful problem to have,' Caroline smiled. She had long blonde hair too, but lacked that mannerism of flipping her hair affectedly, unlike Jennifer. Today, Caroline was wearing faded jeans with loose seams, oblivious to athleisure fads like Spanx, Lululemon leggings, or skintight jeans that many mums at school currently favoured. Caroline's family were the majority shareholders of a telecommunications company in the South and she led the corporate social responsibility or CSR side of the business. She also co-chaired an alliance of socially responsible and environmentally conscious companies in Metro Atlanta, further expanding the already large network of her family. It was Caroline who had referred Tintin to the Universal Group of Hotels, or UGH, a hotel conglomerate headquartered in Atlanta. She lived in an eight-bedroom house at Tuxedo Park, the wealthiest zip code in Atlanta—a fact that she downplayed whenever one of the nosy moms asked her about it. But even in her ordinary outfit, she effortlessly exuded that aura of old money that many moms at Gems aspired for. Unfortunately, some tended to go over the top, calling attention to their branded outfits and flashy jewellery, even in broad daylight, something that Caroline frowned upon.

'This top isn't meant for me, so never mind,' Tintin said, returning the blouse to its rack.

Tintin and Caroline left the department store empty-handed, though not for the first time, given their track record of having done more window shopping than actual shopping. They walked to the parking lot toward Caroline's hybrid car. Caroline swore off big cars and high-end sedans because of their negative impact on the environment, and never jumped into Tintin's Audi Q7 because of this. After their failed shopping mission, they drove off to the Atlanta History Center. The café here had become their default destination whenever they ran out of ideas. At their 'regular' table in a corner, Tintin told Caroline about her recent meeting with Jennifer.

'Really, she said all that?' Caroline raised her right eyebrow. 'What a hypocrite. Do you know what's the latest buzz about her?'

'I'm totally clueless. I haven't kept up with any of the volunteer groups. You know how they are.' Tintin snorted, thinking about the group's thinly disguised 'gossip sessions'.

'She's been spotted around town with her young gym trainer,' Caroline said, almost cringing.

'Isn't she married?'

'To an old geezer, twice her age,' Caroline said, sipping coffee from the personal mug that she brought with her to the café. 'You know what, I'll pop into your next committee meeting. I'm curious what she'll do when she finds out that we're thick.'

'Why bother?'

'She's so pretentious. It's high time someone told her as much,' Caroline laughed.

At the next charity auction committee meeting, Caroline breezily swept into the parents' room, waving cheerfully at the volunteers. She went to hug Tintin, who sat at the back of the room, busily labelling a new set of donated items. Caroline winked at Tintin before turning to Jennifer. 'Jennifer, is that you?' she said.

'Caroline, what a surprise. I didn't see your name on the list.' Jennifer suddenly straightened her back.

'No, I didn't sign up for this one. I was driving by, so I thought I'd say hello to Tintin,' Caroline placed her arm on Tintin's shoulders.

Jennifer looked perplexed as she glanced at Caroline, then at Tintin, before smiling at Caroline. 'How have you been? How are your folks?' She asked in a tone sweeter than her normal one. She wore a black turtleneck sweater over skintight jeans that were tucked into her knee-high boots, her bangles and bracelets jangling as she wrapped a gift item.

'Basking in the sun in Antigua and escaping the dreary winter that we lesser mortals have to bear with. I should tell Dad to invite Hugh next time,' Caroline said. 'Hugh is Jennifer's husband,' she explained to Tintin.

'They know each other?' Tintin looked surprised.

'They were together at school,' Caroline said with a poker face.

Jennifer bit her bottom lip perhaps to avoid saying anything.

'By the way, I've read about this environmentalist who has set up a green school in Bali,' she told Tintin before turning to Jennifer. 'I'm thinking of going this summer. Have you been there, Jennifer?'

'Of course, Hugh and I spent our honeymoon in Bali,' Jennifer said, looking confused.

'It must have been an unforgettable trip. How long were you there?' Caroline asked.

'A week or so,' Jennifer replied, her brows knitting.

'Oh, I remember Hugh saying you also went on a cruise,' Caroline said. 'Was it on the same trip? Where all did you go?'

'Bali, Singapore and then to another island, somewhere in the Philippines? I can't recall the name,' she said.

'And China?' Caroline probed.

'China? We did that much later, on another trip.'

Tintin was seething inside, but quietly glared at Jennifer who now had her fake smile plastered on while answering Caroline's questions.

'Hey Tintin, weren't you looking for a trainer?' Caroline asked.

At first, Tintin was baffled but eventually realized Caroline's intention. 'Yep, I am. I need some toning here,' Tintin replied cheerfully, raising her right arm and rolling up her sleeve to show Caroline her bicep.

'Perfect.' Caroline turned and now faced Jennifer squarely. 'Could you recommend a trainer? I heard you're quite the gym rat,' Caroline smiled.

'OMG. I'd totally forgotten I've got an appointment with my hygienist,' Jennifer was blushing suddenly. 'Tintin please say hello to Wendy. She'll be here shortly—actually, never mind. I'll call her from the car.' She belatedly waved at Caroline and Tintin before grabbing her coat on the way out.

Caroline could not suppress her laughter as soon as Jennifer was out of sight.

'What did you do that for?' Tintin said, also chortling now.

'I hate people who take advantage of others, you know that. And she is too pretentious for my comfort,' Caroline said.

'What do you mean?'

'People can't blame the circumstances of their birth. But what I can't accept are those who deceive, dissemble and lie about their beginnings,' Caroline whispered, looking around in case other volunteers could overhear.

Tintin was restless that night. She had finished reading the news and all the relevant feed on her Facebook account; she had put her phone on her bedside table, and yet she couldn't sleep. She couldn't forget what Caroline had said about pretentious people. Wasn't she pretentious, too, at some level? Why did she not talk about her family in the Philippines, specifically her rift with her sister, Tonette? Why couldn't she tell Caroline about Tonette?

Chapter 4

Harvest season was a festive time in the province. That was how Tintin remembered it. She wanted to visit her childhood home during this season, in the hope that she could recreate and recapture the happiness that she had once felt. More importantly, Tintin wanted to settle how the remaining family inheritance was divided, to prevent any more sporadic selling without her knowledge. The ancestral house was the crown jewel of their real estate portfolio as a family. Marina had tried to broach its impending sale during every call, but Tintin had intentionally evaded the discussion. Selling the only house that she had known since birth was unacceptable. There shouldn't be any selling, as far as their ancestral home was concerned.

After landing at the Manila airport, Tintin took an immediate connecting flight to Iloilo City. In a little over an hour, the plane began its descent and Tintin peered out of her window at the vast and azure sea. As the gap between the plane and the ground narrowed, the deep blue of distance gave way to the emerald green of the Gulf of Panay and the provinces along its coast including Iloilo, the neighbouring Aklan, and the island of Guimaras. At 10,000 feet above sea level, the plane zoomed into the more urban areas of Iloilo. Rows of houses with roofs made of galvanized iron sheets, occasionally interspersed with colourful tiles, came into view. A few high-rise buildings made of steel and glasses dazzled in the midday sun. Gradually, the plane landed and Tintin rushed through and out of the terminal, retrieving her luggage from the carousel. She looked around for Inday, Marina's helper, and saw her in the pick-up lane, waving at her. Inday rushed towards her and took the luggage trolley from her.

Marina was waiting in the van. She pushed her large-framed sunglasses over her hair upon seeing Tintin. Marina still coloured her bouffant hair dark brown and she had also tattooed her eyebrows in the same shade. She alighted to hug Tintin. 'Mama, you look as fashionable as ever.' Tintin looked approvingly at Marina, who wore a black pantsuit and a matching silk sleeveless blouse topped with an embroidered bolero in a mix of lavender, purple and pink floral design.

'Thanks, hija. I don't want the local folks to start thinking I'm down and out.' Marina replied.

'Why bother about other people? You're a private citizen now, you don't need to woo them for their votes for Papa anymore,' Tintin said.

'San Agustin is a small city and the folks still seem to watch my every move,' Marina sighed. 'Anyway, how are Patrick and Jamie? I miss them a lot, why couldn't they come with you?'

'They're both fine. It's peak season at Patrick's office so he couldn't take a holiday. And Jamie still has school. Mummy Gina is in Atlanta, taking care of him,' Tintin said, referring to her mother-in-law who had flown in from New Jersey to be with Patrick and Jamie while Tintin was travelling.

'I'm happy that *balae* lives in the US now, at least you can travel like this and not be too worried about Patrick and Jamie.'

'You should come, next time. Jamie misses you a lot.'

'I'll come as soon as things here are sorted out.'

The drive from Iloilo City to San Agustin was quiet as Tintin and Marina avoided tackling confidential topics, lest the helpers overheard them. Tintin adjusted her neck pillow and rested her head against the window. Marina had dozed off and she wanted to follow suit, but couldn't. Tintin straightened up and peered out the window. They had just passed by a crowded Jollibee fast food branch with a harried attendant directing a long line of cars to an adjacent parking lot. Next to it was a row of small businesses, starting with a pension house followed by a drugstore and a convenience shop. An Inasal restaurant with its bright green signage, occupied the corner of the next block. It served grilled chicken marinated in calamansi, the tiny green citrus fruit indigenous to South East Asia and common in the Philippines, mixed with pepper and other ingredients, resulting in a unique Filipino taste. An ancestral home converted into a museum and a restaurant stood in the next block, followed by an Internet and gaming lounge, where students in high school uniform were queued up at the entrance. Iloilo City was more bustling than Tintin remembered, considering that this particular area was outside of downtown.

After a few minutes of driving along city roads, the van merged with highway traffic. Long stretches of onion and garlic farms, interspersed with other crops, lined either side of the road now. Many farms had sacks of harvested crops piled on the roadside, waiting to be picked up by their buyers. Then a cluster of homes with various façades came into view: new concrete homes sitting next to shacks, high-fenced properties alongside ones with crumbling bamboo fences, and even a few with no fences at all. In between, billboards and placards and corner stores with large signages sponsored by carbonated soft drink companies or mobile network providers vied for passersby's attention. On the highway, all types of vehicles tried to hog the lanes: SUVs and sedans, various models from across the decades, zoomed past; tricycles and pedicabs raced against ten-wheeler trucks; and even *kuligligs*, a two-wheeled trailer pulled by a two-wheeled tractor, tried to outrun new jeepneys plying through the province. Here, everybody was the king of the road.

Visitors might get rattled by this chaotic scene, but for Tintin, this was home—the place she always thought of, whichever hemisphere she was in, whatever the season, but especially in winter, when she longed most for the warmth of the sun in this archipelago of more than 7,000 islands. After an hour of such eclectic scenes, they turned onto less busy but narrower roads, lined mainly with residential houses like the crumbling bungalow with its paint peeling off, its corner converted into a neighbourhood mom-and-pop store. Then came the three-storey homes built close to the roadside because of limited lot size, most likely owned by overseas Filipino workers' or OFW families.

Soon, the van entered San Agustin's town square. Tintin craned her neck at the familiar landmarks. Even though she had seen them hundreds of times before, her excitement each time still felt like the first time: the 400-year-old Catholic church at the centre of town, the plaza across from it, the city hall and the health centre, adjacent to the park. The place was bursting with colour. It pulsated with its own unique brand of chaos. Marina stirred and opened her eyes, surprised that they were almost at their destination. 'Welcome home, hija.' Marina's eyes beamed with joy.

'Thanks, Mama,' Tintin smiled as she loosened her seatbelt and adjusted the long grey cardigan that she wore over her black slim jeans and matching sleeveless top. She couldn't explain to her mother that currently her heart was pounding, inflating like a balloon. These familiar landmarks of her childhood never failed to overwhelm her at every homecoming. She remembered how she used to skip sideways on the church steps on their way to and from Mass on Sundays. She remembered running to the city hall's balcony and singing the national anthem with Tonette at the top of their voices, when they visited their father at his office. She remembered the fairs in the park during the city's foundation day celebrations. She remembered these things and many more. She closed her eyes and tried to focus on the present.

After a few blocks, the van turned right and gradually slowed down in front of a gated compound. Before the driver could honk, a helper in white-and-blue gingham uniform unlocked the white gates. Tintin alighted from the vehicle and surveyed the manicured front garden with its roses, hibiscuses and other ornamental plants. Reminded of her childhood habit of walking barefoot on the grass, she absent-mindedly stepped on the well-trimmed Bermuda grasses that filled the gaps between the plots, then realized she still had her shoes on and had more urgent things to attend to. A sitting area that consisted of four chairs and a round table, lay under a host of palm trees in a corner of the lawn. Tintin followed the mosaic path that led to the steps of the spacious porch wrapped in ornate floor-to-ceiling wrought iron. Tall jars and vases were clustered in one corner. A white rattan sofa with fluffy cushions in botanic designs took up space on one side of the porch. Tonette and Tintin used to play jackstone on this spot. The ball would roll over to the console table on the other side, and both of them would run after it, but always, a helper would get there ahead of them, picking up the ball and handing it over to whoever reached her first.

Inday opened the ornate double-door to the hallway. And there, above the mantelpiece at the centre of the living room, stood a large portrait of Tintin's family, serenely welcoming visitors into the room. Roberto in his powder-blue coat and tie, sat beside Marina, who exuded her characteristic glamour in a floor-length lavender dress. Tonette, who was nine at that time, and Tintin, who was six, were both wearing pale pink chiffon frocks in Empire waist designs. Roberto draped an arm around Marina's shoulders while holding Tintin on his lap with his other hand. Marina held Tonette at her side, while clutching a bejewelled purse. Tintin moved closer to the portrait and scrutinized the face of her father. He must have been only in his mid-thirties in this portrait but was already wearing thick-framed glasses. Tintin's memory of her father always included those glasses, such that the eyewear became a mnemonic for whenever she wanted to conjure his image in her mind. He used to wear them everywhere, even when they were out swimming at the beach.

'Inday, take the suitcases up to Tintin's room,' Marina instructed the helper. 'Come, hija. I've asked Lina to prepare some of your favourite food.' Marina led Tintin across the living room, into the adjacent dining room. A sumptuous spread filled the eight-seater dining table with native delicacies like bingka, the Ilonggo version of baked rice cake, to bichocoy, a bread made of sugar-rolled and deep-fried dough, like a doughnut, but rectangular in shape. As though all this wasn't enough, a box of colourful macarons, another box of butterscotch and tubs of ice cream in several flavours, covered one side of the table.

'Mama, this looks like a dessert party. This is too much if it's just for me.' Tintin found the spread excessive. As a child, she remembered complaining about the huge dining table when there were only four of them in the family. Her father had explained that someone was always dropping by at mealtimes and he naturally had to invite them to stay. It was expected in a politician's house, he had said.

'I know, hija. But it's been two years since your last visit. We're simply overjoyed to have you again after such a long time. Tonette and the kids will be here soon, too. And you never know who else might drop by.'

'But I've asked you not to tell anyone about my visit. You know I'm in no mood to socialize right now.' Tintin wanted to focus on family matters on this trip.

'I haven't told anyone other than Tonette, but as they say, the walls have ears,' Marina said. 'Anyway, just sit back and relax in the meantime. Why don't you start with this buko juice?

I'm sure you haven't had it fresh in a long time.' Marina pointed at the young coconut, split open on top. She inserted a red straw into it and handed it over to Tintin.

Tintin's first afternoon back home turned into a hectic one with several unexpected visitors dropping by. Tonette and her two teenager children, Gino who was in town for his semestral break from university, and Mika who came straight from school, joined her for the *merienda* or afternoon snacks. Later on, two of Tintin's distant aunts, together with some family members, also came by. Then three of Tintin's high school classmates arrived in the late afternoon, which prompted Marina to invite them to stay for dinner. All this exhausted Tintin. She excused herself and requested Marina to go up with her to her room. 'Mama, you know the reason why I came home, right?' she said.

'Of course, hija. But let's talk about that tomorrow. It's late now and I'm sure you're more tired than any of us here,' Marina said, kissing Tintin on the forehead before leaving the room.

Tintin surveyed her room. It hadn't changed much since her last visit, or since she had left for university, for that matter. The only major change was her former sleigh bed having been replaced by a queen-size one. The room still had the same dresser, the same settee by the window, and the same secretary desk that she had inherited from her paternal grandmother. The windows were still the same—three frosted rectangular glass panels with a half-moon design above each panel. A door led to a balcony that had off-white concrete balustrades topped with spiral wrought-iron grilles in tiny leaf designs. The balcony ran across the entire side of the house, all the way to Tonette's room. On balmy nights, the sisters used to lounge on their customized wooden deck chairs, with their names carved on the backrests in Edwardian script. Marina decorated the chairs with fluffy cushions in covers back then, that had evolved over time—initially they had flora and fauna designs on them, then princess and fairytale figures, and eventually, unicorns or other designs. The balcony looked out into the backyard, where there was a *bahay kubo*, or nipa hut, that served as Lina's so-called 'dirty kitchen', where she cooked most of their main meals. She only used the kitchen inside the house to prepare breakfast and light meals. A vegetable and herb garden occupied the lot beyond the nipa hut, with trellises dividing the inner part into plots. Tropical fruit trees ranging from avocado, mango, to pomelo and other citrus trees, lined the perimeter alongside the high concrete fence. Shorter vegetable trees, too, like moringa and papaya, that Lina must have planted, grew behind the bahay kubo.

A simple two-bedroom house stood in a corner of the backyard. Lina and her husband, Dodong, the family driver, lived there. They had two daughters: Rita, the older one, was now a helper at Tonette's house, while the younger one, Gladys, worked as a sales assistant at SM Department Store in Iloilo City. When they were kids, Tonette and Tintin used to invite the two girls to play with them, but Lina would always tell her girls to go back home and mind the house.

Tintin returned to her room and took a long shower. Now the weariness that she had tried to ignore earlier had set in and she fell asleep as soon as she hit the pillows, only to wake up at two o'clock in the morning to extreme quietness, which felt almost eerie. Tintin switched on her bedside lamp and noticed a serving tray that held a glass and two bottles of water, on the nightstand. Inday might have brought them in when Tintin was already sound asleep. Inday had a habit of moving around so quickly but quietly, that Tintin and Tonette used to call her Flash, like the DC superhero, behind her back. Tintin drew the curtains and peered out of her window. The lights along the fences emitted a warm, albeit flickering, glow. Tintin could barely figure out the *kubo*'s outline. Nighttime here was darker than in bigger cities, perhaps because of lesser light pollution and lower bulb wattages. It was also quieter because of fewer vehicles on the road and since the neighbours with televisions and sound systems switched off their devices by late evening. Tintin, who by now had been living in cities far longer than she had lived in the countryside, felt uncomfortable at the deafening silence and utter darkness.

However hard she tried, she couldn't go back to sleep and instead, ended up tossing around in bed. She was hoping the helpers would be up soon, so she could at least have a cup of coffee. She couldn't remember where things were kept so she didn't bother venturing into the kitchen on her own. By five o'clock, Tintin heard Inday open the back door for Lina. She immediately descended the stairs. 'Yes, ma'am. I'll make your coffee right away,' Lina said, surprised that Tintin was awake this early.

Tintin bumped into Inday, who was holding a rag and a broom, ready to clean the living room. 'Good morning, ma'am. Why so early?' Inday asked.

'Good morning, I couldn't sleep anymore. Lina is making coffee and will bring it up soon,' she said. Upstairs, Tintin sat on the tan leather sofa, hugging one of the fluffy cushions that Marina had covered in accordance with the latest fabric trends. The covers had large green leaf prints, echoing the botanical theme downstairs. All the rooms opened into this family room at the centre of the second floor. As a child, she spent more waking hours here than in her own room. Here, she could see her family entering or leaving their rooms and could easily ask any of them for a quick hug, anytime in the day. The spaces downstairs were more public, and with the constant stream of visitors during the mayoralty of her father, Tintin wasn't comfortable sitting in any of the rooms there. Meanwhile, access to the second floor was limited to the family members and trusted helpers like Inday or Lina.

Tintin's eyes rested on a cluster of souvenirs on the large square coffee table. A ceramic tray at the centre held some of the souvenirs from their family holidays, while a stack of their family photo albums sat neatly under the glass top. A tall display shelf holding more keepsakes stood across from the sofa. Framed photos from their trips to Bacolod, Cebu and other cities in the region, as well as to Manila and Baguio, lined an adjacent wall. A blown-up photo of their first trip to Hong Kong took centre-stage. She was eleven then and Tonette was fifteen, though she was already almost reaching Marina's five-feet-four-inch stature. Tintin looked around the room once more, taking in every detail. All the memorabilia were portable. She could easily carry these items to the US with her. So why didn't she want to sell this house?

Despite being married for many years now and having her own family home, Tintin had always indicated her ancestral residence as her permanent address in the many documents that had required that information. Even if she didn't visit regularly, this house was her refuge, assuring her that she always had somewhere to return to. She had lived in a series of dwellings, starting with her university dormitories, up to their current home in Atlanta, but all those were temporary for her. At university, she knew that her stay was transient when she moved from a freshman to an upper-class dormitory. After university, she shared a condominium unit in Makati City with her cousin. When she got married to Patrick, they moved into their own condominium unit in the Fort Bonifacio area in Taguig City, which they subsequently left when they moved to Japan. Then they relocated to New York, and finally to Atlanta. All the earlier residences were a blur to her now, reminding her of a required literature reading on Proust at university, who had said that 'memories of . . . houses were as fleeting as the years'. Some people could live like turtles, carrying their homes on their back, and could feel at home wherever in the world they went. Unfortunately, Tintin wasn't a light traveller. She tended to accumulate things.

Whenever she had to move, she invariably packed and sent some items to her childhood home for safekeeping, scared that they might get lost during relocation. She stored all types of memorabilia in this house, filling up her walk-in closet and built-in cabinets with boxes of photos, cassette tapes, costume jewellery, and even a tiny cat-shaped pillow that Issa had gifted her at their first Christmas exchange party.

And to this family room, she had added souvenirs that she had collected on her own travels: a framed Jim Thompson scarf from Bangkok, a Japanese doll in Kabuki costume, a Miro print from Spain, and a few trinkets from other destinations. She could easily sum up her life in the mementos she had stored up in this house. She didn't consider them as things 'left behind', but rather as memories that were safely kept there; her additions to the family tapestry. This room itself represented precious moments like when her family would sit together before bed, listening to how everyone's day went, the only time when no one else distracted her father or took him away from them to attend to various requests made by his constituency members. This was a sacred place.

After breakfast, the next day, Tintin immediately broached the purpose of her visit with Marina. 'But Mama, I don't understand why you want to sell this, the only family home I've known since birth.' She finally released her pent-up emotions.

'It's too large for me, hija. I'm all alone here, with only the helpers for company,' Marina said, standing up from the sofa in their family room and spreading her hands to indicate the spaciousness.

'This is Papa's legacy. It holds so many memories,' Tintin pointed at the different items, 'And not just physical ones. Don't you remember all those moments we spent here, right here in this room? They're precious to me, Mama.' Tintin paced back and forth behind the sofa.

'I know, but we can't be shackled to the past forever,' Marina returned to the sofa and picked up a snow globe from the tray that she absent-mindedly fidgeted with.

'Where will you stay? Don't tell me you'll be staying at Tonette's? I don't think you can have peace of mind there,' Tintin involuntarily wrinkled her nose in distaste.

'No, I'm going to buy a house in Palm Square. You've seen the development there, haven't you?'

'But aren't the units there a lot smaller than this house?'

'They are, but I can't manage staying in this house on my own for much longer. It's too large and not sustainable, both practically and emotionally,' Marina crossed her arms over her chest. 'I'm not getting any younger.'

'What if I don't agree to the sale?' Tintin turned to face Marina. 'I won't sign any deeds of sale.' She added, clenching her hands.

'Hija, I'm begging you. Please try to understand,' Marina said, her voice quavering and her hands starting to shake. 'Tonette needs the money as much as I do. Gino still has internship and residency. Mika will also soon start university.' Marina clasped her hands together.

'When you talk about Tonette's kids, it's as though they don't have a father,' Tintin said.

'We've already talked about Tom so many times.' Marina was frowning now, her wrinkles more pronounced than Tintin remembered.

'I won't agree to the sale just because Tonette and her kids need the money. They've already taken so much,' Tintin almost stomped in anger.

'Tintin, try to be more compassionate. If not towards Tonette, then at least towards me.'

'Why are you like this, Mama? I couldn't stop you from selling the other properties, earlier. But this is the last straw.' Tintin didn't want to blackmail Marina emotionally but felt she had to give her an ultimatum. 'I will not sign the affidavit or any deeds of sale. If you still insist after this, I will stop visiting altogether.'

'Hija, you can't do that to me,' Marina begged. 'Besides, I'm sure Gino and Mika will repay you someday. Please help them get a leg up.'

'That's not the point, Ma. Look at them, they're living in luxury. How many SUVs do they have? And why do they have a driver when both Tom and Tonette don't have a job?'

'You don't want the kids to suffer, do you?'

'No, but their parents should stop being delusional and start living within their means. They should stop depending on you. You know what, Mama, maybe you're part of the problem. You've been enabling both Tom and Tonette. You're an enabler,' Tintin's nostrils were flaring in her anger. 'Mama, this is our ancestral home. From Papa's parents. I will *not* sign any affidavit and I will hire a lawyer, if it must come to that.' She turned in the direction of her room, intending to walk out on her mum, but Marina got up quickly and held Tintin's arms tightly.

'Hija, I wanted to spare you this detail, but there's another reason we must sell this place,' Marina pulled Tintin gently back to the sofa.

'What is it, Mama?' Tintin was suddenly concerned upon seeing that Marina seemed to have lost all her energy. Marina was now slumped on the edge of the sofa, her shoulders drooping, and her eyes in deep sadness, the saddest ever that Tintin could remember.

Chapter 5

The festive harvest season, that she had initially looked forward to, was now lost on Tintin, who was deeply mired in her recent discovery about her family. She stayed for longer than the three days she had planned for this trip, but couldn't attend any of the festivities in the community. She merely watched one of the parades from a window in the family room, gazing at the floats that were decked out with different crops as they passed by: a life-size angel with wings made of garlic; lanterns made of onions; cars out of corns. Tintin smiled to herself at the ingenious decorations made by the locals. After the parade, she returned to her room, still muddled, but relieved that one thing had been achieved on this trip—she had understood Marina's underlying reason for wanting to sell their crown property.

Roberto had been a general practitioner who had left his medical profession to become the mayor of his city for nine years, which was the term limit for a mayor. Though he had shifted from family medicine to the city government, he had continued to help patients, especially in far-flung villages, who had barely any access to healthcare providers. He had developed San Agustin's health centre into a model unit for the Visayas region, and had hosted several young doctors, especially members of the Doctor of the Barrios, a programme that encouraged fresh graduates to practise in rural villages. Because of his support and sponsorship of the programme, San Agustin and its neighbouring towns always had a doctor ready to serve the residents, however remote their villages may be. Tintin was proudest of this legacy, which she had highlighted at an earlier exhibit at the city museum.

But Tintin was devastated to learn that Roberto was no hero after all: he had been unfaithful to Marina. He had had an affair with a fellow medical student. At that time, Marina had just given birth to Tonette and had stayed back with Roberto's parents in San Agustin while he had returned to Manila to complete his internship and residency. The affair had lasted for more than a year and resulted in a son, Robbie.

Marina had discovered this only a few years ago, when Robbie, already a grown man, had appeared at her doorstep one afternoon, three years after Roberto's death. He had inquired about the estate left behind by Roberto. After that visit, Marina suddenly had a compelling need to sell off the properties from Roberto's side, those that he had inherited or acquired before his marriage. That would be simpler than getting into a legal tussle over the properties, even if she knew that the law was on her side as the legal and principal heiress and conservator of Roberto's estate. Marina wanted to keep only the properties they had acquired together after their marriage.

'How long has Tonette known about this?' Tintin was appalled at this disclosure.

'She's known about it for a few years now,' Marina said, looking away from Tintin.

'Why didn't either of you tell me sooner?' Tintin felt scandalized.

'You were away, busy charting your own destiny,' Marina pleaded for her understanding. 'Tonette was here when Robbie visited for the first time. He knows Tom's brother, and that's how he found us.'

'Seriously. That Tom. As though his encroaching on our properties wasn't enough, now he brings other predators into the fray,' Tintin exhaled loudly in exasperation.

'Robbie is a big factor in my decision. But it doesn't change the fact that Tonette is in dire need of money,' she looked at Tintin. 'And my moving into a smaller place is another valid reason. I'd like to start living the life I'd always wanted to.'

The last reason caught Tintin by surprise, but as Marina already looked drained, Tintin decided to probe another time.

Ultimately, Tintin agreed to the sale of their ancestral house, not because of wanting to help out Tonette, but because she understood Marina's desire for peace of mind, and to prevent any other claimants from appearing to grab a share of their estate. Tintin felt for Marina, who had suffered so much throughout her marriage to Roberto and been shackled to the outdated traditions that came with living in his ancient house. Tintin used to adore her father, whom she had believed to be a model citizen. But now, Tintin could feel that hatred was gradually replacing love in the space where it used to dwell.

Having come to terms with the impending sale of their residential property, Marina and Tintin started planning the purchase of a unit in Palm Square Residences. Marina showed her a brochure of the development project and the different options available. Tintin suggested that Marina buy a larger unit and that she would share in the expenses so that she always had a place whenever she came to visit. And a space for keeping all her memorabilia.

When Marina took a break from reviewing the documents and looked more relaxed, Tintin remembered to ask: 'Why didn't you take down all those framed pictures and portraits of false harmony, especially that huge portrait of our "happy family" downstairs?' She flexed her index and middle fingers to make air quotes as she mentioned 'happy family'.

'I've thought about it, but it would invite questions from the people here who had no idea about his other woman. Or even from you—you always look at that huge portrait first thing whenever you arrive,' Marina said, patting one cushion on the family room sofa into shape before placing it back beside her.

'How did Tonette react when she first learned about this extramarital affair?'

'She was naturally shocked. Who wouldn't be, right? But Tonette has the capacity to forgive easily. She understands that we're but human, that we aren't perfect, that we're fallible.'

'Of course, she is the authority on that, having made a huge mistake herself,' Tintin rolled her eyes.

'Tintin,' Marina said in a reprimanding tone.

'Sorry, Ma. I can't help it. Anyway, what will happen now, will you give Robbie a portion of the sale?'

'I already gave him a huge sum because he said he needed it badly. He has two young kids. But then he kept coming back for more. I told him there's nothing left.' Marina was now looking at the framed photos on the wall. 'Besides, he had no legal rights over all that and this house. His mother never listed your father's name on his birth certificate.'

'So what made you believe his story in the first place? He could be a con artist. And I wouldn't be surprised if he were, given his association with Tom.'

'I think he genuinely needed help. At least initially. His mother never finished medical school because of him. That's his story.'

'It could be anyone's sob story. You could have been scammed, for all you know.'

'He looks exactly like your father,' Marina suddenly looked defeated as she glanced at a photo of Roberto on the wall.

For once, Tintin was at a loss for words. She hated her father even more. Her mum didn't deserve any of this pain. 'It must have been difficult for you, Ma,' Tintin stepped closer and held Marina's hands. 'You must have detested Papa for what he did to you . . .'

'At first, yes. I cursed him a thousand times in the privacy of my room. The hardest part was that I couldn't even ask him why. That's one question that will never be answered,' Marina said, the corners of her eyes glistening now. 'And while he was busy doing all that, I was probably going through postpartum depression,' Marina wiped her tears off. 'Do you know how difficult it was for me, being a first-time mum, never having any say in how to bring up my own daughter? Your grandmother meant well, but she wanted to control everything.'

'I'm sorry, Mama. I didn't know all these things,' Tintin hugged Marina tight. A lump was now forming in her throat, but she repressed any tears—she wanted to be strong for her mum. 'It must have been horrible for you, Ma.'

'It was, hija. But I can't change anything in the past. It's wrong to carry grudges against the dead. You can't murder people who are already dead to begin with.'

'I know,' Tintin said, patting Marina gently.

'Anyway, I don't want Robbie to abuse my generosity.' Marina straightened her shoulders and lifted her chin up. 'I'm not letting the past, or remnants of the past, hold me back now.'

'I've been telling you that, Mama. Make yourself your priority. You deserve to live the life you've always wanted for yourself.'

'I've been thinking about that since Robbie's first visit. Then more signs pointed in that direction, including the launch of Palm Square.'

'I'm excited for you, Mama.'

'But you and Tonette will always be my first priority,' Marina said kissing Tintin on the forehead.

'It's been sometime since you last visited us. Why don't you come back with me?' Tintin asked in a sweeter tone.

'Some other time, hija. After I've settled into the new house,' Marina ruffled Tintin's hair gently.

Chapter 6

Tintin relied on routine to anchor her day, however much she despised what went into it, at times. She had been back from the Philippines for two weeks now and her mother-in-law had returned to New Jersey. Tintin had resumed her chores at home, pick-up and drop-off, and her work at UGH. Yet, she felt restless and disturbed.

Tintin had kept Patrick posted as things had unfolded in the Philippines, and now that she was back, she filled him in on the details of her discovery. Patrick seemed unaffected by it all. For him, all that had happened was immaterial to them now. 'But don't you want to meet your half-brother?' Patrick asked while packing for yet another trip.

'That didn't occur to me. But what's the point of meeting him, right?' Tintin said, handing him his toiletry bag.

'Curiosity?' he asked, inserting the small pouch inside the suitcase before closing it and pulling it to a corner of the master bedroom.

'I'd been ignorant of his existence until two weeks ago. It was bliss, as they say,' Tintin shook her head. 'Knowing about him now doesn't change anything. I don't want to be unnecessarily curious. What if I learn other things I'm not supposed to know?' she said, coming to the settee at the foot of the bed.

'Like what?' Patrick asked, sitting beside her.

'Maybe I should ask Mama or Tonette about a few things. Now I'm starting to wonder what his relationship with Papa was like. How often did they see each other? What are his memories of Papa?' Tintin said. 'But again, what good would knowing all that do to me? Nope. I don't want to open another Pandora's box.'

'Right. The past is irretrievable. It's immutable. Whatever happened then lies there for a reason. We are now in the present, in our own reality.' Patrick squeezed her hands gently.

It bothered Tintin that Tonette had kept the knowledge of Robbie a secret all these years.

But then, Tintin and Tonette had stopped confiding in each other when Tonette had started dating Tom. Tintin had heard rumours about Tom and she had cautioned her sister about him, but she had ignored her. Tintin had felt betrayed. She had assumed that she was the most important person in Tonette's life. And suddenly, Tonette had taken the side of someone with a questionable reputation over her. It had shattered Tintin's relationship paradigm. In response, she had ignored Tonette. She had refused to be a bridesmaid at Tonette's 'shotgun wedding' and even her parents couldn't persuade her to reconsider. She had insisted that she was too young, at thirteen, to be a bridesmaid. And that was exactly how her parents explained her absence in the entourage to people who dared ask why. Her parents did their best to hide any discord between their daughters.

The sisters' strained relationship persisted through their adult years, which was exacerbated by another row during Tintin's earlier visit to commemorate Roberto's death anniversary. Tintin couldn't forget what Tonette had said to her at the height of their argument. 'That's the problem with you, Maria Christina,' she had snapped at her. 'Just because I've made a mistake earlier, doesn't mean I'm incapable of making better choices anymore. Having a university degree doesn't make you smarter at life. And my not having one doesn't make me an imbecile. It's because of judgmental people like you that people like me find it difficult to recover in a society that prizes superficial success like yours.' She had banged the bedroom door shut before Tintin could reply.

Their quarrel started when Tonette gave a suggestion on how they should portray Roberto's legacy in the museum and the health centre named after him. Tintin had insisted on showing only his public side—his accomplishments as a mayor, including the establishment of the health centre during his term. These, to her, were the most relevant themes for the event. They should be single-minded with their message. In contrast, Tonette had also wanted to present Roberto as an attentive family man, which meant including a few family photos. Tintin felt this encroached on their privacy. She didn't want people to gawk at memories of their precious and private moments. The sisters' relationship had deteriorated further after their screaming at each other over this. Marina had intervened and begged them to patch up their differences. They had agreed to be civil to each other for Marina's sake, and pretended to talk to each other whenever Marina or Tonette's kids were around. But left to their own, they scarcely spoke to each other. They never regained their earlier bond as sisters.

'Have you ever thought of redeeming yourself?' Tintin asked Tonette once, breaking one of their uncomfortable silences after Marina had left the room.

'I'm doing my darned best to ensure my kids don't become like me. Gino will one day be a doctor like Papa. And Mika is doing well too, academically. They are my redemption. I'm crossing my fingers and kneeling every single day, fervently praying to God that my children don't end up like me,' she had said, lifting her chin up before leaving Tintin alone in the family room.

Chapter 7

Friendship transcends seasons. Her friendship with the Room 216 girls was a constant that Tintin was grateful for. During her regular call with them, she revealed her discovery of Robbie's existence.

'How's your mum taking it?' It was Issa who reacted first.

'She's better now, but she had an awful time when she first learned about it,' Tintin said.

'I can imagine. It must have been difficult to be so devoted to the memory of your father, mourning him all those years, and then belatedly discovering this,' Sandy chimed in.

'Exactly. Mama said that even if she'd wanted to avenge that injustice, she couldn't, because the guilty is now dead,' Tintin said.

'I'm sorry to hear this, Tintin,' Serene said. 'Have you met your half-brother?' she asked.

'Oddly, I'm fine with not meeting him at all. There's nothing wrong in that, right? It's not my moral responsibility to make nice.'

'I don't think it's your responsibility, moral or otherwise. You don't have any emotional connection or bond to begin with. You know what they say about that sound in an empty forest,' Sandy said.

'My thoughts, exactly,' Tintin said.

'Sandy's right. You're under no moral obligation to introduce yourself,' Issa said. 'However, under humanitarian conditions, if he needs help, and you're in a position to do so, you should reach out.'

'That's a great way of putting it. I'll definitely help if required. But I don't have to meet him now,' Tintin said.

'You've got to take care of yourself first before you could take care of others. You can only share your light if there's enough oil in your lamp,' Sandy said.

Tintin felt relieved after the call, grateful that she had this tight group of friends who had her back. With them, she could be her true self, she didn't have to conceal anything. She recalled the first time she had had this type of dilemma back in university, when she didn't know how much she should divulge about herself. It wasn't so much about lying, but rather not knowing where discretion ended and honesty began. How much of the truth should be revealed?

Chapter 8

It was the era of university rock bands. The four roommates had just returned from watching a concert at the campus's traditional post-Valentine's fair. Big acts that had been successful outside the campus—Eraserheads, After Image and *Parokya ni Edgar*—headlined the concert that night at the Sunken Garden, singing one hit song after another. Tintin and her roommates screamed, danced and even jumped along with the crowd. But she stopped suddenly when she saw her thesis adviser, Daniel Macaraeg, a few rows ahead of them. When After Image played a mellow song and the audience sat on the ground listening, Tintin saw Daniel drape one arm around a woman with long straight hair held neatly in place by a slim, black hairband. The woman turned around to check what was written on Daniel's back. He was wearing a black shirt with a four-digit logo embossed on it. Just then, Tintin caught a glimpse of her face. Somehow, she looked familiar. In the middle of 'Next in Line', as the audience lit up their lighters and held them up in the air, Tintin suddenly recalled where she had first seen that face. It belonged to Ginny Pelaez, who taught Communication II at the College of Arts and Letters. Tintin had heard the buzz from her male batchmates a year or so ago, when they had all wanted to be in Ginny Pelaez's class. They had described the teacher as the ultimate '*crush ng bayan*', or everybody's crush. Attractive.

45

Confident. Carefree. And definitely more than just a pretty face. She had completed her undergraduate and graduate degrees with top honours at Brown University in the USA. But right then, Ginny Pelaez placed her arm around Daniel's waist and hooked her left thumb into his belt loop. Tintin's jaw simply dropped at this. And when the next band, Eraserheads, played '*Alapaap*', Daniel pulled Ginny closer to his side, cradled her head, and kissed her on the lips for what Tintin felt like was forever. Tintin's stomach grumbled. She couldn't focus on the concert anymore, even as her three roommates were screaming at the top of their voices during the chorus. Tintin couldn't wait to be back at the dorm. She needed to go to the bathroom urgently.

When they reached the dorm, Tintin rushed to the bathroom, where she tried to throw up but couldn't. She wept in one of the cubicles, covering her mouth with her palm to stifle any sounds, lest the other residents heard her. The girls were waiting for her back in Room 216. Issa was the first who noticed how pale she looked. 'What's wrong?' she asked.

Tintin told them about Daniel. She had just started going out with him, two weeks prior. It all began after one of her thesis consultations, when Daniel had remarked at how interesting her pendant was—a miniature design of the *Dinagyang* logo that Marina had purchased for her at that year's festival. He had asked if he could touch it. Tintin, who had a huge crush on him, had promptly nodded. He had been careful not to touch her white sleeveless blouse or her exposed collarbone. After that, he had invited her to discuss a chapter of her work at a coffee shop. Outside the campus. Naïve as she was, she had agreed immediately. Daniel had picked her up from her dorm's parking lot. He had taken her to a coffee shop on Katipunan Avenue, which was known for its exquisite cupcakes. They discussed her thesis outline in depth during the first half an hour of their meeting. But after that, he had again asked to touch the same pendant that Tintin had still been wearing. This time his hand had rested on the edge of her crew-neck top. And his hand had lingered there even as he had shifted his gaze from the pendant to her eyes. Tintin had felt herself blushing heavily by then, but she had held his gaze. 'I love it when you laugh and your eyes crinkle a little bit at the corners. You're endearingly pretty,' he had said.

'Thank you,' she had replied in a somewhat tremulous voice.

'I wish you weren't my student,' Daniel had said, still holding her pendant and her gaze. 'Do you mind if I keep seeing you? Outside the campus, to avoid any talks. I hope you understand that I have a position to protect.'

'I'd love to see you too,' she had nodded meekly. For a couple of weeks after that, Daniel had waited for her at the parking lot at the designated time and taken her out to Katipunan or the Scout Area. It had been a blissful two weeks, with her getting excited every time she rushed out to meet Daniel in his car.

But now, Tintin knew that Daniel Macaraeg was a mistake and those two weeks with him were a sham. At the concert, Tintin had realized the real reason why Daniel had kept their relationship a secret. It wasn't for the job that he had wanted to protect. He was simply a two-timer.

Her roommates had every right to be annoyed at Tintin for concealing this relationship. But when they realized how hurt Tintin was, they immediately huddled and drafted a plan of action to avenge her. To be fair, the relationship was in its early stages and Tintin said they hadn't gone past necking.

Tintin planned to break up with Daniel immediately. But she was also worried about its impact on her grades. 'What if he makes it difficult for me to graduate? What if he flunks me?' she said.

'Is it too late for you to change your adviser?' Sandy asked.

'I'm not sure. I only have one semester left. And I'm more than halfway through my draft,' Tintin replied.

'Could you still work with him after you've broken up?' Serene probed further.

'I don't know. As it is, I'm always nervous whenever he's around. I guess I'm too overwhelmed by his mere presence,' Tintin said.

'In that case, you should change your adviser. I'm sure it's possible. We can find a valid excuse,' Issa said.

Tintin asked Daniel to meet her at an ice cream house near her dorm. 'Is something wrong?' Daniel rushed to meet her as soon as he saw her entering the shop. He led her to a far corner, even though the shop was never crowded and even less so after school hours, like just now.

Tintin didn't want to order anything but Daniel said they needed to justify sitting in there. He ordered a pinipig crunch that he unwrapped mindlessly. 'I'm not really in the mood for this,' he said, grabbing a paper cup from the centre of the table and placing his ice cream stick in it. 'Now, tell me what's bothering you?' he asked. 'You look paler than usual,' he attempted to touch her chin, but Tintin swiped his hand away.

'I saw you with Ginny Pelaez,' she said without preamble.

He inhaled sharply and looked away. He stared at the wall for a few seconds. 'We had broken up, some time back. We both needed space,' he crossed his arms over his chest. 'We got back together only recently,' he looked at Tintin with a blank expression, as though he was merely reciting data or numbers.

'Why didn't you tell me sooner?' Tintin was mentally cursing him.

'We've just gotten back together,' he repeated. 'It happened rather fast. I couldn't have predicted it earlier,' he said solemnly.

'But shouldn't you at least have broken up with me before resuming your relationship with her? Wasn't that the proper way of things?' she glared at him.

'I know, I'd been meaning to tell you when we met for your thesis next Tuesday. But then at the concert . . .'

'You just happened to be there, sitting quietly, I assume,' she added sarcastically.

'I'm sorry . . .' he said, and was about to explain further but Tintin cut him off.

'I can't work with you anymore under these circumstances.'

'I understand. I will transfer you to another adviser. I'll take care of it,' he tried to assure her. 'I'm truly sorry,' he said again.

'And how will I explain the transfer to the next teacher?'

'You can tell them the truth. I made a mistake in my judgement. It's my fault and I'm sorry for putting you through this. Needless to say, I'll talk to the next adviser so that they don't ask unnecessary questions.'

'How could you calmly assume that all these things would be sorted out without any scandal?'

'I haven't crossed any line. I truly felt something for you. And if Ginny didn't come back, I would have gone on seeing you,' he said. 'Of course I would have waited until after you graduated before we became official. I'm not stupid, I know what's at stake.'

In the end, Tintin was assigned to an older professor for her thesis. She didn't ask her any awkward questions. The professor, who was in her sixties, treated her like a granddaughter and patiently worked with her to turn in one of the best theses in her batch. In that paper, Tintin had tackled the role of body language in communication, specifically in the context of conflict resolution. It even won her a certificate of appreciation from a university panel that recognized the top fifty theses in the system, annually. The paper helped Tintin eventually land her first position as an editorial assistant at a large publishing house in Makati City.

During her last term at the university, Tintin stopped hanging out at the College of Mass Communication or the CMC building, after class. She had successfully evaded Daniel

Macaraeg or even his shadow. Years later, she heard from a
batchmate that Daniel and Ginny had got married eventually.
At that time, Tintin had still been avoiding dating, despite a few
potential matches that her former roommates had lined up for
her. Had it been because she was still in love with Daniel then?
But had she ever loved him or had she merely been infatuated
with him? She remembered, though, that it had taken her some
time to recover from the hurt, not because of despair from the
rejection, but because of regret. She had wept for countless
nights, blaming herself for not having asserted herself back
then. Why had she not slapped Daniel hard when she had the
chance, at the ice cream parlour? Why had she made it easy
for him? She could have enjoyed her time at her *tambayan*, the
space designated for academic organization members, instead
of acting like a fugitive, rushing out of the building as soon as
her class or thesis consultation was over, just to avoid bumping
into Daniel. Why had she been the one to suffer? Why not him?

Her failed relationship with Daniel had taught Tintin to
be extremely cautious when it came to the male species. She
had remained wary of dating even after Sandy and Serene had
got married and Issa had started living with Enrique. It took
Patrick's, her colleague, extreme persistence to get Tintin to
even just watch a movie with him. After Patrick had overcome
the initial hurdle, it took an equally copious amount of patience
and many more dates before they got together. 'Why do I have
to suffer because of the mistakes of another guy?' he had said
out of frustration, one time.

'How do you know it's because of a guy?' Tintin had
stopped in her tracks while they were strolling in Greenbelt, a
mall in the Makati Central Business District.

'Could it be otherwise? You respond to me, so this isn't
about chemistry. It must be someone you haven't told me about
yet,' he had said glumly, his shoulders drooping.

'You're right,' Tintin said. 'There was someone. It's almost irrational, but I've been burnt acutely because of my naïveté.' They had found a bench they could sit on. She had told Patrick about Daniel.

'That was a long time ago. You should have gotten over him by now,' Patrick had said, crossing his arms. 'Are you still in love with him?' he had looked at her intently.

'I don't think I ever loved him in the first place. I might have been merely infatuated with him.' Tintin remembered how Daniel was likewise a 'crush ng bayan' at their college. Most of her female classmates used to vie for his attention, employing one ruse or another to get it, pretending to swoon over him whenever he passed by their tambayan. Many of these 'swoons' occurred when he changed into his tennis outfit and on his way to a match with his friends. One of the popular national players happened to be Daniel's friend, further raising his esteem in the CMC community. That women openly desired him was probably why Tintin had felt nervous in his presence. She had put him on a sort of pedestal that he clearly didn't deserve. 'I was young, inexperienced and impressionable. And there he was, extremely confident and assured of himself,' Tintin had sighed. 'Whatever I had felt for him then was definitely not love. But that episode was terribly unfair to me.'

'Definitely. And much more unfair to me,' Patrick had said. 'But never mind, I'll help you forget that chapter in your life,' he had said, helping her to her feet and leading her toward a pavement across the courtyard near the chapel.

Chapter 9

Though most flowers bloom in spring, some, like the eastern red buds, blossom earlier in the season, while others, like magnolias, bloom only much later. But when magnolias bloom, they do so conspicuously, owing to both their size and fragrance. Marina was like a magnolia—a late bloomer—as far as her passion for interior decoration was concerned. Marina was unusually excited around the sale of their ancestral property and even more so with her purchase of the Palm Square unit. She couldn't wait to move into Palm Square. She immediately hired a contractor and immersed herself in the interior design in the months that followed. 'We're officially shifting tomorrow,' Marina announced excitedly over the phone.

'Wow, that's fast. How will you fit everything into the new house?' Tintin knew from the floor plan and having viewed the model unit earlier, that it was half the size of their family home.

'I followed your suggestion and donated most of the furniture to the town museum and the church. Tonette wasn't too keen on keeping any of it,' Marina said.

'Please ensure that my things are intact. Have you marked my boxes so that nothing is lost in the transfer?'

'Of course, hija. It's the first thing I attended to.'

'Will you video call me when you enter Palm Square tomorrow?' Tintin felt guilty that she couldn't be with Marina, but she could still be part of it, even if only virtually.

'I was planning to anyway, hija. It would be eight o'clock, your evening, so set an alarm for it.'

'I am, I'm doing it now as we talk.'

'We'll start with the prayers. Father John is coming to bless the house.' Marina was almost breathless with excitement.

The next day, Marina called Tintin for the housewarming ritual. She passed on the phone to Inday, who remained on the video chat while the priest and other attendees went about the blessing of the house. Tintin could see Tonette standing beside Marina. Tonette even waved at her upon realizing that she was on the video call. Tintin smiled and waved back, though it somewhat surprised her that Tonette was this friendly when they still had a 'cold war' going on. Marina then showed them each room as she completed setting it up with the furniture brought in by the movers. Marina was clearly enjoying the process, despite it being physically taxing, especially at her age. 'Mama, please don't overdo it. You're not that young anymore,' Tintin said.

'I'm not lifting a single thing, hija. We have a few helpers for that. But I need to be there to tell them where exactly to put the furniture. Aside from the movers, Inday, Lina and Dodong are taking care of the actual shifting,' she said.

'By the way, where will they stay?' Tintin asked, suddenly remembering the long-standing helpers.

'There's a staff room for Inday. Dodong and Lina finally bought a house of their own, in Barrio Villasanta,' Marina said. 'I gave them the seed money and guaranteed their loan. I can't tell you how happy they are to finally have something of their own.'

Tintin couldn't help but admire Marina's organizational skills. A large part of Roberto's success as a politician was due to Marina, who had efficiently organized many of the events that had supported his programmes, from chairing various civic organizations tasked with maintaining parks and public spaces, to feeding programmes for malnourished kids. She had also never heard Marina complain about the numerous dinners and frequent parties at their house in support of Roberto's career. A woman of lesser calibre would have easily crumbled. But in Marina's case, she was always on top of situations, efficiently handling get-togethers, regardless of their scale—be it festive and grand bashes for thousands of townsfolk or intimate but high-level dinners for heads of the provincial government or visiting senators. Roberto didn't have to worry about any of the logistic requirements and could then focus on the schmoozing part of his job.

Chapter 10

Atlanta and Iloilo, 2017

Tintin and Patrick were enjoying one of the better weathers of Atlanta on their backyard patio while Jamie slept in. Patrick brought out sunny-side-up eggs and toasted bread to the round table near the fountain in their backyard. Tintin followed him out with a tray of coffees and jams for their Sunday breakfast, when her phone, which she had left on the kitchen counter, rang. 'Just leave it. If it's important, they will call again,' Patrick said, wanting to savour quiet moments like this with Tintin. With his hectic schedule nowadays, moments like now came by rarely.

'Okay, fine.' Tintin said, settling in her chair and picking up her coffee mug.

But then, the phone rang again. She looked at Patrick, who nodded at her. Tintin rushed to the kitchen. It was Marina.

'Hi Ma, what's up?' Tintin asked cheerfully, though she had a feeling that this wasn't going to be one of their usual cheerful chats. Marina didn't usually phone her repeatedly like this.

'Hija. I'm okay, hija. But there's bad news,' Marina inhaled sharply. 'It's Tommy.'

'What about him?' Tintin couldn't help but roll her eyes.

'He died this morning.'

'Oh my God, how did it happen?' Tintin almost dropped her phone. Though there was no love lost between her and Tom, she was shocked to hear this. Earlier, when she had rolled her eyes, she was expecting a less tragic update, like his jumping out of the car to escape rehabilitation.

Apparently, Tom was with his fellow Harley Davidson bikers, riding along the highway in Bukidnon, a province in Mindanao. He fell behind the convoy and was trying to catch up, when he hit an oncoming ten-wheeler truck at a sharp curve.

'How is Tonette holding up?' Tintin asked, genuinely worried about her sister.

'She's distraught, naturally. She needs me more than ever, so I'm heading back to their house,' Marina added.

Tintin couldn't eat the remainder of her breakfast. For all her criticisms of Tonette or Tom, she had never wished a tragedy like this on them.

'Why don't you call Tonette?' Patrick encouraged her.

'What if she rejects my call?' Tintin said, while absent-mindedly wiping her hands on the napkin for the second time. She wouldn't be surprised if Tonette never picked her call up again, considering her constant verbal accusations. But right now, she simply wanted to hear her voice. She couldn't imagine what Tonette was going through.

'Give it a try. Let me get your phone,' Patrick said, returning shortly with the phone. 'Go ahead, call her. I'll just prepare Jamie's breakfast,' he said, kissing Tintin's forehead before going back into the house.

Tintin stared at the fountain for the longest time before picking up her phone. She called Tonette. There was no response. She kept the phone back on the table and went over to pick up a fallen twig near the edge of the fountain. She picked up dried leaves and even pulled a few errant weeds. She truly understood if Tonette never wanted to speak to her again, but the mere thought of it saddened her so much. A wave of weakness came over her and she had no more energy left to pull another weed. She let her shoulders droop as she stared listlessly at the pond. Then her phone rang.

It was Tonette.

'I'm sorry to hear about Tommy,' Tintin said. She couldn't help but say Tom's nickname. 'Please, please accept my sincerest condolences,' she almost sobbed.

'I still can't believe this is happening. We couldn't even say goodbye to him. They flew him to Davao City Hospital. But by then it was too late,' Tonette cried. She shared more details forgetting that she and Tintin weren't supposed to be on speaking terms.

'Where is he now?' Tintin asked softly.

'His body is at the funeral parlour. I'm just waiting for Mama. We're heading there as soon she gets here,' she said.

'And the kids?'

'Mika is inconsolable at the moment. Gino is about to board his flight from Manila. We're still in deep shock. The house is a chaos with all the relatives streaming in. So I've locked myself in our room for now, until Mama arrives.'

'I'm sorry, I wish I could be there for you. I know we have our differences, but know that I'm truly saddened by this and I'm sincerely sorry. I really want to be with you right now.'

'I understand. But let's talk about that at a better time,' Tonette said, sobbing.

'I'm sorry again for your loss, if there's anything I can do, please let me know. I'll call the kids separately.'

'Thank you. I think that's Mama knocking on the door. I must go now,' Tonette said before hanging up.

Tintin could not attend Tom's funeral, given the distance, but she ordered flowers that were promptly delivered to the wake. She also wired money through Marina to help with the funeral expenses. Tintin called Tonette after that, and while they spoke a few times, Tonette was more reticent in their subsequent calls. In the end, it was Marina who kept Tintin posted on how Tonette's family was coping with Tom's tragic end.

Chapter 11

Iloilo, 2018

10,000 miles. Twenty-five flight hours above the Pacific Ocean, plus layovers somewhere. Like a pilgrim, Tintin had to traverse the distance wider than the maximum width of the Pacific Ocean, just to remain connected to her family, friends and her homeland. But unlike a pilgrim, she had to make this trip more often because just once wasn't enough to sustain a connection. She had made several of these trips by now, in the fifteen years she had been away from home. This time around, Tintin wanted to check how Marina was settling into her house at Palm Square.

On the ride from the airport, Marina excitedly filled Tintin in on how wonderful things were in the gated community, how it had all the modern amenities, including an Olympic-sized swimming pool, tennis courts, picnic tents and barbecue pits. The estate also had a clubhouse with function rooms, a gym and a twenty-four-hour convenience store. Marina had chosen a standalone unit in a quieter part of the community, away from the entrance and the clubhouse.

Tintin's smile widened as she alighted from the car and looked up at the split-level Mediterranean-style house in pale ochre and with a terracotta roof. As with her earlier homecomings, Inday rushed out to open the carved wooden double-door for her. It led to a spacious drawing room with wide windows, which kept the place bright. A new five-piece set of sofa, chairs and coffee table in tan colour occupied the centre of the room. A large seascape painting in soft hues and evoking calm that complemented the colour scheme of the house, now hung behind the sofa. It was by an emerging Ilonggo artist, whom Marina had met at an exhibition. Select furniture from the ancestral house found new life here as accent pieces, like the newly varnished camphor chest that now shone brighter in one corner. The dining room had a six-seater birch table with matching chairs, a departure from the dark and heavy design of their former one. The kitchen had an open design, that made it airy. An island counter stood in the middle, surrounded by sleek fixtures and appliances. Gone were the dark and ornate cabinets that had made their old kitchen seem dated and gloomy. Tintin returned to the dining room and opened one of the doors that led to a patio at the back of the house. The customized lounge chairs from the balcony of their old house had made it here but had been updated with nautical-themed cushion covers. Other than the select pieces, there was barely any trace of the old house. In fact, it was only then that Tintin remembered the family portrait that usually greeted her back then, realizing it had no place here. 'Mama, I love the ambience, it's light and relaxing. And where's my room?' She asked excitedly.

'Come upstairs, it's next to the master bedroom,' Marina led her up the steps to the upper floor of the house. The second floor had three bedrooms and an alcove with a cozy sitting area, where Marina also kept her curved sixty-five-inch television. 'And welcome to your room,' Marina opened the door to a familiar set of furniture: Tintin's queen-sized bed, secretary desk and settee. Though the furniture was all in a dark veneer, Marina had painted the walls and built-in cabinets in complementary but calming shades of blue and chosen dove-grey Thai silk curtains that had tied the overall look together.

'I feel like I'm in a Mediterranean resort,' Tintin smiled.

'I'm truly glad that you like it.'

'Great job, Ma. You obviously love it, too.'

'Yes, indeed. I'm loving it too much, I guess. I might just have reinvented myself in the process of simplifying my life,' Marina lifted her chin as she said this.

'This house is undeniably yours. It's stamped with your calm personality.'

'Thanks, hija. I think this is my most significant accomplishment. After you and Tonette, of course,' she said. 'And you know what? My friends have started asking me to help them redesign their homes.'

Tonette dropped by Marina's for dinner. Initially, Tintin didn't know how to greet her, as this was their first meeting after Tom's death. But Tonette didn't have any hesitation, rushing to Tintin, hugging her tightly as she said a warm 'welcome home'. Noting Tonette's cheerful tone, Tintin avoided asking about Tom. Tonette looked thinner than before, but it could also be because she wore a black shirt-dress with a thin leather belt. She still wore her hair long and with light brown highlights. Her eyebrows were also lined in the same colour. But other than her seeming fragility, Tonette, with her more glowing skin, exuded a more relaxed aura than before.

The dinner conversation revolved mainly around Marina's discovery of her passion for interior decorating. After dessert, while waiting for their coffee from Inday, Marina stepped out of the dining room to answer a call.

'How are you?' Tintin asked Tonette once Marina was out of earshot.

'I'm better now,' she said. 'The first few months were torturous. I tried to make sense of things, not just of his death, but also of what he had been reduced to over the years,' she said, looking at the door to the patio.

'I'm sorry,' Tintin said, at a loss for the right words to say in moments like now.

'By the way, thanks for helping Gino with the CDC application. I heard it's highly competitive, but his department had encouraged and endorsed him. It would be a great opportunity for him,' Tonette said.

'Please don't be too formal. We're family.'

'But we haven't really talked like one in a long time.'

'It's largely my fault,' Tintin reached out to hold Tonette's hands.

'It's equally mine. I should have been more understanding. I'm your elder sister, after all. But then I had Tom to take care of. I realize now how much of my life went into that.'

'I should have been there when you needed me,' Tintin said. 'I'm your only sibling. I should have been there in your most trying time,' she stopped upon seeing Inday approaching with their coffee.

'It's all water under the bridge now. I had all the support I needed from the folks here. I also understand that you felt strongly about Tom, may he rest in peace now,' Tonette replied as soon as the helper left the room.

'How are you feeling, really, about Tom's passing?' Tintin asked. The hallmark of her relationship with Tonette had always been their frankness with each other. They never masked their feelings towards each other, be it tenderness or anger or even hatred.

'It's inexplicable,' Tonette sighed. 'I miss certain aspects of him. He was caring in his own way and I certainly needed that, at times. For a time, I remembered only his tender side, to the point of delusion. But later on, I felt as though a cloud was lifted and I saw things for what they truly were. I couldn't save Tom, however hard I tried. His last couple of years had been tumultuous. He swung between paranoia and utter depression.

I knew he was suffering a lot, but I couldn't reach out to him at all. Sometimes, I think that his premature death could be God's way of ending his suffering too,' Tonette said.

'I truly admire you for carrying that burden gracefully,' Tintin said.

'I'd been going to a therapist in Iloilo City. I always said I was going to the parlour, which also I did, but in truth, it was primarily to visit Doctora Grace. Of course, the visits to the parlour helped, too,' Tonette chuckled.

'Both deserve the credit,' Tintin couldn't help but laugh too.

'As Mama says, we must play with the cards we are dealt. I now have more time to think about others,' Tonette said. 'I just wish that Tom had conquered his demons so that he would have known how to truly live,' she added wistfully.

Soon, Marina returned to the dining room and resumed talking about her upcoming 'projects'. 'Your Auntie Conching is about to renovate her place. Tintin, she's the one who owns the Fresh Bread bakery chain, in case you've forgotten. She's visiting tomorrow. She said she wants to learn from me,' Marina smiled.

'Oooh, cool. Who knows, she just might be your first official client,' Tintin said.

'Exciting. I'll be your sales manager, Ma. I can find other clients for you,' Tonette joined in.

Tintin had never seen Marina this cheerful when engaged in projects. She knew Marina could manage events and programmes efficiently and effortlessly, as she had demonstrated many times over as a First Lady of the city. But this time, Tintin could see more energy in Marina's steps. Tintin also understood now that Marina never had any real freedom in their ancestral house. They had never renovated it, ever since it was passed down from her grandparents. Most of the furniture was also from the first generation of Pestaños. Perhaps this helped explain Marina's fixation on fabrics and cushion covers—they were the only things that she could control, as most of the furniture and permanent structures embedded into the house virtually had an invisible 'do not touch' stamp, similar to the notices in museums. Somehow, Tintin likened the old house to an intransigent spirit, never changing, year after year, even when fashion changed, season after season. She initially thought that Marina was simply disinterested, but now she knew better.

That night in her new room, Tintin heaved a deep sigh as though to expel all the negative energy trapped in her chest. Even the ambience in her room radiated comfort and calm, reassuring her that she wouldn't be frightened if ever she needed to get up in the middle of the night. Tintin smiled to herself as she remembered how fulfilled Marina looked these days. Marina was having a vocational awakening, however late in life that might be.

Tintin also felt less encumbered now that she was speaking more frequently with Tonette. She realized how much she had lost in those years of conflict. She had been carrying the weight of guilt, and proud as she was, she hadn't attempted to reconcile with Tonette. She had simply allowed conflict to grow and attach itself like barnacles to the base of their relationship, flourishing unimpeded until it attacked the core of their sisterhood. But now, as they started to strip the barnacles away, layer after layer, Tintin gradually rediscovered the beauty of that bond. She would restore this bond to its original lustre. She couldn't help but recall their honest conversations as kids and teenagers. How she would run to Tonette with questions she couldn't ask her parents. Tonette had always answered her openly, without restraint. It was also Tonette who comforted her when Tintin had her first period.

Setting aside biases and prejudices, Tintin remembered Tonette as beautiful, generous and caring. If Tintin had been less self-absorbed and been listening to her, she would have understood that Tonette was messianic and it was this tendency that had sent her into Tom's orbit. Tom needed care, and Tonette undoubtedly thought that she was his saviour. Unfortunately, Tom had spoiled what could have been a beautiful life for Tonette. But that was water under the bridge now, as Tonette had said. And all wasn't lost. Perhaps Tonette could still have her chance and live a beautiful life.

The next day, Tonette picked Tintin up for a joyride to the villages. 'What happened to your driver?' Tintin asked after settling into the passenger seat of Tonette's Mitsubishi Montero.

'Manong Dan has decided to retire. As Gino and Mika are in Manila, there's no point keeping a driver. I know how to drive anyway,' Tonette replied. 'Okay, shall we?' she asked, adjusting her rear-view mirror before pulling back her sunglasses.

Tintin was amazed at the pace of real estate development in her city. A tourism boom seemed imminent, as had been predicted by the buyer of their old property. Aside from their ancestral house being turned into a bed-and-breakfast, Tintin also saw a couple of new pension houses cropping up in their district alone. As they turned onto the main street, she saw a new Jollibee branch, the first in their city, and a few blocks later, a newly opened McDonald's store. 'That's somewhat new, it opened about six months ago,' Tonette said, noticing Tintin's amused expression.

'I suppose it's the most objective sign that San Agustin has levelled up. I remember that the likes of Jollibee and McDonald's only opened a branch if they are assured of viable footfall.' Tintin knew this from her years working at an advertising agency. 'This is a big deal for our good ol' San Agustin,' Tintin smiled. 'Who owns the Jollibee franchise?'

'Tom's sister,' Tonette said, almost too softly. Tom had two brothers and one sister. The latter was married to a real estate developer in the region.

'Really?'

'Yep, really,' Tonette sighed.

'And they didn't give you a single penny when you were almost evicted from your house?' Tintin was frowning now.

'Precisely. You know the drama at their house. Whenever we needed help, they would say, all they have left is their good name. But then you hear about Stella getting this franchise and that,' Tonette said. 'I suppose they just got lucky with the seed money from my in-laws. Anyways, I don't want to talk about it now.'

'And McDonald's?'

'Don't raise an eyebrow, but it's owned by the mayor's son. You remember Angelo?'

'Angelo as in the Angelo Ledesma in my batch?' Tintin couldn't help but arch one eyebrow.

'Yep, the same Angelo.'

'No way,' Tintin said in disbelief. Angelo used to be the slowest boy in her primary school class. He stood out for being a show-off, but also notorious for scoring the lowest in the exams, across subjects.

'Yes way,' Tonette laughed.

'How did that happen? This is the height of injustice.'

'Don't ask me. If I knew how, I would have bought a franchise too. Remember how we had a good laugh because of his gross grammar errors in that letter he sent you?' Tonette laughed again.

'Oh God, please don't remind me. I'll never go near McDonald's again. Let's not talk about that anymore,' Tintin put her palm on her forehead exaggeratedly. 'So what district is this? It looks like an exclusive community to me,' she said, looking at the newly built houses.

'This is Barangay Santa Ana. Thanks to OFW money, it looks like a private subdivision, indeed.'

They drove farther out to the next town, where they passed by a theme park that was apparently popular not just among the locals but among tourists from other regions as well. Having a theme park a few kilometres from their small city was unimaginable when Tintin still lived here, or even just ten years ago. Tintin couldn't take her eyes off the fenced property. She could see the ziplines, canopies and other structures from the road. On their way back to San Agustin, Tintin tried to look at her hometown from the eyes of a tourist. San Agustin, in particular, had apparently been getting considerable spillover tourists, especially during the peak seasons, both in the summer and around Christmas. The city itself was worth a visit: it had architectural heritage, including the Catholic church at its centre that dated back to the 1700s, and several ancestral houses built in late 1800s and early 1900s; San Agustin had beaches, though not the white-sand variety, but less crowded ones; it had a marine sanctuary, something unique to this locality; and the much sought-after local cuisine. It also celebrated local fiestas, revolving mainly on the feast days of the Catholic calendar, and a satellite version of the famous Dinagyang Festival, a cultural celebration of faith and devotion held in January each year. 'Can we go to Coral Beach? We don't have to stop, we can just drive by, I just want to see how it looks now,' Tintin said, referring to a childhood favourite resort of hers in one of the coastal villages of San Agustin.

'Of course. Even that has changed a lot, as you will soon see.' Tonette turned onto a narrower road lined with vines and tall grasses. Soon, they approached a sandy clearing lined with palm trees.

Tintin's heart beat faster upon seeing the stretch beyond the palm trees. From a distance, the sea looked like a smooth, soft, blue blanket. But as they drew closer, she could see gentle waves that shimmered at times when the sun's rays hit their crests.

It was at once familiar and strange. It was the same body of water that she had swum in regularly, years ago, though each wind brought a different wave of water to the surface. She hadn't been here in a decade now. Most of her earlier trips were shorter ones, three days on average, and she hadn't had the luxury of coming to the beach.

Soon, a row of tents and beach huts along the shore came into view. A couple of the huts sold snacks and drinks, sunblock lotions and sundry items. 'It is more crowded than I remember,' Tintin noted.

'Our population has grown and we get many visitors and students from nearby towns, and even from Miag-ao. They come for the marine sanctuary and then spend the rest of the day swimming here,' Tonette explained. 'Let's go for a short walk,' she said, parking the car near one of the larger huts.

They walked along the beach all the way to the cove, where they used to spend many weekends swimming with their father. This part of the beach was less crowded, perhaps because the resort charged a higher fee than the others. 'I'll go get us something to drink,' Tonette said. 'You can sit on this lounger, I know the owner of this place,' Tonette pointed at the row of white loungers facing the sea. After seeing that Tintin found a clean lounger, Tonette turned in the direction of the house behind the cabanas.

Tintin took out a tissue packet from her bag and wiped away the water droplets and leaves on the lounger before sitting back. She looked out at the sea. This part was nearly empty but for a couple of boats, farther out. Now and then, clouds would pass by and the sea would reflect that greyish-blue colour, unlike the deep aquamarine that she remembered from her summers here. But the water was clear and inviting. She remembered wading through this body of water, the Sulu Sea, that would join the Panay Gulf, further down. Once, she even got caught in a 'massive' wave. She couldn't see anything but the swirl of water and she felt as though she was being churned along with the swirl and was about to see the end of her short life. But it was just a fleeting moment caught in a passing wave, and her father had held her tightly and pulled her up right then. Her saviour. Her father explained to her that the 'eternity' she had felt inside the swirling water was just a split second in real life. As she grew older, she became less frightened by the waves. She would run to meet them and pretend to surf and jump over their crests. Meeting each wave headlong became a thrill for her. The bigger the better.

Tonette came back with a young attendant carrying a tray of fresh buko juice in green coconut shells, a plate of bibingka, or baked rice cakes, and another plate of biscocho, Iloilo's version of sugar bread. 'Andy, the owner, insisted we try this biscocho. Remember how we used to have a competition, biting noisily into the biscochos?' Tonette asked.

'And putting the piayas over our ears like earmuffs,' Tintin laughed at the memory.

'To Mama's irritation,' Tonette joined in her laughter. They ate the snacks amid a flurry of updates from Tonette, especially about the local events and celebrations she had been helping with.

'I've been meaning to ask you something,' Tintin said after she had put away the coconut shell.

'What is it?' Tonette raised her eyebrows.

'Robbie,' Tintin said.

'I never thought that this day would come. Finally, you're showing interest in Robbie.'

'How did you feel when you first met him?'

'Surprised is an understatement. Who wouldn't be, right?' Tonette said. 'But I grew up going with Papa to his campaign sprees and meeting folks of all stripes. So I know how to mask any awkward emotions.'

'But he's related by blood. Did you feel any of that thing, the "call of the blood"?' Tintin asked.

'Nah, nothing like that. I tried to be welcoming. After all, he knew Tommy's younger brother, so I couldn't be mean to him,' Tonette explained. 'Robbie didn't tell Tommy's brother the truth. He simply said that Papa was a former classmate of his mother's.'

'Which is partly true. Tell the truth, but tell it slant,' Tintin couldn't help but laugh at the irony of this.

'Huh, what do you mean?'

'Oh never mind. It's just a random quote.'

'I see, I didn't know that.'

'Mama said you're in touch with him?'

'Yep, he calls regularly. He loves his daughters. A lot. Apparently he tells his daughters about Papa all the time. He's proud of being Papa's son.'

'Was he close to Papa?'

'It doesn't seem like it. I think Papa supported Robbie financially until the end, but he scarcely visited him. I feel bad in a way.'

'How come he waited years before showing up?'

'His mother forbade him from making any contact. But after she passed on, he started finding out about us. His company had a summer outing in Guimaras once, so he made a side-trip here after that.'

'How is he as a person?'

'He's pleasant and sociable. A fairer version of Papa. He's the district sales supervisor of a pharmaceutical company in Northern Luzon.'

'Do you see him as a real brother?'

'Not really. See, we had different upbringings. We're lucky, you and me, because we had both Papa and Mama. And obviously, we grew up in better circumstances. That difference had a lot of impact in how we've turned out as adults. Even two people who had grown up in completely similar circumstances can still have vastly different fortunes. Look at the two of us,' Tonette smiled wanly.

'What do you mean?' Tintin asked.

'We're poles apart, Tin. Maybe it's not obvious because superficially I still behave like I'm well-heeled,' she said. 'Without Mama's support and my inheritance, where would I be? I've barely stepped into university. I'm jobless and I don't have any special skills. I'd been married to a drug addict. All the odds were against me.'

'Oh, please don't talk like that.'

'It's true though, isn't it? Without our parents, I'd be no different from the homeless people begging on the streets,' Tonette sighed.

'You have two beautiful children,' Tintin reminded her.

'They're the only hope that kept me going during the darkest of times.'

'I'm sorry,' Tintin reached out and held Tonette's hands.

'It's okay, I think I've been through the worst. Things are looking up for me now, so I should count my blessings, especially my two kids. Sometimes I feel I don't deserve them,' she said. 'Anyways, let's change the topic, how are you? How does it feel to be you, the jetsetter?'

'It's always fun to travel for pleasure, but it's rather different when you migrate,' Tintin said. 'There's an abundance of material resources, for sure, but people tend to abuse that. They hoard, only to throw things away because they go bad. It's horrible.'

'Really? No wonder those TV programmes about hoarders, which I thought were weird, are still on air,' Tonette replied.

'There's gun violence too,' Tintin sighed. 'On some days, I think living in one's native country, however difficult the circumstances, is sweeter.'

'That's a totally different view from those *balikbayans* who've built large houses,' Tonette said, referring to the OFWs who had returned to the country for good.

'Oh yes, of course. Some people tend to rationalize their choices so maybe they only highlight the positive side,' Tintin frowned. 'But then the fact that they built their mansions back here, instead of there, speaks for itself, right?'

'But isn't it more convenient living in a First World country?'

'In some ways, life here is more comfortable. Look at you, you haven't completed college, you don't go to work and yet you have a housemaid and other helps,' Tintin laughed at the irony of this. 'In the US, I do everything myself, especially when Patrick is travelling. I get a bit of help from the cleaners, the yard service and all, but other than that, I do practically everything, from cooking to washing, all the daily maintenance,' Tintin went on about the drudgery of housework.

'I don't think I'll survive.'

'Exactly. Then if you go out, there's always that risk of microaggressions from narrow-minded people.'

'Like what? I've only travelled out a few times, and that too as a tourist, so I wouldn't know.'

'Some people don't even know where the Philippines is. I'm not kidding when I tell you that some people think it's part of China,' Tintin said incredulously.

'Are you kidding me?' Tonette was flabbergasted.

'And here's the clincher. Many are amazed when they realize I can speak proper English. Even my dentist told me that.'

'Oh my *gulay*, this is totally hilarious,' Tonette laughed so hard that her shoulders shook.

'But I guess all that comes with the territory. After all, I'm just a guest and must respect the rules of my host.'

'So why don't you just come home for good?'

'That's a great question. It's my duty to be with my family. I can be many things, but when it comes to family, I'm clear with my principles, they come first. Unequivocally.'

'I know what you mean.'

'But maybe a little part of me is in it for the adventure, too. I guess I'm also a sucker for the adrenaline rush from the chase,' Tintin said, sitting more upright as she explained further. 'Maybe I want to prove that I can survive away from the comforts of home. Call it earning a badge of survival in less familiar terrains.'

'That's too profound for me, Tin,' Tonette looked at her almost in awe.

'Not everyone who leaves the country behind is raring to do it. Some have personal battles that they think they could conquer in another land,' Tintin said. 'But going by the millions of balikbayans each year, these travellers inevitably realize that there's no place like home,' she added.

'For those of us left behind, we only see the shiny parts— the greenbacks, branded gifts and other *pasalubongs*, well-maintained houses, snow, and all that.'

'All the images that Hollywood has conjured up and served to us. Most of them are just make-believe, pretty much like the movies,' Tintin said. 'Wait, this is too intense a discussion for a pleasant afternoon like this,' she smiled.

'I'm happy that we had this discussion, though. I miss having this kind of talk. I only have Mama to talk with,' Tonette said. 'Now I'm realizing how much I've missed it, and how much I'm missing out on with you being away.'

'What about your friends? Don't you have such real talks with them?'

'Only a few of my friends returned after university. Like you, most have chosen to live in bigger cities rather than resume a provincial life. I'd have probably done the same, had things been different,' Tonette said, looking melancholy again.

'Please don't feel sad. In the end, everything evens out. It's not whether we left or stayed. What truly matters is if we're happy with our choices,' Tintin held Tonette's arm. 'As I've said, those balikbayans, they want to be back, right? So there must be something here that compels them to return.'

'What about you? I know you said you're there for your family, but if it were just you, wouldn't you want to come back? For good?'

'If it were just up to me, I wouldn't hesitate,' Tintin sighed. 'Jamie is still too young, but maybe when he's done with university, who knows? It could be a retirement option, isn't it?'

'I'm crossing my fingers,' Tonette hugged her tightly.

Both Tonette and Tintin only realized the lateness of the afternoon when an attendant came to collect their tray. Tintin pushed her sunglasses up through her hair and looked out at the sea as the sun gradually sank into the horizon. Right at that moment, the sun looked like a round biscuit slowly dipping into a cup of tea. The waning rays shimmered gently on the approaching waves. Tintin slipped off her sandals and walked closer to the edge, where the water, a mix of elements that the waves carried over from faraway places, was now lapping against the fine sands of San Agustin ceaselessly. This was the same Sulu Sea that she swam in as a child, and yet the water that ran through this passage was never the same on any given day. Out of habit, she scooped a handful of sand and let it fall gently back to the sea, its particles being blown away from her. She remembered a passage from Annie Dillard's *Abundance*: 'The average river requires a million years to move a grain of sand one hundred miles.' Soon, the tide rose higher and the last of the ripples caressed Tintin's ankles. She watched as a thin layer of seawater inched toward the shore and then receded to merge with the waters of the sea.

'Ready?' Tonette called out, a few steps ahead.

'I miss afternoons like this,' Tintin said, picking up her sandals and falling in step with Tonette as they made their way to the car, their arms entwined around each other's back.

Chapter 12

Atlanta, 2018

Tintin's friendship with Caroline had, in a way, passed the test of time, having lasted several seasons now. They had been driving around Virginia Highland in Atlanta's Midtown when they spotted a new coffee shop beside a quaint store selling country-house decor. 'This takes care of our venue for this week's catch-up,' Tintin pointed at the coffee shop, Stay Awake, with a steaming cup of coffee as its logo.

'It does look interesting. Let's check it out *pronto*,' Caroline said, turning right into the driveway and following the parking lot sign to the back of the cottage-like stores. She spotted a vacant slot facing a wall. 'Here we are. Don't forget to bring your stuff with you, never leave anything in the car,' she said pointing at the notice on the wall. There had been a series of car thefts and break-ins in Atlanta recently, and Caroline was on the verge of paranoia when it came to car parking and safety. 'Not that they would be interested in my tiny car, but nonetheless, I don't want to go through the trauma of losing any of my stuff or worse, invasion of my privacy,' she added before alighting from the car.

'The things that we worry about. This takes up so much mental space,' Tintin said as she fell in step with Caroline on their way to the shop.

'That's one thing that truly irritates me. All this just makes Atlanta look bad. I love this city and it hurts me so much when I hear about another theft or break-in or any of the other crimes that seem to have become more prevalent. Why can't people just be honest? Why do they have to take someone else's belongings? And what for? To support an addiction?' Caroline looked exasperated. 'Next time, stop me when I rant too much. Anyway, let's just be careful,' she said as she opened the door and led the way to the counter. 'Now I don't want to talk about depressing topics.'

Tintin found a space by the window. 'I've been meaning to tell you something about my family in the Philippines.'

'What is it? Obviously if it's something about family, however depressing, we must talk about it.' Caroline quickly put her eco-friendly cross-body bag on the empty seat next to her and turned to face Tintin, ready to listen to her story.

'I'll get our coffee first,' Tintin said, before going to collect their coffee orders.

'Here you go,' she placed Caroline's personal mug on her side of the table and carried her mug to her side.

'Now, tell me,' Caroline said.

After a sip of her coffee, Tintin recounted her discovery of Robbie and how she had a long-standing conflict with Tonette.

'It's a tough situation and I obviously feel for you,' Caroline said, holding Tintin's hand and patting it gently.

'Sorry if it's bumming you out right now.'

'No, don't be sorry at all. I'm glad you told me. We're friends for a reason.'

'I wanted to tell you earlier but I wasn't sure about how much to divulge and all. I don't want to be dumping trivial stuff on you, if you know what I mean. Even after all these years in America, I have yet to fully understand the culture part.' Tintin had been reserved when it came to her internal landscape.

'Oh please,' Caroline patted Tintin's hand again. 'Honesty should be borderless. Any culture appreciates honesty. Besides, these things happen all the time,' Caroline said. 'Millions of families have graver problems. There's nothing to be ashamed of.'

'Not that I'm ashamed of it. It just doesn't define me, so I don't think it's relevant and it doesn't even occur to me to bring it up.'

'I get you. Anyway, I'm here anytime you need to bounce things off.'

'And now, moving on to the weather report for this week,' Tintin joked as she changed the topic.

Caroline almost sputtered out the coffee she had just sipped. 'Oh please, be mindful of your timing next time,' she laughed.

After coffee, Tintin and Caroline moved to the quaint shop next door. It sold linens, dish towels, bric-a-bracs, and even handmade cards with greetings that were somewhat wittier than the typical Hallmark cards. They had a good laugh reading out some of the hilarious dedications. This time around, however, each of them found something to buy, even if it was just a tiny item. Tintin picked up three greeting cards, while Caroline bought a small bottle of responsibly made hand cream.

Chapter 13

Atlanta, Spring 2019

Despite the vast Pacific Ocean dividing them, Tintin somehow felt that their consistent phone conversations helped reduce the great physical distance between her, Marina and Tonette. Tintin was now more plugged-in with the events and social circles in San Agustin. Tonette had become more engaged in civic activities, helping organize community events, especially after Gino had completed his residency and Mika was more settled in university. It was because of this greater involvement with the community that Tonette had decided to run for a seat in San Agustin's city council. She campaigned heavily on the issue of drug abuse prevention. Tintin put together a brochure on the facts about drug addiction for Tonette. In the process, Tintin was shocked to learn that methamphetamine or 'shabu' use had become prevalent in their city. It had penetrated even far-flung villages and destroyed the fabric of family and society as they knew it. She explained to Tonette how methamphetamine, heroin, cocaine and fentanyl could alter the brain. How a dose of those drugs could send a person swinging from euphoria, or 'high', as the lay people called it, into crashing depression. How long-term use of the drugs could lead to health issues like kidney malfunction and metabolic diseases. Tonette had seen these patterns in Tom: how his mood swung and how he would stay awake for days and nights in a row, oblivious to hunger, walking around at all hours as though floating through the house. Then when the effect of the drugs would wear off, he would sit in a corner crying like a kid, remorseful, regretting all the wasted opportunities. How he would promise to go clean and reform, but then wouldn't be able to resist the temptation. He would sniff it all over again whenever he met up with his so-called friends, the same people who supplied him with the drugs. Tintin knew that drug abuse had broken up families, led to other crimes, caused traditional values to be trampled on, and that their effects rippled into the next generation. Tonette experienced some of these first-hand and suffered from the consequences.

Tonette came out with her story about Tom, telling the public how life would have been better had Tom not been addicted to dangerous drugs. How he had inherently been a good person, inevitably destroyed by drug abuse. How he had assumed that a tiny amount of shabu occasionally couldn't lead to addiction, but in the end, had even had to pawn his jewellery for buying drugs. It pained Tonette to share all this, but she genuinely felt it was her duty to give a testimonial from her own life to help prevent drug addiction, especially among the youth of San Agustin. Initially, this revelation had stirred some controversy, especially from Tom's family, who had ignored Tonette's pleas for intervention in the first place. They tried to stop Tonette from 'washing dirty linen in public'. And when they had failed to silence her, they started supporting other candidates to block Tonette from getting a council seat. But ultimately, the residents had decided for themselves and had elected Tonette to office.

'Congrats, I'm so happy for you!' Tintin screamed excitedly when Tonette answered her call.

'Now you can be proud of me,' Tonette said. 'I hope I've levelled up and am now worthy of your esteem,' she said. Her voice was gentle, so Tintin doubted if that was a sarcastic remark.

'Tonette, I'm sorry if I've been harsh to you and if I haven't been of any comfort during the most difficult chapters of your life. But I'm literally jumping with joy for you right now.'

'I'm many things, but one thing I'm not is someone who holds grudges. I always remember that I'm your *ate*, even if you don't call me that anymore. I don't even remember when you stopped calling me that.' Tonette said, referring to the Filipino term for older sister.

'I also don't know. Maybe in high school? Does it even matter now?'

'No, it's not that relevant. But I'd assumed it's because I'd lost your respect that you didn't see the point in calling me ate anymore.'

'I have so much respect for you; not just now, but before you ever even ran for a seat in the council,' she said. Tonette was quiet at the other end. 'I'd feel awkward calling you Ate now. It won't feel natural after all these years.'

'Exactly,' Tonette laughed. 'Anyways, I just want to share that I have greater control over my life now and I'm happy about how things are with Gino and Mika. Now I have more time for others instead of always being the burden that I used to be.'

'You weren't exactly that. Being a mother is truly difficult, whatever the circumstances. In your case, it was doubly so. But look at how wonderful Gino and Mika are. And that's all because of you.'

'I shouldn't be bringing this up now, but I remember that look you had on your face when I was begging Mama to sell some of our properties to pay for my house loan.'

'I didn't mean to be so insensitive and without compassion. I had my own problems. I'm not proud of this but I know I have an attitude, at times. But I hope I didn't come off as imperious,' Tintin could feel her eyes glisten.

'It's more disapproval and definitely not imperiousness. But I understand where you're coming from. You had a stricter yardstick. And that's okay, you're still my little sister,' Tonette chuckled. 'Anyway, I hope you could come home soon so we can spend more quality time together. I've been remembering those midnight snacks we shared on the balcony, whispering so as to avoid waking our parents up,' Tonette sighed.

'Now you're making me nostalgic,' Tintin said, wiping her tears with the back of her hand.

'Come soon. This time around, I can say this in all honesty: I miss you,' Tonette said before hanging up.

Tintin regretted all the time that she was cruel to and judgemental of Tonette, who was so down-to-earth, easily admitting to her weaknesses and embracing her fallibility. Tintin's eyes brightened just thinking about how Tonette's prospects were now looking up, especially with her kids growing up to become responsible members of society. Tonette could now attend to her own dreams. For the first time in a long time, Tintin looked up and felt grateful for Tonette.

Chapter 14

Atlanta, Spring 2019

Tintin's weariness from the winter gradually evaporated as the temperature started to rise. It was now springtime and she could sit outside and be in nature—it had always revived her. Today, she could indulge in her 'nature bathing' in their backyard, as Patrick was in town and could drop Jamie off on his way to work. That alone freed up an hour of her time, giving her this breathing space in the morning, which somehow made the afternoon pick-up less of a drudge. As Patrick had completed his travel assignment for the quarter, they now had time to play board games or watch old episodes of *Big Bang* after dinner, before tucking Jamie into bed. And now that the days were longer, they could play badminton in their backyard or go for a short walk around the block in the early evenings. This helped Jamie settle into bed easier.

Tintin discovered that Jamie wasn't that sulky in the presence of his father. Earlier, she had felt it was unfair that Jamie made things more difficult with his tantrums, but later on she realized that even she was less cranky and less likely to nag Jamie when Patrick was around. Never again would Tintin take Patrick's presence for granted. His absence created negative energy and only his presence could decrease the entropy in the house. Even he himself was happier to be home, in the comfort of his own bed and his own pillows. He had shared this with Tintin as they were about to turn in, last night. 'What a vast difference being together makes to everyone's disposition, isn't it?' he had asked before switching off the nightlight.

Lately, Tintin wanted to be a birdwatcher, observing the variety of species of birds in their backyard. She considered joining a birdwatchers' society, like Audubon Society. Just now, a northern cardinal came pecking at a few crumbs nearby, while she was sitting on her white Adirondack chair. It didn't linger; it flew away when it sensed even the slightest of movement, a testament to how they operated on optical flow, convincing her that birds had powerful peripheral vision. Tintin looked up at the yellow pine tree above her—a flock of Georgian swallows called out in pleasant notes before leaving their perch on the bough and flying to the west. These birds, they were migrants like her. They had arrived from hundreds of miles away and were possibly just passing by this side of the world as well. And like those birds, she could feel happy about her fate. She could sing happy notes and be a grace for others who longed for the sounds of springtime. She had grumbled enough like a cat, and it hadn't been fruitful. Things could have been different; she could still have been in that rift with Tonette, but why should she carry a grudge to her grave? Isn't life more fun when lived without bitterness? She looked to her left and took in the greenery around her, from the Japanese maple tree at one corner to the pines that lined the stretch all the way to the back. This reminded her of her university days. How she and the Room 216 girls spent some weekend mornings under the leafy trees in the Sunken Garden after their walk around the Academic Oval. She couldn't wait for her next monthly call with them. This time, she could truly say that she was in a much better place.

A pair of bees buzzed around; they had most likely escaped from the neighbour's hive or had simply taken a break and ventured over to this side of the fence. A giant elm tree towered over the garage behind the fountain, its branches swaying in the wind. Now Tintin could hear the wind passing by; she could feel the morning breeze and could see it in the rustling leaves. To her right was an eastern redbud, now ablaze with its deep magenta blooms. Tintin let the mild spring breeze play with her hair.

Part II

Sandy

Chapter 1

Singapore, 2013: Departure

Sandy felt like a thief as she quietly inserted her key into her own front door. She had arrived at their Singapore home earlier than expected, wanting to surprise her husband, Steve. From the Changi Airport, she had taken a cab and told the driver to drop her off a few metres away from their gate on Mountbatten Road. The house seemed empty, though—not surprising as her son, Alex, was still at a friend's house for a sleepover. Sandy placed her black Tumi suitcase carefully beside the black Italian leather sofa in the drawing room. She slipped off her white sneakers and tiptoed across the dining area to the back of the house. The glass door to the patio was ajar. Sandy stepped out expecting to see Steve having his morning coffee there, but the patio was empty. She could hear splashes from the pool. Steve could be doing his weekend laps. She took a few more steps outside, her back close to the wall to ensure that Steve wouldn't see her.

But what greeted Sandy was the sight of Elena, their helper, frolicking in the pool in a two-piece red swimsuit. Sandy didn't want to disturb Elena if that was how she wanted to spend her rest day, after all it was a bright day and the pool shimmered in the sun. It struck Sandy, though, that this was the first time she was seeing Elena swimming. And in a skimpy bikini, too. Sandy was about to return inside when she heard another splash from the far end of the pool.

It was Steve jumping in and swimming in broad strokes until he reached the gutter on the other end. Then he splashed water at Elena, who initially protested but was soon laughing and retaliating with bigger splashes. Steve swam underwater and emerged from behind Elena. Sandy blinked hard to clear her vision. When she opened her eyes, she clearly saw Steve and Elena holding hands. Then Steve drew Elena closer to him, his hands moving to her lower back. Elena, in turn, wrapped her arms around Steve's neck, tiptoed and raised her lips to his.

Sandy was frozen on the spot. She clamped her mouth to prevent any sounds from escaping her mouth. Her eyes widened in disbelief as Steve and Elena deepened their kiss. Sandy wanted to shout a long list of invectives at them but held her breath. She belatedly realized that she had uprooted a monstera plant in anger and was now tearing at it. She looked at the empty pot, wanted to pick it up and hurl it across, wishing it would hit those scumbags smack in the head. But instead, she squeezed her eyes shut and breathed deeply, tapping into her years of meditation and mindfulness practice.

When Sandy opened her eyes, Steve and Elena were swimming leisurely toward the pool steps. Then they sat side by side, their legs entwined, arms around each other. Sandy fished out her phone from the pocket of her black shirt dress and took photos and videos of the despicable couple. She watched as Elena shifted, moving toward the nearby lounger. Steve followed her there, kissing her first before lying down with his head in her lap. Then Elena began to massage his shoulders. Sandy took one final photo and returned to the house. She tiptoed to the master bedroom where she found Elena's bright yellow negligee still on the bed. She hated the loud colour. She took another picture and threw the offensive nightwear into a corner bin. She unlocked her safe box and pulled out her most important folder of documents and her jewellery box, placed them in her weekend bag, along with any other clothes that she could reach out and grab easily from her closet. She booked a taxi and left the house as quietly as she had entered it.

Sandy vaguely recalled telling the cab driver to take her to a hotel. She didn't remember having mentioned a specific hotel, but the driver somehow dropped her off at The Stamford Hotel. She absentmindedly gave him a fifty-dollar note and was about to alight when the driver reminded her to take her change. Sandy grabbed the change and uncharacteristically shoved it into her purse carelessly. She entered the lobby of the hotel, quickly scanned the room, and as though on autopilot, walked over to an empty seat in a corner. From there, she called out to Tracy, her friend and colleague, who came to her rescue straightaway. Tracy had filled in the check-in form for her at the hotel upon realizing that Sandy had simply been sitting in the lobby all this time, still dazed from the discovery. Later in Sandy's room, Tracy asked all the pertinent questions that ultimately helped Sandy calm down and deal with her situation rationally. Tracy then offered to pick up Alex from his sleepover.

Alone in her room, Sandy simply sat on a chair and peered out the window. She stayed there for the longest time, her mind racing back and forth to the scene from this morning. 'How could he? How could they?' She kept on asking herself. Then she started kicking the floor and the chair, before throwing herself on the bed and crying uncontrollably.

When she finally gathered her bearings, Sandy called Tintin, who was still in Manila. Only yesterday, they were all together, celebrating Serene's wedding. That felt like lightyears away now.

'Oh my God, oh my God!' Tintin exclaimed. 'I can't believe this. What in the world got into him? And with your helper too?'

'I've just left the house and I'm filing for divorce right away. My officemate is now looking for a lawyer,' Sandy sighed.

'I'd do the same, Sands. Steve doesn't deserve you a single bit,' Tintin said.

'But what about Alex? He's everything to me,' Sandy said. 'This is my worst nightmare. I don't want my son to be part of the broken-home statistics. It's not fair to him.'

'I understand. No mother would ever want her child to go through that.'

'Why did it happen to me? Why me? What did I do wrong?' Sandy wept quietly.

'Sands, you haven't done anything wrong. This is not your fault at all,' Tintin said gently.

'I really don't want to put Alex in a difficult place,' Sandy kept rubbing her brows, willing herself to find the best solution.

'I'm coming over, Sands, I'll take the first flight in tomorrow,' Tintin offered. 'I'll call Serene and Issa shortly.'

'Tin, there's no need to come all the way.'

'There's every need. I'll see you tomorrow. I love you, Sands. Just hang on,' Tintin said in a comforting voice.

Later that afternoon, Serene called Sandy. 'Sands, how far are you willing to go for Alex's sake?' she said. 'You know I've just heard of a high-profile couple who live in an unconventional arrangement. The ex-wife is a newscaster and the guy is a well-known businessman. And they still live together, in separate rooms, apparently.'

'I don't think I can stand living under the same roof with him ever again. I can't even say his name now. And I definitely don't want to see his face,' Sandy replied.

'We'll figure something out for Alex,' Serene tried to reassure her.

'I'm sorry that this came right after your wedding. I hope I'm not souring your post-wedding celebration,' Sandy didn't want to bother Serene, but Serene had learned about the situation from Tintin.

'Please don't say that, Sands. Besides, it was more of a ceremonial wedding.'

'Just the same, I didn't want to rain on your parade.'

'Lance and I are more concerned about you now,' Serene said, doing her best to soothe Sandy.

Sandy's phone rang again after a few minutes. 'Sands, are you okay?' Issa asked.

'I'm still in denial, Issa,' Sandy sighed for what seemed like the umpteenth time today.

'You don't deserve this. You've been such a loyal wife, a hardworking partner and a dedicated mother. And yet, what did he do?' Issa was clearly upset. It was unlike her to be this angry at anyone or anything.

'Exactly. I hate him to hell and back. But I'm worried what this will do to Alex.'

'Look, Sands. Alex is a smart boy. Of course, any marital conflict will affect him. But only temporarily. I'm a product of a broken marriage myself. But I think I've turned out well,' Issa reassured her.

'It's just that Alex is so sweet and innocent. I don't want him to go through so much pain at such a young age.'

'You know children are more resilient than we credit them for.'

With Tracy's help, Sandy eventually found an experienced divorce lawyer. The next day, Tintin arrived in time to accompany Sandy to the first meeting. The lawyer immediately contacted Steve, who was clearly caught by surprise. Steve asked to speak to Sandy to explain his side, but Sandy declined. He had been calling Sandy directly, but she had rejected his calls. The lawyer then informed him that the evidence was too damning. He arranged to meet Steve separately to show it to him. Eventually, he convinced Steve to sign the papers before the divorce got acrimonious.

For the most part, Sandy was just following whatever Tintin or Tracy were telling her to do, and signed whatever document needed her signature. She didn't even remember what she was eating at mealtimes. She simply put things in her mouth whenever Tintin gave her something to eat. But one thing she was clear about: she didn't want to talk to Steve.

The days after the divorce papers were signed passed by like a blur for Sandy. She understood only later that trauma blunted memories of ordinary things and heightened those of the extraordinary, especially painful ones.

Sandy terminated Elena's contract and ensured the employment agency deported her straightaway to the Philippines. Sandy and Alex returned to their house as soon as Steve vacated it. Tintin stayed on for the rest of the week. Serene arranged for meal deliveries for the entire week and Issa spoke to a cousin in Singapore, who sent a helper to Sandy's place every other day while she waited for the arrival of her own new helper.

'This is too much of a test. And so soon after Serene's wedding,' Sandy sobbed on Tintin's shoulder. 'Isn't that ironic?' she sniffled.

'I know, Sands,' Tintin couldn't hold back her tears any longer. 'But you'll get through this. You're strong and smart. You've made the right decisions. And we're here for you.' Tintin stroked Sandy's hair, picking a strand and tucking it back into her ponytail. They were sitting in the drawing room, on the sofa that now felt bulky, and the house that now had more empty spaces without Steve and his personal belongings. The house felt quieter too, without Elena's shuffling in the kitchen or around the house, without her singing and her clanging of pots and pans.

'I was so naïve and trusting. How could I not recognize all the signs when they were staring at me all along?' Sandy recounted the cues that she had ignored. She should have listened to her gut feeling. She should have investigated further when she saw too many WhatsApp exchanges between Steve and Elena. But then she prided herself for not being nosy or petty. She should have sensed something was askew when Elena took the longest time to iron Steve's office clothes. She should have questioned when she caught Elena smelling one of Steve's shirts before loading it into the washing machine. But Sandy attributed that to the helper's quirks—everybody had some. And those long glances they gave each other at dinner, with Elena hanging around long after having served their meals. Sandy was more preoccupied with discussing Alex's school activities than concerned with the prolonged exchanges between Steve and Elena. She regretted this lack of attention, or even hiring Elena two years ago, when her long-standing helper—who had been with Sandy since her marriage—had decided to retire and return to the Philippines. She should have vetted Elena more, but in her haste, had blindly trusted her former helper's recommendation.

'They definitely abused your kindness, but these assholes will get their karma,' Tintin said angrily.

Because of the turmoil that the divorce had created in his career, Steve took a new job and relocated to Hong Kong. Sandy completed the lease on their house and eventually shifted to a three-bedroom condominium close to her office. In the end, the hardest part of the divorce was explaining to Alex why he and Sandy were now on their own. There wouldn't be another Christmas or holiday with all three of them together—Alex's nuclear family. It hurt even more when Sandy recalled past Christmases and how jolly they all were, especially the one they had spent in Tokyo when Alex was six. 'Mummy, look outside,' he had pointed at the street below.

'Oh wow, snow flurries,' Sandy had joined him by the tall window of their hotel room. 'Steve, come and see this,' she had called out to Steve, who had jumped off the settee excitedly.

'Wait,' Alex had said, looking at Steve's pajamas, then at Sandy's, and then his own. 'We all have the same pajamas?

Red and white!' Alex had been so amused. 'Can we always be together like this?' he had added sweetly.

'Of course, honey,' Sandy had replied, lifting him. Steve had joined them in a tight family hug as they had watched the flurries that Christmas morning.

Just when Sandy thought she had regained her equilibrium, she would find herself overcome with misery, even without a specific reason. She had this ineffable heaviness in her chest that at times left her on the verge of tears. She hated crying, though; sometimes she willed herself to do so hoping it could lift the weight off. But the tears would refuse to form fully and she would be left instead with this inescapable and burgeoning pain. She even contemplated taking drugs to numb it or perhaps smoking a joint, though she knew very well she wasn't the type to do so, even if it was legal in Singapore. Could this be a residual effect of the trauma she had been through? After all, she was yet to experience full catharsis from her divorce, months ago. Divorce. It was like a curtain that segregated her life into a 'before' and 'after'. She couldn't help but remember flashes of her life before it had happened.

Chapter 2

Singapore, 2012: Roadblocks

Everything in her life was in order. And that was why Sandy found it difficult to pinpoint the source of her anxiety. Her house was uncomfortably quiet after her mother's annual visit to Singapore. Sandy was restless and as per her habit when in such a mood, she resorted to comfort food. She opened the fridge and took out a new tub of Häagen-Dazs's macadamia ice cream. She carried her bowl out to the patio and sat under the umbrella shade, staring out into the pool as she relished her ice cream. She didn't know why but she frowned as she licked the last spoonful from her bowl. She shouldn't be worried about her family. Alex had been doing well in school, getting exemplary grades in maths and science. This was a big source of joy— seeing Alex reach great milestones in school. Steve was also looking more relaxed lately and was less conflicted after his recent promotion. Sandy's family in the Philippines was fine; she had just spoken with her mother, who had arrived home safely and had, characteristically, resumed her volunteer work at her parish immediately. Similarly, her brother, Chris, was enjoying his new life back in their hometown. Sandy shouldn't have anything to worry about. Even her workload was relatively light and there were no upcoming reviews or pitches. So what was bothering her?

Sandy had met Steve, a cheerful expat, at an Executive MBA class, twelve years ago. More than his height and athletic build, it was Steve's carefreeness that had attracted Sandy. How he laughed at jokes so easily. How attentive he was to their classmates. How he was always game for Friday night-outs despite his many responsibilities at the office. Steve always cheered her up with his light-hearted disposition. When they first started going out, Sandy had thought they were the most compatible couple. They were both career fast-trackers and they understood well the demands of getting ahead in the office. Long hours at work was par for the course, as were travels on short notice. They didn't blame each other when a date was cancelled because of a pending work commitment, but rather accepted cancellations as part of their reality. After all, their careers were integral to their lives and helped define them.

When they decided to settle down after a few years of dating, they managed their wedding preparations like a business project, complete with Gantt charts of daily and weekly timelines, to Sandy's relief. This was how they avoided any surprises. A friend once asked Sandy to illustrate how they balance work and life using a Venn diagram, and Sandy had replied that Venn diagram was not applicable to them because in both their cases, the 'work' circle completely swallowed the 'life' circle. Steve had jumped in and explained to their friend how work was like Pac-Man, a hungry monster that ate everything it could get hold of. The seconds, minutes and hours of the day vanished easily whenever Pac-Man was around. It could even eat their entire weekend if they let it.

After their wedding, Steve and Sandy went about their lives accepting the fact that Pac-Man could intrude at any time, even on weekends. There didn't seem to be any liminal stage between personal and professional life. The boundaries were completely blurred. Their corporate style even influenced how they communicated privately. For one, they had key result areas or KRAs for each relationship milestone. They also did a Strength, Weakness, Opportunity, Threat or SWOT analysis of their relationship regularly.

As a young husband, Steve had been supportive of Sandy's career and clearly acknowledged Sandy's financial contribution to their household, which had helped improve their investment portfolio significantly. At home, they had both shared in the house chores, though there weren't that many chores, as they had a live-in helper. Sandy was comfortable with the power balance in their early years. Later on, though, when Alex came along, the equation changed drastically. Although Steve pitched in with childcare, the greater weight of it fell on Sandy, as Steve began to have a more hectic schedule at the office. Sandy also noticed that along with this, his light-heartedness gradually dissipated and his laughs became few and far between.

When Alex got a little older and Sandy resumed work projects that involved greater travelling, Steve started to complain about how she seemed to be spending more time on the road than at home. He even suggested she quit work so that she could focus on Alex and him. Sandy simply stared at Steve when he said this, dumbstruck at the absurdity of his suggestion. Was he mad? Didn't he understand that she had to compensate for earlier times, including her maternity leave, if she wanted to progress in her career? Yet, despite all this, she was still doing more heavy-lifting at home. Her calendar could easily be filled with work as a mother, a wife, and household manager. Childcare, even if it involved just one child, took an incredible amount of time and energy. Sandy herself prepared Alex's breakfast every day because she wanted to ensure that Alex ate his quota of nutritious food first thing in morning. In the evenings, she sat with Alex to go over his homework. Then she had to remind him to bathe on time, get ready for bed on time, and be in bed on time. This routine of reminding, or 'nagging', as Alex would say, wore her down in a way. As though this wasn't enough, she also had to attend various parent and volunteer meetings at school, and organize or coordinate parties and playdates on weekends.

Meanwhile, Steve increasingly took up more of Sandy's time when he needed her inputs on his work presentations and in editing his speeches and messages. As for the house per se, maintenance required a long list of chores that could fill up a whole month. Her role, as the 'reminder-in-chief', of 'reminding' what needed to be done, didn't stop at Alex. Sandy had to do the same thing with Elena. She always had to remind Elena to wipe the bookshelves and the turntable thoroughly. Despite the helper's claim of doing this chore daily, Sandy couldn't help but see a line of dust whenever she ran her index finger on top of the furniture. And how many times did she have to remind Elena to sort the laundry and separate light from dark colours? This recurring mental load annoyed Sandy, at times, and yet she kept going without much complaint. The responsibility of holding things together for her family and household rested squarely on her shoulders. At times, she didn't know how she managed to do anything at work, with all the family and house responsibilities.

Sandy couldn't imagine quitting work. She had been building her career progressively since leaving university. While her work impinged on her personal time, she didn't know of any other way of life outside of it. She needed the intellectual stimulus she got at work. She needed the interaction with fellow professionals—she needed it like air. Her social circle also largely overlapped with her work circle. She knew of women who gave up their careers to focus on family and she often wondered how they could so easily walk away from their careers. And worse, how could they become fully dependent on their husbands, financially? Over time, some of these marriages had collapsed and in the aftermath, the women had suffered the brunt. A few couldn't pick themselves up afterward. This train of thought somewhat startled Sandy.

Then all of a sudden, Sandy remembered how Steve had become even more preoccupied with work recently, which she had initially attributed to his now more senior role at the office. He had also become too formal around her, even when they were alone in their bedroom. When had this started? Sandy counted the months on her fingers. It had gone on far longer than what she had initially thought. But what could she do about it now? Sandy got up from her chair and picked up her bowl. 'Stop this paranoia,' she murmured to herself on her way to deposit her ice cream bowl in the kitchen sink. To begin with, she by herself was financially stable. She had earned enough and made wise investments over the years of working non-stop. She, Sandy Sanchez, would never be that divorced woman who couldn't recover from a marital disaster.

Then she remembered she had to remind Elena about something. 'Elena, please wash the dishes immediately once you are done with the laundry,' she told her helper.

'Yes, ma'am, in a few minutes,' Elena replied from the adjoining laundry room.

'Don't take too long because dirty utensils invite ants,' she emphasized. She didn't like utensils left in the sink. It annoyed her that she had to remind Elena about this repeatedly.

Chapter 3

The Philippines, 2014: Recalibrating

The only traffic on the road as Sandy turned right onto the main street of her hometown, was a brown mutt crossing from the town's sole pharmacy. Perhaps six o'clock was too early for the townsfolk to be out. After all, even the sun hadn't risen fully yet and the fog still hung in the early morning breeze. Not that she would recognize many of the townsfolk anyway. Sandy was spending Christmas here after a long time. She had been home only a few times, and only once on Christmas, ever since she had moved to Singapore, nearly fifteen years ago.

In Sandy's mind, the streets of San Joaquin were wider and the stretches longer. But now, the main road consisted of just two lanes and it took her a mere five minutes to get from her childhood home to the town's main street. She had read somewhere about this discrepancy between recollection and reality, how our brain could sometimes trick us into believing that our memory of a place was reality itself, when in fact that memory was already a biased rendering of reality.

As had become her morning routine in the past few days, Sandy had got up early, driven out in her mother's car across the town centre, past the church, and the winding road up the hill. Midway through her drive, she passed by the cemetery. Here in this town, the dead would always be saved from flooding as they were interred at the highest point. She shook her head to dispel these strange thoughts. She let out a long exhale as soon as she crossed that stretch. The morning mist gradually dissipated and the road ahead slowly brightened. She smiled to herself when she approached the junction that led to a narrower but tree-lined road. She rolled down her window and basked at the zephyr; it was still breezy and Sandy wanted to breathe in the scent of fresh morning dew.

Sandy turned into a gravel driveway, parked the car in front of an off-white bungalow, and strolled through the garden on the right side of the house. Roses in various colours, large-petalled hibiscuses and orchids were in their best bloom. Sandy took in the wild mix of yellow, purple, red and all the shades of pink. Her brother, Chris, soon stepped out from a greenhouse behind the flower garden and rushed over to greet her. 'I still can't get over this, Chris, it's a real paradise. Even better than Giverny,' she smiled, recalling how Chris loved those paintings by Claude Monet.

Chris, a former bank executive, had returned home two years ago and ventured into organic farming. 'I've got a green thumb, remember? Come, enjoy these beauties now. As lovely as they are, they are also ephemeral. So yes, luxuriate in their gloriousness while you can,' he opened his arms wide to welcome her to the garden. 'But speaking of colours, will your coffee be black as usual?' he asked.

'Yep, and I will have it over there,' she pointed to the little thatch-roofed hut at the base of the sloping farm, a tranquil spot hidden from view by a thick vine.

'Give me a few minutes then while I go and brew your cuppa,' Chris said before heading back to the house. He preferred to brew his own coffee and one of the few luxuries that he had brought back with him was his nifty Italian espresso machine with a built-in bean grinder, to make his coffee truly fresh.

Sandy strolled over leisurely to the hut, where she found a smooth wooden bench. She faced the eastern side and sat cross-legged as she waited for the sun to rise higher. She listened to the cacophony of nature: hens clucking, dogs barking and goats bleating as though they were in conversation. Every now and then, the faint sound of motorized tractors would travel through the air and intersperse with farmers' bellowings from afar. Then there was a lull, which according to old folks, meant that an angel was passing by. Her reverie was broken when the hens resumed their clucking.

Soon, Chris joined Sandy at the hut, carrying a tray laden with two cups and a pot of coffee. A helper, Nana Maring, followed him with freshly baked bread rolls, omelette, sausages and even rice cakes. 'Now, you have to try this biko, not sure if you remember, but it used to be your favourite. Nana Maring made it,' Chris pointed to a slice of caramelized baked native rice cake. Sandy nodded and thanked the middle-aged woman. Nana Maring smiled shyly and quickly bowed before leaving.

'Hmmm, I've forgotten how amazing these cakes are,' she said, savouring the cake and registering the burst of flavours in her mouth. Now at least she could remember the taste of what she was chewing, unlike that time around her divorce when she didn't have any idea what she was eating—she wouldn't have noticed it even if it were sawdust.

After breakfast, Chris excused himself to talk with the farmhands, who had started trickling in for work, giving Sandy some time to herself. She wrapped her hands around her cup and sipped her coffee slowly while evaluating yet again how her erstwhile 'orderly' life—that stretch of time before the curtain of divorce had fallen on her—had changed irreversibly. She had thought she had a handle on things. Everything had been in her control, until it hadn't. Why was life so incomprehensible?

Over the past two years, Sandy had tried to balance her role in the office with her 'new normal' at home as a single parent. She had ensured that Alex didn't miss any of his extracurricular activities, birthday parties and sleepovers, even if she had to skip an office meeting or two so that she could do drop-offs and pick-ups. During this time, Sandy had avoided business trips so that Alex wouldn't be left alone with just the helper. She had created a detailed work plan, ruthlessly pruning out activities in her calendar that added little value, but also making sure she allotted time for self-care. She had declined get-togethers that made no sense to her, but had ensured that she didn't skip her salon appointments. She had delegated tasks such as grocery shopping to the helper, so that she could go to her yoga class. She automated most bill transactions so that she didn't miss any payment deadline. Sandy had done her best to look put-together, such that any outsider didn't have a clue of what she was going through.

Her phone alarm brought Sandy back to the present. She needed to call Alex, who was spending the holidays with Steve this time around. She quickly fished out her phone to speak to Alex, who had gradually accepted their situation. She missed Alex a lot, but she put on her most cheerful tone throughout their conversation. Alex seemed in a good mood as well, telling her about his recent shopping trip for Funko Pops and posters of his favourite comic heroes. Though Steve had failed as a husband, Sandy knew that he genuinely loved Alex and would take care of him well, especially during the holidays.

Sandy got up from her bench and went to look for Chris, who was in the greenhouse, showing new members of his team around. A pink rose by the entrance caught her attention; it looked more delicate than the rest and its petals were still dewy. A small spider web had formed under its sepal. Its threads held a tiny dewdrop, hanging so precariously that a small breeze could easily shake it off. Sandy sighed. She was almost like that dewdrop, suspended, hanging by a thin thread. So much in life could be blown out of balance even by the slightest wayward wind.

Chris broke away from his team and joined Sandy by the doorway. 'So are we on for our road trip of the decade?' he asked.

'Of course. I haven't been to this part for years. I wonder how much of it has changed,' she replied, leading the way back to her car.

'Oh you'd be surprised. What might have been inconceivable just a few years ago, is now very much a reality. New buildings have sprouted in almost every corner. There are now four malls in our district. But in a way, it's good because now I can get my coffee beans without having to go all the way to Baguio or Manila.'

'Well, you're getting the best of both worlds then. You can have your peace and quiet at the farm, at the same time, you're just fifteen minutes away from urban comforts.'

On the drive back to her mother's house, Sandy remembered the dewdrop holding on to the spiderweb. It might have fallen on the waiting soil by now, in which case it would have been absorbed by the roots and become integral to the life of the pink rose. Something good could still come from it. Something good could also come from all this, her current predicament, she thought, as she pulled into the driveway. Just then, her phone flashed a reminder. She had to attend a reunion in two hours. She started pepping herself up for the luncheon party that was being organized by three high school classmates of hers, who were based in Union City, the provincial capital. One classmate now owned the largest electrical appliance store, the other headed a department at the Capitol, and then there was Marian, now a nun at their former Catholic school. Sandy was never keen on these high school get-togethers, having been out of touch with most of her classmates, and she wouldn't have attended this one either, if it weren't for Marian. Sandy found it difficult to say no to someone who wore a habit and a big cross pendant.

Just before noon, Sister Marian picked Sandy up and they drove to a hotel in the city's downtown district. In the ballroom, Sandy was ushered to a table that she shared with Marian and a few other classmates. The programme opened with remarks from their former principal and faculty adviser, followed by a dance number from the organizing committee. Dennis, their host and master of ceremony, soon introduced a video showing clips and collages of their high school pictures and played it while they proceeded to lunch. They were all laughing at one of the clips when Marian suddenly gasped. Then a rush of excitement quickly spread like wildfire across the room. Sandy followed Marian's gaze but before she herself could ask, Dennis grabbed the microphone and announced: 'Well, well, well, look who's here!'

Everyone who wasn't already looking at the door, soon turned their heads toward it. Paul, their class valedictorian who had never confirmed his attendance, was standing there, waving at everyone in the room. He had been so elusive that none of Sandy's batchmates had seen him since their high school graduation. In fact, the room had buzzed with the where-is-Paul-now guessing game just before the programme. When the euphoria subsided, Paul went from one table to the next, greeting their classmates. He came to Sandy's table last, eventually pulling an empty chair between her and Sister Marian.

In high school, Sandy had performed better than Paul academically, but she hadn't got the top award partly because she had refused to join extracurricular activities that could have earned her extra points and boosted her overall class standing. She hadn't been one to humour teachers and had turned down invitations to activities that didn't interest her, even when the teachers had urged her to represent the school in some competitions. She also didn't bother to run for office in their student body organization, which Paul had led in senior year. But their academic rankings aside, Sandy and Paul were more friends than arch-rivals, back then. They used to work together on many projects and even studied together for major exams. In fact, they were oblivious to the ranking system when on their own.

After the customary greetings, Paul updated everyone on their table: he was with a non-profit organization, helping impoverished villagers, women, children and other marginalized groups in and outside the country. He had been to the poorest regions of the Philippines, some parts of Africa and Latin America, as part of a project monitoring and evaluation team that included counterparts from donor agencies like UNICEF, World Bank and Overseas Economic Council for Development, better known as OECD. He also spent some time with OFWs, nurses and domestic workers in the United Kingdom and Italy. But recently, he had taken a sabbatical from work to pursue further studies in community development. Sandy was quietly impressed by all this. In fact, she once thought that Paul might have become a store manager of a fast food or pizza chain, after not having heard from him after their graduation, and knowing that he didn't make it to the state university.

'You haven't said anything about yourself. What's up in your corner?' Paul asked.

'It's a long story.' She didn't want to talk about herself, especially with people she wasn't close to, even if they happened to be her high school classmates. None of the people at her table was Facebook friends with her, except for Marian. But then Paul kept looking at her, waiting for her response. 'So where do I begin,' she said hesitantly.

'How about 16 March 1994—was it? I haven't seen you since then, can you imagine?' Paul shook his head in disbelief.

'Coincidentally, I happened to look at my high school album the other day and I saw this photo of us on the stage, taken after we had received our medals and certificates. It has that date at the bottom of the photo. How could you remember it after all these years? Before this reunion, I couldn't even remember what year that was,' Sandy said.

'I remember it for many reasons, some of them a bit too personal,' he replied.

By then, Marian had joined the exchange and made an effort to fill Paul in about Sandy, who clearly didn't want to say much about herself. Sandy was the only one in their batch who had attended the country's top state university. Over time, she had lost contact with her classmates, except for Marian, who used to visit her at her dormitory. After college, she and Marian emailed or called each other regularly if they couldn't meet up. Sandy hadn't found any compelling reason to reach out to her other classmates.

'Wow. But then again, I'm not surprised at how much you've achieved and early in your career, too,' Paul commented after Marian mentioned that Sandy was a 'big-time' regional director at a global nutrition company.

'It's all the hard work and sleepless nights,' Sandy replied, still embarrassed at people thinking that she was a big fish just because she had the word 'director' in her title.

'Still, it's a regional role and that's no mean feat. And what about your family? I heard you have a son?' Paul asked.

'Right. I have a twelve-year-old son who means the world to me. But I'd rather not talk about family now,' Sandy replied before taking a sip of her nearly empty glass of wine.

'Oh it's okay, we can talk about it another time,' Paul said, refilling her wine glass. 'Do you want to check out the courtyard garden?' He offered, seeing that Marian had left her seat to coordinate the programme with Dennis. Sandy nodded. Paul carried her glass for her while she got up from her chair and they both stepped out into the nearby garden, catching up with their other batchmates who were also out for fresh air.

'I've always wondered why you were out of touch all these years, as though you've completely vanished from the face of the earth,' she said when they reached a quieter spot.

'Look who's talking. We all know who's the real elusive one here,' he replied.

'At least people knew where I was.'

'Fair enough. In my case, I just felt that although I was the class valedictorian, somehow the batch didn't have faith in me; they didn't believe that I could be successful after high school.'

'Really? That's odd. And why would you think that?'

'You probably haven't heard the whispers and rumours. Fortunately, or unfortunately, I have Dennis who updated me regularly,' Paul explained.

'What kind of rumours?'

'Like I only became valedictorian because my mum used to curry favour with the teachers. They made a big deal about her bringing tubs of ice cream on teachers' day.'

'That's nasty.'

'Actually, that's a milder one. Do you want to hear the really nasty ones?'

'I'm not so sure . . .' Sandy avoided gossip as much as possible.

'Oh but you should. Here's another example. They said that however much I'd put my feet on a block of ice to stay awake and study, I could never match your intelligence and cleverness.'

'What?' Sandy almost choked on her wine.

'Yes. For years, those rumours hounded me and, in a way, have somewhat impaired me.'

'What do you mean? Like you had a meltdown?'

'Not like a nervous breakdown. I still had control of my mental faculties. But I lost confidence in myself. I avoided mingling with my college classmates. I barely talked in class for fear of being judged. I started having social anxiety. Fortunately, I met this mentor who helped me gradually overcome my insecurities.'

'But who started all those rumours? And why would you believe them in the first place?'

'I must confess that I felt they held a tiny grain of truth. It's true, for example, that I've tried many tricks to stay awake at night,' Paul laughed at the memory. 'But as most rumours go, the spreader only needed a dash of truth for it all to be believed. And this tiny bit was added to a cauldron of balderdash to make it sound credible,' Paul said.

'I stayed up countless of nights, too.'

'Right, I remember we compared notes on that also,' he chuckled. 'But listen to this. Not only did I place a block of ice under my feet all night, apparently I also padded around our balcony in my white pajamas in the dead of night, shouting out mnemonics for the periodic table in chemistry.'

'Seriously? This is beyond nasty.'

'They were mostly fake news, of course. But anyway, that kind of talk doesn't hurt me anymore. I've realized that even if I could never be as clever as you, I have my own strengths and could do meaningful things, too.'

'I can't believe this. I'm far from brilliant. And I never thought I could unknowingly cause someone so much heartache,' Sandy's eyebrows furrowed.

'It wasn't your fault. You just happened to be the yardstick that people compared me to. Anyway, I got over it a long time ago. I felt so liberated after that,' Paul smiled. 'So now, let's talk about you.' He waited for her to say something. 'Come on, Sands, it's just me, your old pal. Remember the old times?'

He reminded her of those moments during their study breaks when they would talk about random topics and occasionally confide in each other about their apprehensions.

Sandy looked away before saying, 'I divorced my husband last year.'

'I'm so sorry. But is that even allowed here?' Paul asked.

'We got married in Singapore. So yes, it's possible and it has happened to me. Here I am, Exhibit A,' she pointed at herself.

'I'm sure it's not solely your fault. It takes two to tango as they say.'

'My friends said the same. Anyways, enough about me. Back to you, do you have a family?'

'I have a partner. Livia is a Polish nurse whom I met in the UK. She is at my parents' house now. I'd asked her to come along but she thought I'd be better off doing this on my own.'

'Kids?'

'Nope. I've not been lucky in that department,' he said. 'Until when are you here?' he asked, changing the topic as they joined other classmates on the way back to the ballroom for the next part of the programme.

'This Friday.'

'Great. Then we can still meet up early next week and talk like old times?'

'Yes, of course,' she said as they exchanged numbers and promised to stay in touch.

At their meetup, Paul encouraged Sandy to talk. When Sandy started, she couldn't stop and before she realized it, she had told Paul about how her marriage had unravelled.

'He's such an idiot. I don't know him but I feel like hitting him hard on the head,' Paul clenched his fists as he said so.

The talking didn't solve her problem, but Sandy felt somewhat lighter after.

Early the next day, Chris picked up Sandy for their 'epic' road trip, which was really just an hour's drive from their town. But then again, distance was relative. Without the traffic jams of the big cities, the car could easily traverse about eighty kilometres of countryside scenery. They zoomed by treelined highways, mangroves and the sea, that at times, looked like a blur. Sandy was reminded how fun road trips were with Chris. They listened to a Café del Mar playlist, at times singing along and breaking into a duet. In between, they reminisced about their childhood trips to the nearby beach in the summer. How Chris craved the colourful fruits of summer like watermelons, mangoes and pomelo. They used to stop by roadside fruit stands, where their mother, Solita, would haggle hard with the vendor, but would eventually buy most, if not all, of the produce, which she would later share with their neighbours. The thought of Solita trying to be tough while negotiating made Sandy feel proud of her mum. Solita had single-handedly raised Sandy and Chris after her husband, an army colonel, had died in an ambush.

After an hour or so of greenery, they stopped at a newly opened resort. Chris took Sandy for a quick tour before leading her to the restaurant at the back of the property, where he had reserved a table facing the beach for them. The mere sight of the variety of fishes at the buffet table excited Sandy. She could never find this variety of dried fishes elsewhere, the tiny ones that tasted like dilis, and the medium-sized ones that were slightly longer than danggit, but much saltier. Here in her province, they normally fried the small fish with lots of onions and tomatoes to reduce its saltiness. This being a day of decadence, Sandy decided to scoop out fried rice to go with her fried fish.

Chris' eyes widened when he saw the heap of food on her plate and Sandy simply shrugged her shoulders. After coffee, they spent the best part of the afternoon simply lounging by the quiet beach, a well-kept secret of surfers in the region.

'Ah, this is life as it should be.' Sandy grinned in her cozy position on her lounger. She had taken off her wide-brimmed rancher's hat earlier and kept it beside her drink on the side table. She pushed her sunglasses up her head and turned to look at Chris.

'Indeed, this is one of the reasons I came back. Life doesn't always have to be a busy highway,' Chris answered, removing his shades and pressing his index and middle fingers on his nose bridge.

'I'm happy you finally acted on that long-standing wish,' Sandy blew him a kiss. She put her sunglasses back and leaned back on the lounger. They both looked out at the sea. It was mid-afternoon and still a couple of hours before the surfers started trickling back in. The air was still and the waves lapped at the shore gently and rolled down into the sea at regular intervals. As though lulled by this rhythm, both Sandy and Chris stayed quiet for some time, each resting in their own mental space. Sandy simply stared into the blueness of the water, letting her thoughts drift like the waves. This kind of blue calmed her. It made her feel as though everything was alright with the world, even her own world. Sandy instinctively raised her chin and straightened her back. She had stored enough courage to brave the world that awaited her in the new year.

Chapter 4

Singapore, 2015: Restarting

Back in Singapore, Sandy had expected her first two weeks after the Christmas holidays to be calm and uneventful. The office had this uncharacteristic lull as many of her colleagues extended their holidays, making this time conducive for assessing the prior year and re-strategizing for the year ahead.

While all was quiet in her office, Sandy was surprised to hear that Steve was in town and was begging to meet her. After two years of avoiding him and ignoring his telephone calls, Sandy eventually agreed to meet him at a café near her office in Tanjong Pagar. As soon as their coffee orders were served, Steve immediately begged her to remarry him, if only for Alex's sake. 'I won't stop asking until you say yes,' he said, leaning forward on the table.

'Look, Steve, it's been some time. We're doing perfectly fine without you.' She silently blamed herself for breaking her resolve to stay away from him. If only her visit back home had not calmed her and that she hadn't put down peace and reconciliation as her resolutions for the year, she wouldn't have found herself in this position.

'But don't you think Alex needs my presence? He's at an age when the presence of a father is ever more crucial,' he said earnestly.

'You should have thought of that before frolicking with your maid,' she snapped.

'I've already suffered enough because of that. I'm not stupid enough to do it all over again. Besides, I've tried, but I truly can't live without you, Sands,' he clasped his hands together as he begged.

Sandy looked him in the eye. 'Steve,' she said in her most serious tone. 'I'm sorry, but I've moved on,' she deliberately spoke slower to ensure Steve understood. 'Reconciliation is out of the question. Not even for Alex's sake.'

Steve gulped the remaining coffee in his mug. 'How could you react with so much equanimity. I was hoping that the last couple of years would have made you kinder. But it's done the opposite. You are heartless.' He stood hurriedly, took out a fifty-dollar note from his wallet and left it on the table before huffing away.

Sandy stayed on at the coffee shop long after Steve had left. Over the past two years, she had forced herself to keep on recalling things that had led to her divorce Steve. This had kept her steadfast in her resolve not to reconcile with him, despite his constant pleas. For the most part, she had successfully blocked memories of the Steve that she had loved—the Steve from their earlier acquaintance and marriage. But sometimes, a moment of weakness would overwhelm her and she would remember. He used to be dependable and truly attentive to her and Alex. How he would come home early on some days and would cheerfully cook dinner for the family. And how on some wedding anniversaries, he would blindfold her and take her to some of the places she could only dream of. One time, she had casually mentioned a much-talked-about rooftop restaurant and the next thing she knew, Steve flew her to Bangkok and took her to the famous Michelin-starred restaurant for their anniversary celebration. And how he would surprise her with a gift certificate for some craft classes that she had been wanting to enrol into. Occasionally, he would also buy tickets to theatres for her and a friend if he could not watch plays with her. Steve did really pay attention to her earlier on in their relationship. So when did the love end? Sandy considered mapping their relationship timeline year-by-year and month-by-month to know when exactly his love started to wane. That is to assess if love had declined gradually and not abruptly. And what was her role in all this? Wasn't marriage a two-way street? When did she stop loving? Was it at that particular moment when she caught Steve with Elena in the pool? Did love die instantly on that shameful Sunday morning? What did that say about her love for Steve? Or had love begun to wane much earlier in their marriage, when their power balance shifted with the addition of a child to the equation?

Sandy asked the waiter for the check and left Steve's fifty-dollar note, even though their bill only amounted to a fraction of that. 'Let one person be happy today,' Sandy thought on her way out as she acknowledged the server who thanked her profusely.

Chapter 5

Singapore, 2015: Side-trip

Sometimes it still amazed Sandy how some people who had long been absent from her life would suddenly reappear and be ever more present. In April, Paul came to Singapore for a conference and arranged to meet her for dinner. She chose a Japanese restaurant on the ground floor of the Marina Bay Sands Shoppe for this, so that they could sit outside if the weather was pleasant. When she arrived at the restaurant, Paul was already sitting by their reserved al fresco table, going over the menu. 'Great to see you again,' Sandy extended her hand in greeting. She took off her maroon Jim Thompson scarf, sensing the balmy weather. She draped her scarf carefully over her Prada tote bag and straightened her black DVF wrap dress before sitting on the chair that Paul had pulled out for her.

'Thanks to the work conference, we get to meet again,' he greeted her cheerfully as he passed the drinks list to her. 'What will you have?'

'I'll have their house tea for now. With lemon,' she said, closing the leatherbound list.

Paul placed their beverage order and resumed poring over the dinner menu. After he had given the rest of their order to the waiter, he straightened in his chair and focused his full attention on Sandy. 'So how have you been?' he asked.

'Same old, same old. It's peak season at work and I'll be travelling a bit. In fact, I have a flight tomorrow. Good thing we're meeting today, otherwise I wouldn't have been able to make it,' she shared.

'Oh wow, I'm truly lucky then. It's just my first day here, so I thought I'd meet you before anyone else,' he said before taking a sip of his cocktail. 'Where are you off to this time?'

'London,' she replied. Paul frowned suddenly. 'What happened?' she asked.

'Livia. She's back in London.'

'Until when?'

'I don't know.'

'Why aren't you with her then?'

'She said she needs some space. She might have been overwhelmed by her visit to the province. Not by the place, but more by the family. I don't think she's used to staying with an extended family. I mean, as it is, I have my quirks. Multiply that by six, and they were all there for her to see,' he added.

'I don't see anything wrong with that. Everyone has quirks. But I'm sorry to hear that she reacted that way.'

'I don't know. I guess she's a bit conflicted. On the one hand, she says she needs space. On the other hand, she also wants us to get married soon.'

'Marriage is a natural progression in serious relationships. So what's stopping you?'

'I know I'm way past marrying age, so I can't even say I'm too young for it,' he sighed. 'I've realized that I'm not the marrying kind. There are some things I can't give up.'

'When did she say she needs space?'

'After I told her that I'm not ready for marriage.'

'Give her time. If she truly loves you then she'll be more patient,' she said, though in the back of her mind, she doubted if love was truly patient.

'I can't explain it but I feel drained. Our on-and-off relationship can get tiring, at times. I've never felt like settling down and I don't want to do something I'm not 100 per cent sure of.'

'Maybe you just haven't met the right girl yet?' She blurted and instantly wanted to take it back because it sounded cheesy.

'Maybe that's the problem.' He told her about similar patterns with his earlier relationships. 'Lest you think of me as a womanizer, I want you to know that I'm a monogamist and in my previous relationships, I've always been very focused and I've loved my partners deeply,' he said.

'How did you get over your past relationships?' she probed. 'And don't they ever come back to haunt you? Not physically, but mentally, for example. How do you deal with the memories? And in your case, overlapping ones, perhaps?'

'Sands, you know what this reminds me of?' He pointed at the two of them talking seriously. 'Study breaks. When you used to grill me about anything under the sun,' he chuckled. 'Anyways, I don't have the answer to all your grown-up questions. But let me tackle the easiest one. I've had memory floods—and jumbled ones, at that. I try to dull them with a drink or two. I can't count the number of nights I lay wide awake trying to drown out unwanted memories.'

'That sounds tough.'

'It is, and it's not something I'd wish on anyone. How I wish everything was still hypothetical like it used to be when you asked me questions during our "cafeteria series",' he added.

'How did you get over your past relationships?' Sandy reminded him of the first question.

'I don't think I've ever got over any of my past relationships. I still carry the scar from my first one. And the second one. And from all the others. Each of them is a part of me now that I can't undo,' he stared at his palms.

'Do you have a favourite among your past girlfriends?'

'I do, but I can't tell you who.'

'Oh you don't have to tell me, I don't know any of them anyway. I'm merely curious about what made her your favourite.'

'I guess it had something to do with my life stage at that time. I had fewer worries about work. I was less insecure and more carefree. I had the headspace as much as the heart space for my partner, then.'

Soon, the waiter served their food and for a while, they talked about their travel experiences before resuming with their topic *du jour*: failed relationships.

'At what point did you feel ready to start anew? Like what were the cues?' she asked.

'I try not to overanalyse things, Sands. I guess in most of the cases, the opportunity presented itself and I simply grabbed it. I let the waves carry me. Maybe that's why I keep drowning when it comes to relationships,' he said, reaching out for his drink. 'What about you?'

'I've only had one relationship so far. And I can't seem to get over its failure. I blame myself, most of the time. I should have paid more attention to it,' she said, putting away the rest of her panna cotta.

'Are you regretting leaving the person or your concept of the perfect marriage?

Sandy drew a question mark with her index finger.

'You might be blaming yourself if you've considered marriage as another project. A project that you could excel at, just like in school or at work,' he explained. 'But relationships are different. They involve people. And emotions. You can't control them.'

'I still can't accept the fact that I failed.'

'Would it be easier to accept if you had failed at work? Or at school?'

'I came to terms with the fact that I didn't graduate as a valedictorian in high school.'

'Oh that was different. The stakes were much lower. Besides, everybody knew that you were the smartest one. You didn't need a certificate for that.'

'I'm not sure that's true. But what's true is that because of what happened, I strove much harder in university and at work. I wanted the validation so much.'

'Precisely. Which brings me back to my point. Would it have been easier if you had failed at work instead?'

Sandy sighed deeply. She was starting to understand herself. But before she could say anything, the waiter came with their check and Paul quickly grabbed it and paid for their dinner.

'Thanks for the dinner, though, I should be taking care of it because you've come to Singapore. You're my guest,' Sandy explained.

'Oh please,' he insisted. 'I did the inviting. Next time will be on you. Besides, I truly appreciate our chats. You've made me think about my past relationships. I wish I'd have evaluated things earlier. I could have avoided lots of missteps. But better late than never.'

Sandy felt the conversation was illuminating for her, too, as she got glimpses into Paul's experience that could hopefully shine a light on her situation.

On her flight to London, the next day, Sandy remembered Paul's question. Had she really prioritized work over marriage? Was she ever fully in love with Steve? Did she ever make any of her sacrifices for him out of love, rather than out of duty? Did she ever consider marriage as a secondary project? She certainly put in more effort into being a mother than a wife. But why couldn't Steve support her more? Make it his priority, too, to help her succeed as a mother and as a professional?

How did Steve see her in this marriage? Did he expect her to subordinate her needs to his? And didn't Sandy expect him to do that for her, too? After all, she was used to getting support from people around her, starting from her mother, who had made it her priority to provide whatever Sandy needed in school, to her assistants in the office who promptly delivered whatever inputs she requested from them.

Was Paul right in pointing out that perhaps Sandy considered her marriage as just another trophy, an extension of her academic and professional achievements?

The entire week while she was in London, Sandy managed to push aside thoughts about her relationship status or the lack of it. It was easier to do that when there were more urgent requests to attend to, not to mention physical reminders in the office like the timelines on the whiteboards, the constant ping of alerts and emails, the conference calls and the back-to-back meetings that stretched on late into the evening. By the time Sandy reached her hotel in Knightsbridge, she barely had energy left to drag herself to her room and take a quick shower before bed. She would send a quick message to Alex, reminding him to call her before he left for school, and then would hit the pillows immediately. The days after that were simply a repeat of this. When she left London on Friday midnight, she realized she hadn't even stepped into Harvey Nichols, even though it was right next to her hotel and she walked past it every day on her way to and from the office.

Back in Singapore, all the thoughts that Sandy had temporarily pushed aside, came flooding back, especially when Alex was at football practice and the house felt quiet and empty. She had been pacing around their flat for probably the fifth time now. Her helper, Rona, even asked if she was searching for something when Sandy went into the kitchen several times within an hour. Sandy wasn't looking for anything specific. Not for material things, anyway. She was searching for a resolution to her current emotional state. She was contemplating reconciling with Steve, though she knew that this was only hypothetical. With their combined income, they could live in a larger home again. She also didn't have to worry about Alex constantly. Steve could do the pick-up from school when Alex couldn't take the regular school bus because of extracurricular activities. But then again, did she still love Steve? Did she ever love him in the traditional sense? She hadn't been longing for him in the past couple of years. She also enjoyed having the bed all to herself. She didn't need to adjust and accommodate another warm body. She didn't have to keep on cleaning the bathroom. Steve had a tendency to be messy, he used to leave trails of his clothes and socks in their room. He splashed water everywhere whenever he used the bathroom. He was too much of a mental load, actually. And he didn't carry his weight around the house, especially towards the latter part of their marriage. Sandy only needed to remember this to be fully convinced for the nth time that she made the right decision when she refused to reconcile with him.

But why was Sandy considering the pros and cons of getting back with Steve at all? Was she ready for another relationship? Was she over that liminal space after her divorce and the long gap before the next relationship, whether with Steve or someone else? What about Paul? Not that he had ever explicitly expressed romantic interest in Sandy, though she couldn't help but think of him in that light anyway. After all these years and after his many travels, Paul didn't seem to have gained much outward polish. He wore old-fashioned clothes. When every other fashionista his age proudly went around in slim jeans and the latest colourful trainers, Paul could be seen in his old-fashioned, wide-seamed Levi's jeans paired with black leather shoes. He also carried a nylon cross-body bag when he would have appeared more polished with a man purse. Sandy pinched herself. She shouldn't be mean. But when it came to the quality of their conversation, Paul wasn't as provincial as she had initially thought. He was insightful.

He was also a good listener and didn't hog their conversations, unlike others who pretended to listen but were actually mentally rehearsing their responses. Sandy shouldn't judge people by their physical appearance or packaging. She took another sip of water and finally stopped pacing around the house. She switched on her turntable and sat on the cocoon chair near the balcony as she listened to her favourite Miles Davis album.

Her condo wasn't as large as their earlier house, but Sandy was contented with how things were arranged neatly, according to her own liking. She still had their old sofa, but she had done away with the heavy chests from earlier. She disposed of Steve's recliner, his glass and leather display cabinet, his cocktail-serving trolley, among others. The palette around the house was also a more soothing shade of bluish grey, with less of the darker tones that Steve favoured. For now, Sandy would focus on creating a loving home for Alex and herself. She wasn't ready to share this space with another person, whose quirks she would have to adapt to. Sandy wanted to be free to write the next chapter in her narrative. She had several roles to play—a mother, a career woman, a friend and a daughter, to name a few. She would continue to be all these. But what she wasn't ready for, was to be another person's shadow. She was about to go deeper into her introspection when her phone alarm went off—a reminder for her scheduled call with Tintin. She could not wait to flesh things out with her, who normally had the best relationship advice among all her roommates. After all, Tintin had the right to be the relationship guru, having had the longest relationship among the four roommates.

Chapter 6

Happenstance isn't always what it first seems, in the same way that a collision or an alignment of heavenly bodies is sometimes seen as a 'miracle', but is, in fact, an inevitable and deliberate course, following an unseen force and an unseen timeline. Sandy thought this applied to life, too. Later that year, Paul travelled for a United Nations project conference in Bangkok, where Sandy also happened to be, for her company's event. On her last night in the city, she met Paul for dinner— her treat, this time, as they had agreed earlier. Then they went to a bar that featured a live band, which turned out to be composed mainly of Filipino musicians. Both enjoyed the band's repertoire so much that they decided to stay on until their last song.

Without realizing it, Sandy leaned cozily onto Paul when the band changed their tempo and played Eraserhead's '*Ang Huling El Bimbo*'. Paul pulled her closer to him, lifted her chin gently and looked deeply into her eyes. 'Isn't it weird how we become more sentimental when away from the motherland,' Paul said.

'I know. I used to ignore this band, but here I am now, trying my damnedest best to recall the lyrics of this song,' she said, her fingers tapping the table gently to the tempo of the song.

'It must be the distance; it makes us more aware of how far we are from home.'

'Absence makes the heart grow fonder, as they say,' she chuckled. She couldn't help but giggle. Perhaps it was the effect of her third or fourth glass of margarita, she couldn't remember anymore.

'And do you believe in that?'

'Not by a long shot. I prefer presence. I need presence. I need someone to be present for me to love him or her.'

Sandy might have drunk more than she could manage because she almost tripped over when she got up from her seat after the band's performance. Paul rushed to her side and put his arm around her waist as he led the way out. He insisted on seeing her off to her hotel, given her condition. At that point, Sandy didn't argue anymore and simply revelled in not having to make a decision.

On her return flight to Singapore the next day, Sandy peered out her window and was soon absorbed by the shifting scenes on the ground. As the plane took off, Bangkok's buildings and towers were gradually reduced to miniatures. One of them was the hotel she had stayed at—it was in the middle of all those concrete high-rises, indistinguishable in this urban sprawl. Soon, the entire city was shrouded by the thick clouds that were now below, as the plane soared 20,000 feet above sea level. The flight attendant came with her trolley and Sandy mindlessly accepted the white wine she offered. It was unlike her to drink on a flight, and even more so on a short flight. But she wanted something to quieten her jumbled thoughts, and this was the only thing that came to mind within the confines of the plane. She sipped her wine slowly and held on to her glass for some time. She looked out the window once more and wished that some memories, too, would now be blurred by distance, in both time and space.

Sandy reclined her seat and closed her eyes. She couldn't help but think of Steve and her situation again. It occurred to her that if ever they got back together, they would run into another power imbalance. After all, in their marriage, one party had been clearly in the wrong. Any future misunderstanding would likely be blamed on Steve because of his earlier guilt. It would be a relationship of supplication. It wouldn't be based on equality, which was the hallmark of an enduring relationship. But what if both parties were guilty of wrongdoing, wouldn't that reinstate the balance? Could two wrongs make a right?

Chapter 7

Hong Kong, 2016: Detour

When she was younger, Sandy thought that two years was an infinite stretch of time, like an endless highway that led to nowhere. Two endless school years filled with ennui, broken only by a few special occasions, like her birthday and Christmas. Now that she was much older, two years could pass by easily like a blur. In that stretch of time, she had reconnected with old acquaintances and disconnected from a few, too. It had been almost two years since Sandy had last met Steve at a Tanjong Pagar coffee shop near her office. Since then, Sandy had asked him to talk straight to Alex. After all, Alex was now fourteen years old, self-possessed, and mature beyond his years. Any other communication that didn't directly involve Alex, were routed through Sandy's lawyer. She then found it strange to receive a call from Steve, especially during office hours, midweek.

'Sands, there's something I need to tell you,' he said almost too softly, and Sandy had to press her mobile phone closer to her ears to hear him better.

'Steve, what a surprise. How are you?' she asked without giving away any emotions.

'Sands, I'm not well. I've just gone through a series of medical tests,' he replied.

'Tests? For what?' she asked, suddenly concerned about Steve. 'Steve, you've got to tell me whatever it is. What did the doctors say?'

'I have cancer,' he replied.

'Say that again? What kind?' She grabbed the edge of her desk for support.

'Prostate.'

'Aren't you too young for that, Stevie?' She called him by his nickname without realizing it.

'I don't know, Sands. I thought I'd been extremely conscious about my health and nutrition, so I don't understand any of this,' Steve said. 'I haven't told anyone else,' he started sniffling.

'Oh God, Steve, don't cry. What stage? Never mind, we'll figure out something,' she tried to reassure him. 'I'm sure it can be treated. There's so much progress in cancer treatment and technology nowadays.'

'I hope so too. I couldn't take everything in, so I asked for a break from my consultation with the oncologist. Sands, I need your help,' Steve begged. 'I can't do this alone. Please, could you come? I wouldn't ask this of you if I had another person in mind. I need to ask the doctors about treatment options.'

'I'll be right there,' she said instantly.

'Thank you. You have no idea how much I need you now. Please don't tell Alex any of this without me,' he pleaded.

'I won't. I'll tell him it's a business trip so that he won't get suspicious,' Sandy said, still leaning on her desk. She sighed, deeply unaware that it was audible on the other end.

'I'm sorry, Sands, I didn't want to put you through any of this.'

'Steve, I might be cruel as you had said earlier, but not in situations like this. Regardless of what we have against each other, we still have Alex between us.'

The following week, Sandy found herself disembarking in Hong Kong. She hadn't wanted Steve to come and pick her up from the airport, but he had insisted. She saw him near the gate as she was heading toward the arrival door. He stood there in his long black coat and was looking gaunter than she had expected. Sandy didn't hesitate to hug him when he welcomed her. 'Thanks for coming,' he said before taking her luggage from her hand.

'You don't have to do that for me.'

'I want to. I'm not that weak yet,' he insisted. 'I'm sorry, though, if I'm looking as awful as I feel,' he added despondently. He led her through the exit to the platform for the express train.

'Of course not, you don't look any different from before, except for the weight loss,' she reassured him. After two minutes, the express train arrived. Sandy found a couple of vacant seats and went for the window seat. Steve sat beside her. He patted Sandy's hands gently and thanked her again for coming. Soon, their voices were drowned out as the train hurtled forward. Steve looked straight ahead, constantly checking the beeping of the red dot above the door that indicated the next stops. Sandy looked out of the window. She couldn't remember anymore the last time she was in this city; it was most likely for a short conference, making it unmemorable. The airport express seemed slower than she remembered. Or maybe it was just her. Right at this moment, she felt like running. Running as fast as she could. She didn't understand why, but there were times like now when she couldn't sit still. But soon, they were out of the airport complex and she exhaled slowly upon seeing the more familiar peaks and harbours. She shifted in her seat to get a better view. She liked Hong Kong's varied terrains. It had character that way. For a moment, she forgot about the reason for her visit. She turned to Steve and squeezed his hands, wishing that she could transmit energy and strength into him. Steve nodded and smiled gently, as though he understood.

Soon, they entered Central Hong Kong with its competing high-rises and constant bustle everywhere. Sandy had outgrown that stage when crowded shops drew her curiosity—it was likely an end-of-season sale. Steve soon pointed at the next station, Central Station, where they were to disembark. From there, they took a cab to Repulse Bay. Sandy had insisted on booking herself into a hotel, but Steve had assured her that he had an extra room in his flat. It was just for one night anyway, he had said. Besides, he couldn't be a threat to anyone in his health condition.

That night, Sandy and Steve had dinner at a Cantonese restaurant, a few blocks from Steve's flat. She mindlessly chewed her noodles while Steve barely touched his congee. Even their dumplings lay cold on the table. Back at Steve's flat, neither remembered what they had eaten for dinner. Steve went into the kitchen to make some tea. After a few minutes, he came back to the drawing room and placed the tea tray on the coffee table. 'I still can't understand why this happened to me,' Steve said.

Sandy was standing by the glass window, taking in the stunning skyline along the bay in the southern part of Hong Kong. She turned around when she heard him. 'Steve, you know that cancer doesn't discriminate. It can strike anyone. It's downright unfortunate but it's not your fault.'

'Maybe I deserve it for all the things I've done to you.' He poured tea into a cup and handed it to Sandy before pouring another for himself.

'Come on, you know very well there's no such thing. No immediate karma, anyway. Don't be too fatalistic. It doesn't suit you.' Sandy came to sit on the sofa.

'I still regret whatever I've done to you,' he said from the armchair adjacent to her. 'I regret it every single day,' he looked away.

'It's all water under the bridge now.' The wall adjacent to the sofa caught Sandy's gaze. It was adorned with framed photos from some of their favourite vacations. She stood and moved closer to have a better look. 'I didn't know you had these photos with you,' she said wistfully as memories of their togetherness flooded back.

'I have the same one on my nightstand. It's the first thing I look at every day. Initially, I thought it was to punish myself. To remind me of what I've lost because of my folly and stupidity,' he paused to take a sip from his cup. 'But even after having come to terms with all that, simply looking at the photos gives me utter pleasure,' he smiled pensively. 'Looking at the faces of the two most important people to me, calms me down.'

'We look so young here, don't we?' she noted, staring longer at a photo taken in Tokyo, which was Alex's favourite childhood holiday destination.

'And genuinely happy, too. We didn't know yet that a few years later, I would give in to the dumbest of temptations,' he said sighing.

'I have this tendency to classify things as either black or white. To me, you've made a gross error and that was it. But age brings on a new perspective. I now try to look at things from several lenses,' she said before inhaling. 'I've been meaning to ask you this, how did it happen? You and Elena?' she asked, trying to sound disinterested, though inside, she felt this ineffable weight in her chest that kept growing heavier since she had arrived in Hong Kong.

'It wasn't Elena's fault. I'm fully accountable for that huge mistake and it's mine alone,' he said, looking out the glass window. 'It was a moment of weakness. I was pressured by my ambition, I was too competitive in the office. So I guess on any given day, I'd used up all my energy and willpower at the office.'

Sandy, too, put her empty cup back on the coffee table, and joined Steve by the window. Both of them looked out for some time, quietly taking in the nightscape before them. The bay was dark now, but farther on the other side, the neon lights glittered in the distance. Steve turned to look at her. 'The man who came home at the end of each day wasn't me. He was a worse version of myself. Drained of sound judgement or reason,' he added, his eyebrows gathering in.

'Why didn't you tell me this at that time?' she asked. And why didn't she have a clue then?

'I didn't want to lay any blame on anyone else, especially on you. But at that stage, you were travelling more than usual,' Steve said. 'There were nights when I came home and wanted to simply sit and talk to you like old times.' He put his hands over her shoulders. 'But, alas, you weren't there,' he said sadly.

'I'm sorry,' she said, finally. 'I'm sorry if I, too, was busy trying to get ahead at work.'

'If you remember, I asked you to stay at home. I was already earning enough for the both of us and I didn't want you to work that hard anyway, but then you took it differently,' Steve shook his head. 'You thought I was ignoring your contribution to the household; that I was undermining you. That I wanted you to be a stay-at-home wife so that you would be at my beck and call. Sands, you know I'm better than that,' he explained.

'I was dense and insensitive,' she said, her eyes glistening. She wiped the corners of her eyes with the back of her hands.

'Oh Sands, please don't. It wasn't your fault. Even if you had known all this at that time, it still wasn't a good enough excuse for what I did. What I did was extremely deplorable. And I completely understand why you could never forgive me,' he said, pulling her closer to him.

But she had forgiven him. She couldn't bring herself to tell him that she had, in fact, forgiven him. At what point had she realized this? It was certainly not just last week, because she wouldn't have answered his phone call if she hadn't yet forgiven him then.

In the quietness of her room in Steve's flat, Sandy tried to recall when the exact moment was. It was at Alex's school performance when he had played the drums during the percussion segment of a musical concert. She had been sitting close to the stage and couldn't help but be so proud of Alex's dexterity with the instruments. She had wished Steve were beside her then, like earlier, whenever Alex had a school performance. Sandy had been overwhelmed when Alex had returned to the stage to sing part of the closing song, U2's 'One', and it had struck her how Alex looked so much like Steve. How much he had taken after his father. After that, she had realized she couldn't hate Steve forever, especially after having a gift that they shared, in Alex.

The next morning, Steve and Sandy walked down to a nearby café for coffee and croissant. Steve was pensive and Sandy tried not to distract him and signalled only when she finished her coffee. Steve then booked a cab that took them to Gleneagles Hospital.

'I don't know if this is good news or bad news,' the oncologist said, pausing to gauge Steve's reaction.

'Please go ahead, what's your diagnosis?' Steve asked.

'It's stage-III,' the oncologist announced.

'What does that mean?' It was Sandy. She had to be strong for Steve.

'It means the cancer cells have spread out beyond the prostate. But that it can still be treated. That's the good news about stage-III. There's a greater chance of treatment compared to Stage-IV. I have to be honest with you, though, I cannot guarantee total eradication. I don't want to raise false hopes. Both of you seem well-informed and I suppose you know that prostate is one of the more complex cancer types,' he said.

'I understand. What are the treatment options in this case?' Again, it was Sandy who asked the questions, seeing that Steve remained unusually quiet.

'I've prepared three treatment options here,' the doctor asked his assistant to give the three folders to Steve. 'In all those options, radiation and a course of hormone therapy is a basic requirement,' he said and proceeded to explain the pros and cons of each option, including the cost and time implication. 'But as I've said, regardless of the option, there's no guarantee of 100 per cent treatment. There could be a relapse even after successful treatment. But then again, I could name a hundred or so patients who have resumed normal life after winning their battle against cancer.' The doctor left them for a while to talk in private.

'Let's read through the options thoroughly,' she said, looking at the thick files. 'But from what the doctor said just now, it looks like the second one is the best option,' Sandy said.

'What is the second option about?' Steve said, still looking a bit lost.

'The external beam radiation plus brachytherapy, and a course of hormone therapy,' she reminded him.

'How could you remember all those technical terms?' he asked.

'I work with doctors and scientists on a daily basis, remember? Most of them might be food scientists and nutritionists, but I'm used to hearing all these technical and medical terms as they relate to the impact of chemicals on the body,' she replied.

'You've always had a sharp memory. I remember that from our strategic management class. You could play back whatever the professor said during a lecture.'

'Oh please, only when I'm truly interested in the subject. Anyways, coming back to the options. What do you think?'

'Could we please go somewhere quiet and discuss? I'm worried about the compliance as this will take time and might have greater financial implications.'

'Won't your company insurance cover this? After all, it isn't a pre-existing condition.'

'I know. But I don't know how much they would cover. I have to check with HR. In any case, I also have my private insurance that I continue to pay in Singapore. I can use that to supplement the company's healthcare plan, if required.'

'I didn't know about that,' Sandy said. 'Okay, let's discuss the options in a less depressing environment then.' She noticed the light blue motif of the clinic. 'Blue is supposed to be soothing, but not in this case,' she commented.

'There's a coffee shop around the corner.' Steve pointed to the right before opening the door for her.

'I'll call Serene. I need to get her opinion, if that's okay,' she asked.

'Of course. I have high regard for Serene's medical opinion. And among your friends, she's the most knowledgeable in this matter,' he replied.

In the end, Steve and Sandy decided it was best for Steve to come to Singapore for the treatment, as he could use both his company's and his personal insurance to cover the costs at a hospital affiliated with Gleneagles, which could take on Steve's case. Steve didn't really have anyone in Hong Kong to look after him. His part-time Chinese helper couldn't speak proper English and had no training as a caregiver. While he had the option to go back to Sydney for the treatment, his insurance policy could cover only a small portion. Besides, his mother back in Australia now stayed in a care facility, because of her dementia. There was no point worrying her about Steve's condition.

Chapter 8

Having gone on a few detours, in one way or another, Sandy now felt this tendency to overcompensate for the unexpected turns in her life. She needed to resist the temptation to hasten things. She had to remind herself that life wasn't a race. She took a mental note of this again as she joined Alex for their Friday night dinner. She reminded him that Steve would be arriving tomorrow and they would pick him up from the airport.

'Mum, are you getting back with Dad?' Alex asked. He was now aware of Steve's condition and that Steve would be staying with them on some days over the course of his treatment.

'No, honey,' Sandy replied. 'But Dad and I'll always be your family. We're both adult enough to know that in times of need, we must unite and help each other.'

'Have you stopped hating him for what he did?'

'I'd forgiven him sometime back, Alex. We're but human and fallible. Your Dad deserves a second chance, and so we're friends again. But we're not getting back together as a couple.'

'That's definitely better than hostility. I had a horrible time translating for you when you refused to speak to him.'

'I know. I can be stubborn and inflexible, at times. I'll try to be a better version of myself from now on, honey.'

'Thanks, Mum. I know you're doing this for me, more than for Dad or anyone else.'

'You're everything to me, honey. You already know that I'd do anything for you. Besides, I couldn't live with myself if I left your Dad alone in his condition. Also, I still care for him, though not necessarily as a partner.'

Sandy and Alex picked Steve up from the airport the next day. It was the first time Alex was meeting Steve since learning about his cancer. The two men hugged each other tightly and cried like kids. At nearly six feet tall, Alex certainly towered over Sandy and was now almost as tall as Steve. It also seemed that Alex had grown and become an adult overnight. He had stopped saying he was bored and had become more proactive about his studies, initiating things on his own and conscientiously preparing for his International General Certificate of Secondary Education, or IGCSE exam. Sometimes, Sandy felt an inexpressible pain looking at him. How could someone so young, barely fifteen, go through so much? First, the divorce, and now, Steve's cancer. The previous night, Sandy had wept into her pillow, blaming herself for not having done enough for Alex. She knew that suffering was inextricably linked to existence. Everyone, without exemption, suffered one way or another. But couldn't she at least have cushioned Alex a bit from all the pain? Wasn't that her primary role as a mother? Had she failed in this area as well?

'You've grown taller, young man,' Steve ruffled Alex's hair after releasing him from his embrace.

'I've missed you so much, old man,' Alex replied.

'Come on, let's get going before it starts pouring again,' Sandy said, noting the dark clouds looming over Changi Airport.

Over the next eight weeks, Steve stayed in a cancer facility on weekdays for his daily radiation but joined Sandy and Alex on the weekends, during a break in his therapy. The three largely stayed at home to prevent Steve from being exposed to any germs outside. Being at home together, cooking or simply playing board games or watching Netflix after dinner, had somehow strengthened their bond. Steve also sat with Alex to help him revise for his mock IGCSE exams. One weekend, they were sitting together and started talking about university options for Alex. 'Isn't it too early to talk about that?' Steve asked.

'Of course not, Dad. It's never too early. In fact, some of my classmates have already made some campus visits over the summer,' Alex said.

'Really? I thought we had to do it only in Grade 12,' Sandy said.

'No, Mum. That would be too late. Where have you guys been?' Alex wrinkled his nose.

'And what are you planning to major in?' Sandy asked.

'I really want to do life sciences, Mum, Dad,' he said.

'I'm all for it, honey,' Sandy smiled.

'Same here. So what universities are you considering?' Steve asked.

'I have yet to come up with my top ten. The school requires us to come up with the list. Anyway, my top two are Cambridge and Stanford,' he replied.

'Those are great choices,' Sandy noted.

'There's no harm in aspiring this high, right?' Alex said, raising his arm over his head to demonstrate that it might be beyond him.

'Why "aspiring"? Isn't "aiming" a better term? Those are realistic targets, aren't they?' Sandy asked.

'From academic performance perspective, yes, it's definitely attainable, Mum. Most of my grades are exemplary. But I'm not sure about the financial side . . . I'll apply for financial assistance and scholarship, but the chances of getting one are, as what you old folks would say, like finding a needle in a haystack,' Alex said.

'Why don't you focus on the academic performance, the IGCSE and IB exams, and whatever else is required for you to get in. Let Dad and me worry about the finances,' Sandy gave him a gentle pat.

'I can't, Mum. Especially with Dad's condition,' Alex brows were in a deep furrow.

'Son, you know, regardless of what has happened to Mum and me, we've always done our best, and will continue to ensure you get the best education we can afford. We don't want to deprive you of any opportunities,' Steve said.

'But how will we manage, Dad?' Alex said.

'We will continue to pay the premium of your educational plan, Alex,' Steve said. 'Buying the plan was one thing that Mum and I did right. You make me proud already just by aiming for these lofty goals. I still believe that if you can dream it, you can achieve it,' he said.

'I didn't know about the educational plan. Thanks Mum, thanks Dad,' he said going over to kiss both Sandy and Steve. 'But would it be enough to cover Cambridge?' he said with a wide grin.

'Yes, definitely. It better be, or I'll sell one of my kidneys,' Sandy said.

'Mum, that's a poor joke,' Alex wrinkled his nose in distaste.

'I'm sorry. I didn't mean to be insensitive,' Sandy cringed at her own bad joke.

'Oh please, it still works,' Steve laughed. 'Even in my condition and after hearing it so many times from you in the past.'

After his last radiation therapy, Sandy took Steve and Alex out for dinner in celebration of Steve's 100 per cent compliance with the gruelling therapy sessions. She chose a rooftop restaurant in one of Singapore's tallest buildings.

From the restaurant, they could see the laser light show at Marina Bay Sands. They all revelled at the nightscape and the stunning view of Singapore's central district from this vantage point. It was truly a city of the future.

'I'm so glad I've lived long enough to see this,' Steve teased.

'I'm sure you'll see greater sights in the many years to come, now that your treatment is over,' Sandy said, feeling upbeat herself.

'Dad, you've got long ears. That means you'll live to be 100 or more,' Alex said.

When the waiter came to take their order, Steve stuck to a vegan diet of quinoa, pomegranate and some edible flowers. Sandy ordered pan-seared cod fish with black rice, while Alex opted for his regular burger. And homemade fries. Even in a fancy restaurant.

'Dad, can't you just stay in Singapore?' Alex asked after giving the menu back to the waiter.

'Unfortunately no, son. I have a five-year contract with the company and I still have more than a year to go,' Steve replied.

'But it's so much better with you around. Not that I'm complaining about Mum,' Alex said.

'You better not complain, or else you won't get any breakfast tomorrow,' Sandy joked.

'I need my breakfast, Mum. Every single day,' Alex kissed Sandy on the cheek.

'Why don't you come and stay with me for a couple of weeks after your IGCSE?' Steve suggested.

'Well, I can do that, but that's still many months away,' Alex replied.

'Anyways, I'll be coming down again for the check-ups, for sure,' Steve said.

'Great, I'll get to see you more then. I hope though that they've managed to kill all the cancer cells with all the sessions you've just completed,' Alex said.

'I hope so too. This episode made me realize how precious life is. How short and fleeting,' Steve said. 'But anyway, tonight, let's celebrate this victory and start appreciating each minute that we have with each other,' he said, raising his glass of water in a toast.

'Cheers to life,' Sandy said, raising her glass of wine.

'And my beautiful family,' Alex said clinking his glass of iced tea. At that moment, the laser light show at Marina Bay Sands resumed, and the crystal chandelier in the middle of the room caught Sandy's gaze. She was enthralled by the light's reflection on the chandelier; how the laser lights appeared more multifaceted from this perspective. This chandelier could transform monochromes and make them prismatic. Steve followed her gaze and turned to look at her with his most amused expression. He knew that Sandy was having a 'eureka' moment.

Chapter 9

Singapore, 2017: U–Turn

Reversing and going against the direction of flow negates the distance gained earlier, leading to a loss not just in momentum, but also time—the latter no longer retrievable. But this could be a lifesaving choice. Sandy browsed through a travel magazine while waiting for Paul at a coffee shop at the Changi Airport. He arrived a few minutes later and rattled on about how this airport was far more efficient, compared to all the other airports he'd been to. 'Indeed,' Sandy nodded. 'It absolutely deserves its top spot on those annual airport rankings.'

'How long has it been since Bangkok?' Paul asked, settling on a chair opposite Sandy. He had a stopover on his London trip and had checked earlier if Sandy had time to spare.

'You know what, it feels like a lifetime away. So many things have happened since then,' Sandy said.

'Same here,' he said, pausing when the waiter came to serve their coffee. 'So much has happened, indeed.'

'Do you want to start?'

'Ladies first,' Paul grinned.

'So chivalrous,' Sandy cracked at his one-liner, however cheesy it was. 'I don't mind,' she said, taking a deep breath before recounting what had happened to her and her family, including Steve's health struggle.

'Does that mean you're back together?' Paul asked, leaning forward now, as though not wanting to miss anything that Sandy might have to say.

'We're back to being friends, that's all I can say. I don't want to have any more enemies, Paul. I'm too old for that kind of shit. I've realized that I sleep better when I'm at peace with the world,' Sandy replied.

'Sands, I absolutely agree with you, holding grudges encumbers one on their journey. It drags and slows one down.'

'Right. Take it from the guru. So what's up in your corner?'

'Somehow, it feels like we have been on a parallel journey.'

'What do you mean? Come on, don't be too cryptic. It's just the two of us, you can spill the beans, spell it out,' Sandy continued in her teasing tone. She had been feeling more light-hearted for the past few weeks, since Steve had completed his treatment; now humour came more naturally to her.

'Keep it up, Sandy Sanchez.'

'Don't forget it's still your turn.'

'I'm still with Livia,' he said in a serious tone now. 'Our longest stretch so far.'

'Wow,' Sandy shook his hand. 'Is it for good?'

'Who knows? But I'm hoping. I'm also tired of short-term relationships already. I crave for permanence now.'

'So do I hear wedding bells?'

'You bet.'

'Oh Paul, I'm so happy for you!' Sandy jumped up from her chair and went over to hug Paul tightly.

'I wished we had reconnected earlier, it's so wonderful to have a friend in you, Sands,' Paul said when Sandy settled back on her seat.

'The feeling is mutual. Initially, I thought I don't need any more friends. I have a strong core group in my college roommates. They're more than sufficient. They are my world and they mean the world to me. But then when we started reconnecting, I realized that you offer another perspective.'

'You mean you wouldn't even consider me for a friend if I didn't offer a fresh perspective? No wonder many of our high school batchmates think you're a snob.'

'What, are you serious?'

'And you're so gullible, too. Of course, our poor classmates wouldn't say that out loud, but haven't you noticed that they tend to be mum whenever you're around? They're conscious of what they say in your presence.'

'It never occurred to me. As it is, I have enough on my plate, I don't have the mental space or energy for many other things.'

'That's true, you were never nosy. Even in high school, you had this aura of not caring about others. I'm fortunate, indeed, that I'm back in your orbit and in a positive way.'

'I believe in that old adage that there's a time and season for everything. Had our paths crossed at a different time, we might not have paid attention to each other,' she commented.

'True that. Please come to my wedding?' Paul asked.

'It will be an honour. When is it?' Sandy said.

Chapter 10

Singapore, 2019: Arrival at Destination

Life never comes with a clear roadmap. There might be many routes to a destination, and all of them can be unpredictable. Humps and roadblocks, detours and delays, sharp curves and unexpected turns could be par for the course along one's journey. Sandy felt she had been through all that, but having reached her destination in one piece now, she wouldn't exchange any of her experiences with a predictable, humdrum existence. She was glad she had put Alex at the centre of her map. When the IB examination results came out, Sandy couldn't believe what she saw. Alex had scored forty-four. Not a perfect score, but an impressive one. And what had made her even more elated was the admission letter from Cambridge. It was beyond Sandy's wildest dreams. Steve, who was visiting, was speechless too, looking incredulous. He opened his arms and enveloped Sandy and Alex in them. For both Sandy and Steve, any vestiges of animosity completely dissolved in that moment.

Sandy watched as Alex marched up the stage in the school auditorium to receive his graduation certificate. She sat quietly, trying hard to stem the rivulets of tears that rolled down her cheeks. Steve offered her his handkerchief and held her hand.

'I'm so proud of you,' he whispered.

'He represents the best of both of us. So congrats to you, too,' Sandy replied.

'You've done most of the hard work. And I'm so grateful, Sands. For everything.'

Sandy squeezed his hand, trying to stay focused on Alex, who was now posing for the graduation photos. This milestone transcended their moral failings as his parents—it was as though it completely absolved them from their transgressions. She was profoundly touched by Alex's phenomenal performance. Sandy felt that everything before this moment was now immaterial. The past might be inescapable and would continue to haunt her in unexpected ways, but Sandy realized that her knowledge of the past shouldn't force her into a stasis. She, with her immediate family, could rise above it and live better, despite knowing what they knew. And moments like now made that seem possible.

That night, after Alex's graduation ceremony, Sandy called her mother and Chris, who happened to be together at Solita's house. 'When are you both coming? The graduation party is on this Sunday.'

'Our flight is this Friday. Mummy still needs to have her hair and nails done, we can't miss those critical appointments,' Chris said over Solita's shoulder on the video call.

'Okay fine, you should have got those things done here, then you could have spent more time with us,' Sandy said.

'It's actually Chris who can't leave just yet, he's got a meeting with the provincial government tomorrow, they're going to make his farm into a model organic farm—can you imagine?' Solita excitedly shared the news.

'Congratulations, that's wonderful news! Another reason for us to celebrate,' Sandy said.

'It is, it is. After months of lobbying, it's finally been approved. Can't wait to see you,' Chris said as he blew her a kiss before signing off.

The following morning, Sandy left the house early, while Steve and Alex were still asleep in their respective rooms. She felt overwhelmed and needed time alone to calm herself down. She went for a drive without a clear destination in mind. For some reason, she remembered Paul. In her hotel room after dinner and drinks in Bangkok, Paul had simply sat by the chair near her bedside, holding her hand, waiting for her to wake up. Sandy didn't know anymore how much time he had sat there. But when she had opened her eyes at three o'clock in the morning, she had seen Paul sitting by the window, reading the previous day's issue of *New York Times*.

'Oh, Paul, you didn't have to stay and wait this long,' she had got out of bed in a rush.

'Please, Sands. I didn't want to leave you alone like that,' he had said, handing her the bottle of water from her bedside.

'Oh God, I feel so embarrassed,' she had said after sipping her water.

'Please don't be.' Paul had got up and sat beside her. 'I wanted to be present for you.'

'Paul, I hope I don't read too much into this. I'm a bit vulnerable at this time, as you know.'

'I understand. I'll only go as far as you want me to, I have so much respect for you, as you know,' he had looked intently into her eyes.

Sandy snapped out of her introspection when she realized she had reached a crossroad near Katong Road. She eventually found herself at her favourite church along Sandy Lane. She parked the car and practically ran up the steps to the adoration chapel on the second floor. The room was empty. She chose the pew closest to the altar. She knelt for some time until she could feel tears in the corners of her eyes. Knowing she was alone, she let the tears flow freely. She could never thank God enough for the grace of having Alex. She hadn't failed as a mother, after all—the principal reason why she was here on this earth. It didn't matter if she had failed in other areas, in her other roles.

Part III

Serene

Chapter 1

Life, in its real essence, is shorter than a biological lifespan. As a doctor, Serene understood this only too well, clinically. And though homo sapiens could now live to 100, they still lagged behind some other species, which could live up to 200 years, like Darwin's tortoise, for example. Even if man could reach a century, his 'real life' span could be shortened by illnesses. And regrets. If Serene had to calculate the 'real life' years of a person, she would start with sixty-five years, the average lifespan. Then she would deduct ten years of unhealthy life, a number that was admittedly significant in the Philippines, given the high prevalence of metabolic diseases like high blood pressure and diabetes, that undoubtedly compromised one's quality of life. That left fifty-five healthy years—if one were lucky. Many suffered from years of emotional or psychological issues, which Serene denoted as the 'miserable years' in her equation. According to her 'epidemiological study', these issues were more common in some couples than others, likely induced by arranged marriages or overstaying in a union that had run its course. This further reduced 'real life' to the first twenty-five years—the years before marriage. Whenever someone questioned how Serene could claim that life is short, she would take them through this calculation. Most would lose interest

161

by the time she got to metabolic diseases. Or they found it more convenient to simply ignore the harsh reality.

Years ago, when Serene was still a medical resident working in operating theatres, she had been tempted occasionally to play god and grant the wishes of some families for her patients to live longer. After all, her profession was concerned with the prolonging and extension of life. But Serene had soon realized that she was only mortal, with limited capabilities to prevent some tragedies. When a patient was critically ill, his family members weren't the only ones who were in distress. The entire medical team suffered during the tumultuous period filled with uncertainties. Doctors wouldn't hesitate to deploy everything in their arsenal to restore a patient's vitals to normal. Nothing gives doctors greater gratification than having lifelines restored to green. Conversely, when those lines flatten, the depth of despair is amplified even more by the utter silence of the Intensive Care Unit or ICU, where doctors would be like soldiers in the aftermath of a lost battle. Tired. Broken. Worthless. Some doctors even suffered from post-traumatic stress disorder. Serene was one of them: it broke her heart when her team lost a patient, and this consumed her long after the dead had been cremated. She had been haunted by guilt and blamed herself endlessly for not having had the power to save a life. She couldn't sleep. She lost her appetite. When her medical director had noticed this, she sent Serene to counselling and a crisis management session. This helped for a while, but Serene knew in her heart that she couldn't withstand another tragic case like that. She avoided the operating theatre. She specialized in pediatrics and subsequently set up her own clinic. She was more effective as a consulting doctor, working in the calmer atmosphere of a clinic rather than in the constant high-pressure environment of surgery or worse, the ICU. Besides, she preferred to have deeper and lengthier connections with her young patients, helping them enjoy the healthy years ahead of them. Prevention was more critical to their treatment. Seeing children achieve their growth and health milestones was the most rewarding part of Serene's profession.

Serene pressed the button of the fifth floor for the Pediatric Department at St Luke's Medical Center's Medical Arts Building or MAB. It was Monday morning and Serene should have had a fresh disposition, but she had just read a text on her St Luke's WhatsApp group about a fellow doctor who had died from an infectious lung disease picked up from a patient. Perhaps the doctor's protective equipment had been deficient or inadequate, or perhaps the viral load had been too high for anyone in close contact with the carrier to not catch it. The diseased doctor was known for her empathy, and might have set aside medical conventions and protocols to comfort her contagious patient. There were other conjectures, but they couldn't change the reality of the doctor's death. Despite her gloomy thoughts, Serene put on a smile for the patients and medical representatives waiting in line along the corridor that led to her clinic.

'Good morning, Doctora. You're so poised as usual. How was your weekend?' Maryanne greeted Serene as she opened the door to the clinic. Maryanne, the middle-aged receptionist, looked appreciatively at Serene who was one of the more fashionable doctors in the building. Today, Serene was wearing a smoke grey dress with a thin red belt and matching red high-heeled shoes. One of the mothers in the queue even shot her an admiring glance.

'Quite relaxing. I finally had a chance to go to the spa for my massage,' Serene told Maryanne. She didn't want to share bad news with her staff, especially on a Monday morning. 'What do we have today?' she asked, after checking how Maryanne was.

'We have three routine consultations, then two cough and colds, and one diarrhea. Two others are on the way,' Maryanne said looking at the patient records. 'I've picked up your coffee and croissant, it's on your desk,' she added.

'Thanks. Is Michelle in yet?' Serene asked about her assistant, a registered nurse who preferred to work in a clinic setup because of the more regular working hours. Michelle couldn't manage the irregular working hours, especially the graveyard shift, at the hospital.

'She's in the washroom. She's already done the prep and updated the records of the six patients outside,' Maryanne replied.

'Okay, I'll wait for her,' Serene said, closing the door behind her. She placed her Hermés Birkin bag on the shelf behind her chair, squirted hand sanitizer on her palm and rubbed it thoroughly while checking the food tray on her desk. She picked up her tall Americano and ignored the almond croissant, which was almost impossible to resist with its sweet and nutty aroma. But she had indulged at yesterday's seafood dinner so she should limit her carb intake today. She walked over to the window and looked out at the street below as she sipped her coffee. Her office was on the E. Rodriguez Avenue side of the building so she could see the flurry of activities at the intersection: cars, delivery trucks and ambulances zooming in and out of the hospital complex, pedestrians crossing the street hastily, hawkers knocking on car windows persistently. Rival fast food chain stores stood next to each other. Across the road from MAB, a row of stalls sold fruits and fresh produce while another sold medical supplies and equipment. Behind the stalls, a high wall sealed off a gated community from the main road; only the roofs of the townhomes within were visible from the outside. The road itself was bustling with traffic. Sometimes, like now, the traffic was so slow that the entire stretch was at a standstill, in both directions. Serene returned to her desk when she heard a knock on the door. 'Come in,' she called out. She checked her watch. It was a quarter past ten o'clock. She must buckle down and get to business if she wanted to finish up with the eight or so patients before noon. She threw her empty coffee cup into the bin and put on her white coat before settling into her chair.

'Good morning po, Doctora,' Michelle greeted. Petite and slim, she was wearing her white uniform as usual, her hair tied neatly in a ponytail. She looked like a college student, but was actually in her late twenties and had been working with Serene for nearly eight years now.

'How was your weekend?' Serene asked, straightening her coat collar and putting on her stethoscope.

'I watched a movie with Mark last Saturday night,' Michelle said, referring to her boyfriend. 'And spent Sunday catching up with a former housemate,' she added, opening the folders and placing them on the desk as Serene prepared to review the records. Michelle had arranged the files neatly, starting with the patients who might need urgent care.

'Okay, which one should we start with?' Serene asked. She trusted Michelle's steady and unwavering judgement. She read the file of the five-year-old girl who had been having loose motions and high temperature for the past four days. 'Why did they have to wait for four days?' Serene sighed. She frowned at all the food that the parents had fed the young girl, despite her condition. She looked at Michelle who was also frowning.

And thus began a day in their lives at St. Luke's.

It was past noon when Serene finished seeing the last patient. She removed the protective mask and gloves that she had put on because of the two patients with viral cough and colds. She applied another layer of hand sanitizer, just as Michelle came in with updates on the little girl with diarrhea, whom she had escorted to the hospital for admission.

'Are you going out for lunch? I can drop you off,' Serene asked after their discussion.

'I've ordered in, Doctora. Thanks, just the same,' Michelle said.

'How is it going with you and Mark?' She knew about Michelle's on-off romance with the Chinoy entrepreneur.

'We're in our longest "on" period, actually.'

'So do I hear wedding bells?'

'I don't think it's happening anytime soon. You know what the real problem is,' Michelle sighed.

'Well, I've said my piece about Mark, he should make up his mind sooner than later. I wish I could make him see reason,' she said, picking up her bag. 'I'll meet you at the ward when I do the rounds later in the afternoon.'

On the drive to her lunch meeting with a nutrition company's research team, Serene couldn't help but empathize with Michelle, who had been sticking it out with Mark for years now. But Serene also understood Mark's situation. After all, she had grown up in a similar tradition of Chinese families, with even stricter parents, who were both Chinese. And worse, Serene's mother came from a Binondo clan, the most traditional of all groups of Chinese in Metro Manila. Serene thought that her grandparents had chosen an apt English name for her mother, because Margaret sounded stern, though her Chinese name was supposed to mean 'faithful'. Like many Chinese in the Philippines, and perhaps elsewhere, Serene and her family had adopted an English name for easier recall and assimilation. For Serene, her English name was simply the literal translation of her Chinese name. Henry, her father, had explained to her once that he had chosen 'Serene' because upon birth, she had whimpered only a little and didn't cry as loudly as the other babies in the delivery room. He didn't know then that 'faithful' and 'serene' were going to clash, years later.

Serene had borne more than her fair share of suffering in this world because of her parents' blind obedience of tradition. There had been many instances, but the one that almost broke her, came when she was already grown-up and old enough to decide things for herself. Even now, Serene cringed at the memory of that day when her parents had practically ostracized her.

Chapter 2

Because she believed that life is short, Serene wished that it was easy to erase awful episodes from memory. It was a Saturday morning in January, a day that she didn't want to remember but was now firmly lodged in the innermost part of her hippocampus. 'This is how you repay us after we have sacrificed so much just so you could be a doctor,' Margaret had screamed in a mixed of English and Hokkien, her cheeks reddening in anger. She had turned her back at Serene and refused to utter a single word after that.

'Serene, I'm disappointed.' Henry had looked grimmer, seeing how Margaret was stubbornly and emphatically avoiding talking to Serene.

'But Daddy, I thought you'd understand.' Serene had hoped that her father would be more reasonable. Unlike Margaret, who stayed at home and preferred to interact only with relatives and fellow Chinese friends, Henry seemed more expansive, given his greater multi-cultural exposure at work. Serene had banked on her father's understanding when she had announced her engagement to Lance.

'The fact that I can speak better English than your mum, and that I interact a lot with non-Chinese people, doesn't change my views on interracial marriage,' Henry said. He was the marketing manager of a food and beverage company.

169

Although the company was owned by a Chinese tycoon, it had a global outlook, exporting its products to several countries in Southeast Asia. Henry had far more interactions with people from different cultures and walks of life than Margaret could ever have had.

'Daddy, you've travelled enough and you've met many couples from diverse cultures. You know that interracial marriage can work. It's a global village out there. Even we are not living in China anymore. We are three generations removed from the land of our great-grandparents' birth.'

'Serene, stop it, this is not about our culture. This is about your future,' Henry's lips had thinned further, his back now ramrod straight.

'Besides, if you are so loyal to that land, why didn't you go back? Why did you insist on staying here and making us suffer in the process?' Serene hadn't been able to stop. She had felt like a dam that finally had to release water after having held back the pressure for a long time. 'Isn't it unfair that you force your tradition on us when we are surrounded by Filipino culture and influence? Why are you not making an effort to adapt to the land that has been hosting us for three generations now?' Serene had asked, shaking in frustration. Serene cringed every time she remembered that hers was one among the Chinese families that still pledged their allegiance to China and stuck to their culture and tradition, even when they couldn't locate their ancestral origins in that vast country any longer. Such hypocrisy!

'Don't blow this issue out of proportion. Obviously, we are grateful for our fortunes in this land, but it's because of our ancestry that we've made it this far. Do you think that if we were Filipinos, we'd have it easier, economically? It's because of help from fellow Chinese that we've made it,' Henry had raised his voice and gesticulated uncharacteristically.

'That is so narrow-minded,' Serene muffled in between tears. 'And not everything is about money.'

'It's easy for you to say that because you've been cushioned from the harsh reality and you're a doctor now. But without education and connection, you would be nothing.' Henry had clenched his fist. 'I got ahead in life only because of my Chinese blood. It's the same with you. You also had it easier because of Chinese connections. Don't shake your head like that. Most of your clients are Chinese, aren't they?' Henry had raised his voice now.

'I know. But Daddy, I'm a human being too. I can't get married to someone I haven't even met. I can't spend the rest of my life with someone you've chosen for me, just because he is Chinese.'

'If you are going to dilute your lineage, you will soon see that any child of yours will suffer, down the line. I'm telling you now, they will not have it as easy as you all had. Use your brain, Serene. Meet this guy that your mum has arranged for you.' They had wanted to arrange Serene's marriage with the son of a family friend of theirs, a 100 per cent Chinese with Binondo roots, just like Margaret.

'That's so insensitive, Daddy. I'm not a robot,' Serene had cried uncontrollably.

'Go say that to your mother,' Henry had said, banging the door shut on his way out.

Serene couldn't talk to Margaret, who completely ignored her, leaving the room in a huff after Henry's departure. Besides, even during better times, Margaret scarcely spoke English or Tagalog, and would revert to her Hokkien dialect when talking with Serene, even though she knew that Serene couldn't speak or understand Hokkien properly. As Serene had grown older, she had drifted away emotionally from her mother because of their inability to communicate with each other. It had been easier when she was a child, because she had simpler emotions that she could communicate in sign language, if orally didn't work. But as her range of emotions expanded and she began to experience more complex feelings, Serene could only share so much with Margaret. How did one say 'displacement' in Hokkien? And even if Serene knew how to say it, would Margaret have even understood the context? Wasn't the Chinese language far too prone to mistranslation? Its nuance and meaning prone to getting lost in mere mispronunciation or accent? Over the years, Serene's relationship with her mother had only become further riddled with mistranslation.

Serene had fled their Pasay City home and rushed back to her studio unit in Quezon City, a small but safe place in the Scout area, and near St Luke's, which she had been renting since her medical residency. From there, she had called Lance, who had come to pick her up and take her out to lunch to cheer her up. 'I can't believe they've stopped talking to me,' Serene had said while waiting for the food they had ordered at the L.A. House restaurant along Tomas Morato Avenue.

'You've done your best to get their permission. I also swallowed my pride and went with you last time, but your mum didn't even have the decency to come out of her room and meet me,' Lance had sighed. He had become, by then, a fast-rising executive in-charge of the over-the-counter and consumer health division of a leading pharmaceutical conglomerate. He had met Serene at a forum that his company had sponsored for pediatricians in Metro Manila.

'I know and I'm sorry that you had to go through that,' Serene had said.

'It was pretty awkward, but it's water under the bridge now. We've waited long enough for their permission. It's not even something we need to be doing. This isn't the medieval era and we're both grown-ups now. In fact, we should have started our own family earlier, we're not getting any younger,' Lance had said.

'I was hoping they would understand. I wanted the most important phase of our relationship to start on a positive note, with blessings from our parents.'

'We've long received my parents' blessings.'

'I couldn't be more grateful for their warm welcome. They're so understanding. What a huge contrast to mine,' Serene had started tearing up. 'It was the first time Daddy was furious with me like that. He raised his voice at me. He walked out on me.'

Lance had pulled her gently to his side. 'Your father looks so gentle and mild-mannered. I can't imagine him raising his voice. And I don't like the fact that he raised it at you,' he said.

'I'm more shocked at his reaction than at Mummy's, because she was anyway still giving me the cold shoulder from our last row. She made me feel guilty, saying she sacrificed so much for my education.'

'Don't be guilty on that account. It's the parents' duty to provide their children with good education. Now if they so insist, I will pay them back, every last cent of whatever amount they spent on you.' Lance's nostrils had been flaring by the time he had finished.

'No, that would make it even worse. I know you mean well, but that makes me sound like a commodity which can be bought off.'

'I'm sorry, I didn't mean to sound like that. I just don't like to see you suffer like this,' Lance had lifted her chin and gently wiped her tears away with his handkerchief.

'What should we do now?' She had felt lost. Their waiter had come to serve lunch, but Serene hadn't had an appetite and had ignored the food entirely. The same had been true for Lance, who had also put his untouched plate to the side.

'Well, you know your family better. Weigh things objectively. If there's no hope of them budging, there's always option B, isn't it?' he had said before kissing her on the forehead.

When the waiter had returned, he hadn't been able to help but stare at the untouched food. He had asked if anything was wrong with it. Lance had shaken his head and merely asked for the check, and to have the food packed so they could take it away and Serene would have something to eat, later.

In the end, Lance and Serene had done what was almost inconceivable in Serene's, or even Lance's culture. They had eloped. They had booked a one-week holiday to Koh Samui in Thailand. From there, they had sent out 'Just Got Married' cards and photos to their families, close relatives and friends.

Technically, it wasn't an elopement because they had had a secret civil wedding at the Quezon City Hall, the day before flying to Thailand, though only their best friends and witnesses had been present in Room 11 for the registry of their marriage. Among Serene's former roommates, only Tintin was in Manila, so she had served as witness as well as representative for Issa and Sandy, who lived overseas and couldn't fly in at such a short notice. Lance's two best friends from high school and another close friend from his office had represented his side.

Their friends, who had known about Lance and Serene's situation, hadn't been surprised when they had received the card announcing their marriage. Tintin and Lance's best friend, Alvin, had coordinated and organized a 'Welcome Home' party for them when they returned from their elopement-cum-honeymoon. Even Lance's family had welcomed them warmly and given them a generous present: a check to help the couple with the first instalment for a house of their own.

It had been a different story altogether with Serene's family.

Serene hadn't had the courage to visit their family home in Pasay City and face the wrath of her parents. But a few days after their return from Thailand, Serene had decided to call Henry. 'Daddy, we've got married,' she had said hesitantly.

'Vivi told us,' Henry had said, referring to Serene's younger sister. Earlier, Serene could still talk to Vivi, but Margaret had banned Vivi from calling Serene since the elopement. 'I don't have time for this and I shouldn't be talking to you,' he had added stonily.

'I'm sorry, Daddy. I hope you'll find it in your heart to forgive us,' Serene had said before hanging up. It had proved the most polarizing day of her life—she had been excited to share her happiest moment, only to have been met with indifference by her father. Henry used to champion Serene and cheer her on in many school competitions. He had guided her whenever she had needed help with schoolwork. When she had completed and passed the medical board examination, Henry had even announced it in a Chinese daily paper. He had done the same when she had finished her specialist course and become a pediatrician.

Serene had slumped on the sofa at Lance's condominium unit in the Ortigas area of Pasig City, where they had stayed temporarily. She had been in that position when Lance had arrived from work. He had rushed to her side, full of concern. 'What happened?' he had asked, his eyebrows drawing together.

'I've just called Daddy to share the news,' Serene had said, holding Lance's hands tightly. 'He wouldn't even speak to me.' Her eyes had been puffy from her tears before, but she had dried them out and resolved that she would never cry over this again. Ever.

'This is just the beginning. We need to be tougher and learn to live with this. It is what it is. Now we must focus our attention and energy on building our own loving family,' Lance had said, urging her to nod.

'I know. This is the last time you see me crying over this,' Serene had said with renewed resolve.

'Great. Now, shall we look at these brochures?' Lance smiled, taking out a stack of property brochures from his laptop bag.

Chapter 3

2003

Because she believed that life is short, Serene wished that she could corral, or at least park, unwanted emotions so that they wouldn't interfere with the more pleasant ones. She glanced at the boxes piling up on one side of her studio, the accumulation of her material belongings over the past three years since her residency at St Luke's Hospital. She wished it were as easy to pack away the mixed emotions running through her now. How convenient it would have been if she could simply set aside her tumultuous, unnecessary emotions, even if only temporarily.

'How many boxes in all?' Tintin asked as she helped pack the remaining items in Serene's closet.

'I can't believe I have accumulated twenty-two boxes in this tiny place,' Serene said.

'Where did they all even come from?' Tintin laughed, equally surprised.

'From the closet, I guess,' Serene grinned, opening the doors of the empty wardrobes wider. 'To be honest, I've no idea how all these things found their way here.'

'When will the movers come?' Tintin asked.

'Tomorrow morning.' Serene sank exaggeratedly on the settee.

'Onward to a new life then.' Tintin sat beside her.

'I should be ecstatic. I have the right to be ecstatic, to be a joyful bride, to enjoy the beginning of my marriage. Yet here I am—I can't be fully happy, I can't be fully joyful because of the selfishness of my family, of my mother, especially,' Serene said dejectedly.

Tintin cradled her in her arms. 'You've made the right decision by going ahead with your marriage. This is your life we're talking about. You're a grown woman now, and a smart one at that,' Tintin said.

'Aren't mothers supposed to be caring? Why can't my mother feel any kindness for me?'

'As you've said earlier, your mum comes from an ultra-traditional family. The norms were also different in her generation.'

'It's so unfair. To me and Lance.'

'Have they all banished you completely? Or is someone still talking to you?'

'Only Vivi, and secretly, at that. She's extremely scared that my parents would cut her allowance off if they found out that she was talking to me. She bought a prepaid number that she uses just for calling me.'

'Bless her. She has a good heart.'

'Indeed. I miss her, but I'll just have to wait until the next time she calls,' Serene smiled sadly.

'And your brother?'

'Oh, he is in his own world. He barely talks to anyone, even my parents. So I don't really know what's up with him. He simply sent a text message that said "Congrats". It was so impersonal.'

'Guys,' Tintin rolled her eyes. 'Any word from Issa or Sandy?' she asked, wanting to change the topic, seeing that Serene looked sadder now.

'Though we spoke on separate occasions, funnily, they said the exact same thing: they both wanted to be godmothers,' Serene said.

After a few months of researching and house hunting, Lance and Serene eventually found a townhouse off Wilson Avenue in Greenhills, San Juan, equidistant to Lance's office in Ortigas and to Serene's clinic at St Luke's. Serene soon discovered that Lance was an architecture and design aficionado. He had been heavily involved in both the overview and the tiniest of details of the construction, including the type and size of nails required for each joinery. Lance was now intently comparing the slate teal wall paint with the bluish-grey Thai silk curtain for the large window behind the sofa.

'How did you become so knowledgeable about all this?' Serene asked, watching him from a corner wingback chair.

'I started out as a brand manager, remember? For one to succeed at brand management, one needs to know everything, every detail about the brand, from the chemical components to emotional attributes, from capsule coating to the font size of the dosage instructions. And most importantly, the colour of the product logo,' he explained.

'Even the colour of the logo? I thought no one pays attention to it,' Serene said.

'Nope. The slightest change in its tint or shade, even if it's in the same tone, can result in huge losses. Why? Because loyalists can smell the tiniest change in the packaging. Consumers distrust even the smallest deviation. They might think the product is tampered. The devil is in the details, as they say,' he said. 'Does that impress you enough?' he winked at her.

'Isn't it too late to say no?' she joked.

'Definitely. It's touch-move, similar to a chess game. You made your last move when you solemnly promised to be my loving and loyal wife, back at that temple in Koh Samui.'

'And at Quezon City Hall's Room 11, before that.'

'On that momentous day, when not a single person remembered to bring a pen for the betrothed to make the magical union official,' he said in an exaggerated theatrical voice. 'If it weren't for the clerk next door who had an anemic Uniball, or some other obscure brand of pen, there wouldn't have been a happily-ever-after ending to that wonderful story, folks.'

'I know,' she laughed. 'But where did you keep your Montblanc that you'd always carried with you for as long as I could remember?'

'I hate to admit this, I mistakenly kept it in the kitchen drawer, probably thinking it was a knife. I was too nervous that day,' Lance smiled mischievously now.

'Really? It didn't show,' she asked. She was amused to discover this new side of him.

'Of course. I can pretend to be a cool cat. I have had years of theatre training. It was my extracurricular activity in high school. Would you believe, I even forgot the key inside the car. I was so relieved the car wasn't stolen,' Lance said.

'Oh my goodness. Thank God we were at City Hall. That was probably the only reason it wasn't carnapped,' Serene could not hold back her laughter now. 'But why?'

'Weren't you nervous on that day, our momentous day? I'd be disappointed if you weren't,' he frowned, releasing the curtains now.

'Of course, I was. I even threw up before leaving my place,' she said, remembering that tense morning.

'I didn't know that either. But why?' He asked, mimicking her.

'Please. Seriously now, though. I also threw up this morning,' she said, smiling.

'Oh my goodness, are we . . . ?' Lance rushed to hug her.

'We very much are,' she said, nodding her head vigorously.

Lance was about to carry and twirl her around, but stopped himself from doing so. 'Oops, sorry, I'm not supposed to be twirling you around.' He held her hands and carried her to the sofa and made her sit on his lap instead. 'You've made me the happiest man ever. Again. Thank you for this gift,' Lance held her cheeks and looked at her intently, trying to remember every detail of her radiant face and the expressions passing through it now. He would soon be a father and he wanted to remember every detail of Serene's face as she shared this most wonderful news. Then he lifted her chin and bent his head toward hers. He kissed her lightly on the lips first, nibbling on her bottom lip, before opening her lips and playing with her tongue. 'Can we still do it? You're the doctor in the family so you should know best,' he asked seriously.

Serene felt shy even then but nodded and kissed him back passionately.

Chapter 4

2003

Because she believed that life is short, Serene wanted to savour moments, especially the big ones that mattered. Imminent motherhood had infused her with greater courage and a sudden desire to put things in order. She wanted to fix what could be fixed, even if only within her limited sphere, so that the world that her baby would be born into, would be a kinder one. She had started organizing a room that would soon be the nursery. She worked on this gradually, mindful of her physical condition, and felt rewarded whenever a space was cleared of clutter. She believed in feng shui, and wanted to ensure that positive energy circulated freely in the room, which looked a lot brighter now than when she had started. Decluttering was easier on the physical plane, Serene realized. She had to try harder and put things in order in her relationships. It would be inauspicious for her baby to arrive in a house filled with conflict. Five months into her pregnancy, when she had just learned her baby's gender, Serene had mustered courage to call up Henry again. 'Daddy, I have important news. Could I please, please meet you even just for half an hour?' she had begged on the phone. 'You don't have to tell Mummy,' she had added tentatively.

Serene had walked hesitantly to the Gloria Maris restaurant at the Greenhills Shopping Center for lunch with Henry.

It was a miracle that he had agreed to meet her after six months of silence. Serene had taken a deep breath before entering the restaurant. She had seen Henry sitting by a table in a corner, reading the day's issue of *The Philippine Star*. Serene had wanted to run and hug him tight, but she had held off the impulse as he might not have forgiven her yet for marrying Lance.

'Hi Daddy, how are you?' she had asked awkwardly, not knowing how to approach her father after six months of not seeing or talking to him.

'I'm okay. Sit down. I've ordered some siomai and dumplings for starters.' He signalled for a waiter to come over.

After placing her order and returning the menu to the waiter, Serene had clasped her hands on top of the table and looked at her father pleadingly. 'Daddy, I hope you've found it in your heart to forgive me already,' she had said.

'I can never forget what you've done, Serene. But I've decided that it shouldn't stop me from talking to you. I can talk to you, at least for now,' he had said somewhat sternly.

'Thank you, Daddy. I wish we could all revert to old times, be the family that we used to be. But until then, I'll take whatever you can spare for me,' her voice had almost trailed off.

'I hope you'll soon realize the gravity of what you've done. Only then would you understand why we're reacting this way.'

'I do understand what you mean. But let's not talk about that for now,' Serene had paused. 'I wanted to share some good news.' She had mustered a smile.

'What is it?'

'I'm expecting,' she paused. 'And I'm hoping that you could be a part of my child's future.'

A mix of expressions had passed through Henry's face: first, he had looked excited, then he seemed to have remembered something and had started to frown. 'Well, congratulations are in order then,' Henry had finally said, with the breaking out of a smile that he seemed to have been repressing.

'Thank you.'

'When are you due?'

'In three months.'

'That's not too far away,' he said. 'I didn't notice much change in you so it didn't occur to me that you'd be pregnant.'

'I know, I don't show enough. I'm also wearing a loose dress.'

'But are you sure the baby is okay? Shouldn't you be showing a little now?' Henry looked genuinely concerned now.

'It's just my physical make-up. The baby is absolutely fine.'

'Oh yes, I remember, your Mummy also didn't show that much when she was having you.'

'I wish I could share the news with Mummy. But I'm not sure she'd want to speak to me now. I can't afford emotional tension at this stage, my doctor advised me to avoid stressful situations.'

'I will try to talk to your mother about this, but I agree you should avoid any stress now,' Henry had said, before pausing to let the waiter serve their food. 'Are you allowed to eat all that?' he had asked, seeing the variety of food that she had ordered in addition to the siomai and dumplings: fried chicken with ginger, crispy pork and fish soup with spinach. While the restaurant was known for its shark fin soup, Serene had never been able to bring herself to order the dish since she had watched a documentary programme on how cruel shark finning was on the species.

'Of course I am, Daddy. In fact, I need it more because I'm eating for two now.' Although Henry hadn't been as warm as she had remembered, at least he hadn't been abrasive and antagonistic. They had eaten their lunch quietly. When dessert time had come, she requested for grass jelly. 'Daddy, I hope I can see you again soon, whenever you're available?' she had asked tentatively.

'I have more time now. I don't know if you've heard, but I retired from work two months ago.'

'Oh wow, congratulations, Daddy! Exciting times ahead for you.'

'Too much time, I guess. Now if only I had more friends who I could play golf with, I'd be happier.'

'Hmmm . . . which reminds me, would you like to play golf with Lance sometime? He has a membership at WackWack,' she said, referring to a nearby golf and country club.

'I'm not too sure about that. But shouldn't he be asking me that question?'

'Lance is picking me up shortly, can I ask him to say hello to you?' Serene had asked.

'Yes,' Henry had replied, not showing any emotion.

In the end, Henry had been civil when Lance had come to greet him, but given the circumstances, this instance had given Serene some hope that the ice in her family might start thawing.

A few months after their first meeting, Henry had accepted Lance's invitation for a game of golf. From there, they had gradually become golfing buddies. These days, Henry had got into the habit of calling Lance first, whenever he wanted to check in on the couple.

When Lance and Serene could take Chrystal home after her birth, Henry and Vivi had promptly visited her and joyously welcomed the new, albeit fragile member into their family. Margaret, though, had yet to show up. But after Serene had sent out the official birth announcement of Chrystal with her picture on the card, she had immediately received a call from Henry, who had relayed Margaret's wish to see the baby to her. Lance, with his big heart, hadn't thought twice and when the day had come, had welcomed Henry and Margaret warmly into their house. But even then, Margaret hadn't spoken at all as Serene had led her to the drawing room. Serene had excused herself to go to the nursery and then returned to the room carrying Chrystal. All of a sudden, Margaret had lost her stern composure and run like an excited child towards the baby. Before long, she had been cooing and playing with Chrystal, oblivious to the people around her. All this time, though, she hadn't bothered to even greet Serene. Perhaps she was just naturally awkward. Or so proud that it took her a long while to bend. After the first visit, however, Margaret had called Serene directly to ask for another visit. She had come back with Vivi and had brought bags full of gifts for Chrystal. While Serene and Vivi had caught up, Margaret had busily taken care of Chrystal, babbling and talking with her non-stop. In Hokkien. The sisters had shot each other that 'knowing' look, with Vivi trying her best to repress a bubbling laughter.

As Chrystal grew up, Margaret's pride seemed to have melted gradually. When Chrystal got to preschool, Margaret volunteered to take her to school, even if it meant driving down from Pasay City at dawn to reach Greenhills before the school drop-off time. She also picked Chrystal up from school when Serene was busy at work. By then, Margaret had also started greeting Lance, though she didn't say much beyond her characteristic brief greeting. But she had started bringing along food that she had cooked for him. When she found out that Lance loved the shredded pork she made, Margaret never failed to replenish his stock. It was a quirk that both Lance and Serene had accepted and even laughed about in the privacy of their room.

All this time, Margaret had kept up talking to Chrystal in Hokkien. And to everyone's amazement, Chrystal had picked up the language better than Serene ever had. By the time Chrystal had turned eight, she had become the interpreter for the family whenever Margaret was in the house.

Chapter 5

Because she believed that life is short, Serene did her best to ensure it was never boring. It had been sixteen years since her and Lance's elopement. And so far, there hadn't been any 'miserable years' in their marriage that could be deducted from their 'real life' years. Throughout Lance and Serene's marriage, however busy they both got, they kept Wednesday as their official lunch date, just the two of them, trying out the latest restaurant in town or revisiting an old favourite like Café Ysabel near their place. Sometimes, they would even drive all the way to Tagaytay City on special occasions, like their trip to Antonio's, one anniversary week. This time around, at their weekly lunch date, they chose Las Flores, a new restaurant that had opened at the Podium Mall in the Ortigas.

Serene read all the items on the menu. The paellas and tortillas were quite tempting, but she zeroed in on something in the salad section. She checked her phone and saw a message from Michelle, asking if she could leave early for the day to attend to some errands. Serene promptly replied to this request and kept her phone away after that, to avoid any more distractions. Now she couldn't help but think of how to help Michelle out of her situation. 'Do you remember Michelle?' she asked. 'Michelle, my assistant at the clinic,' she added to jog his memory.

'Of course I do. I've met her a few times. She was there at one or two of Chrystal's birthday parties, remember?' Lance asked, still scanning the menu.

'Right. I keep on forgetting about that. I invited her practically every year, but she attended only a few times,' she said.

'What about her?' he asked.

'I feel bad for her. She's still waiting for Mark to make up his mind.'

'That Mark has no balls,' Lance said. 'Hold that for a moment. Should we try the paella here?'

'Ugh, too much carbs.'

'I've never seen you this diet-conscious. You're on the thin side, in case you're forgetting. You actually need to gain weight.'

'Well, I'll let my natural appetite take over after the grand homecoming at the College of Medicine, otherwise I won't fit into my gown.'

'Oh, I keep on forgetting,' he said, mimicking her way of talking. 'Fine, I'll have one of these combo comidas then. You're free to choose whatever you want. My treat,' he winked at her.

'I'll have the salad for now, but I want to share the leche flan with you for dessert. Will you?' she asked.

'If you ask that sweetly, how can I refuse?' he teased her.

Chapter 6

2013

Because she believed that life is short, Serene wanted to celebrate important milestones in the best way she could. Ten years after they eloped, Serene finally had the wedding ceremony and celebration that she deserved. At five o'clock in the afternoon, on 8 June, Serene marched down the velvet carpet rolled out on the aisle of Santuario de San Jose Church in East Greenhills, with Henry and Margaret by her side. Though this was merely a ceremonial wedding, Serene couldn't help but feel nervous. She felt her knees weakening and she held her bouquet tightly, lest her hands started to shake. But midway through her march, she glanced at her entourage: her matrons of honour, the Room 216 girls, all looking radiant in their champagne-coloured gowns, waving at her enthusiastically, which gave her a boost. Serene quietly heaved a sigh of relief. When she saw Chrystal, her junior bridesmaid, cheering her on excitedly, any traces of nervousness promptly evaporated. Serene blew her daughter a kiss. She marched on almost buoyantly, smiling at the familiar faces along the way: her and Lance's immediate relatives, their close friends, colleagues, and other people dear to them—all looking happy for her and Lance. And there, waiting for her at the altar, was Lance, flanked by his beaming parents, who radiated even more of that characteristic calm and reassuring aura they usually did. Serene could feel the glow emanating from them. Lance looked absolutely dashing in a dark grey tuxedo and a matching bowtie. He had gained a few pounds since their wedding in Koh Samui, but he had the same eager expression, as though he couldn't wait to get married.

After the ceremony, the wedding party proceeded to the Shangri-La Hotel in Edsa for the reception, where Lance promptly received a lot of teasing from his close friends, who noticed his eager-beaver expression. Serene felt weightless when she entered. Peach rose petals were strewn along the path to their table on a dais at one end of the ballroom. The chandeliers that illuminated the room seemed to emit a special glow. A piano and a cello were set up in a corner of the stage. But more than the ambience, Serene could feel the lightness in the laughter and merriment of the guests. Their closest friends and immediate family members sat at the tables by the stage. All the seats were occupied in the huge ballroom. It was as though the 500 or so people that had gathered in the ballroom had left all their worries at the door, and decided that for the next three hours, they would ignore any other concerns. The guests dutifully followed the lead of those at the front tables, who tapped their glasses with their forks, prompting the bride and groom to kiss. And they did this at close intervals, every five minutes or so—to Lance's amusement and Serene's somewhat embarrassment—before the dinner officially started.

Earlier, when they had been reviewing the guest list for this celebration, Serene had been concerned that it was getting bigger than she had wanted.

'I have a large family and so do you, what can we do?' Lance had asked.

'We don't have to invite all of them,' she had pointed at the long list of guests.

'Come on, you've waited ten years for this, we're not going to scrimp now. Besides, Daddy Henry says your mother apparently opened her purse finally, and said she would contribute to the reception.'

'No way. You know I don't want any money from her now.'

'Give her a chance. She's making up for her mistakes.'

'No, let's just say no.'

'I have no problem with that. I can pay for our wedding even if you triple this guest list. That's not an issue for me. But what I'm more concerned about is the peace in your family. I don't want any impasse now. I know how much you suffered when you hadn't spoken with your family for more than six months.'

Chapter 7

Because she believed that life is short, Serene found it in her heart to forgive, even if she didn't entirely forget. Serene had allowed Margaret to come into their lives, mainly for Chrystal's sake. She didn't want to deny Chrystal the joy of having grandparents on both sides. And to be fair, Margaret had been doing her best to be a part of Serene's family. But for all that, Serene was still cautious about trusting Margaret again. She felt betrayed by the woman she had thought was the most important in her life.

For some time now, Serene had been curious about what had motivated Margaret to behave as she had. Had her parents' marriage been an arranged one? Had Margaret not had a say in the choice of her husband? Recalling that painful episode from her own life, Serene felt compelled to understand more about her mother. 'Daddy, I should have asked you this earlier, but I never had the courage. You never told us how you and Mummy had met,' Serene said during one of her coffee meet-ups with Henry.

'It was a set-up,' Henry said, without elaborating.

'But weren't you or Mummy seeing anyone else at that time?' Serene asked.

'No, I wasn't going out with anyone else and I was instantly attracted to your mother. So you see, our marriage was a timely blessing for me. I know your views on this, but for us who grew up in a very different milieu, arranged marriage was the norm,' Henry said.

'What about Mummy?' Serene probed further.

'That's something you would have to ask her,' Henry smiled, though this one was not fully formed.

How did one talk to someone so reticent, especially when they could barely speak each other's language? This became Serene's quandary as she embarked on her 'project' of understanding Margaret better. Now she regretted not learning as much Hokkien when she had had the opportunity. She had been able to learn English, and to a lesser extent, Tagalog, more naturally than her mother's language. Conversely, Margaret could hardly express herself in either of those languages, up to this day. And even if Serene was fluent in Hokkien, she didn't think Margaret articulated her emotions well. She was austere and stoic in both her ways and emotions. Perhaps the only exception was when it came to Chrystal.

After days of devising a strategy to understand the problem called Margaret, Serene decided to employ Vivi's help. Vivi was the baby of the family, and a darling in many ways. She adored Serene and looked up to her, but was also an obedient daughter. Among the siblings, she was the only one who talked with Margaret in Hokkien. Their elder brother, Joseph, couldn't care less about learning the dialect. But his was another story altogether.

Serene called Vivi to arrange one of their salon trips at the Shangri-La Mall. Serene made it a point to treat Vivi to this luxury, knowing her job as a corporate translator wasn't steady and she couldn't afford visits to the high-end salon on her regular paycheck. Vivi excitedly hugged Serene when they met at their so-called 'happy place'. Nikki, their regular hairdresser, or 'senior artist', led them to a quieter part of the salon, and asked an assistant to serve a special-flavoured tea to his favourite clients before preparing the hair treatment concoction for the two ladies. Both Serene and Vivi flipped through the pages of the glossy magazines on their dresser, pausing every now and then to exchange their views on some articles about Hollywood celebrities or luxury homes. After the treatment and styling, Serene and Vivi stood side by side and looked at their reflection in the mirror. They both beamed at each other, relishing Nikki's special touches. They left the salon in high spirits, blowing Nikki several kisses before walking over to TWG Tea Salon for high tea. Vivi enjoyed this more than Serene did, noting the meticulous table arrangement, even the spotless napkins. 'Vivi, there's something I've been meaning to ask you,' Serene said after taking a sip of her French Earl Grey tea.

'Hmmm, whenever you make that intro, I start to feel nervous, as though I'm about to hear something ominous. I wonder what it is this time,' Vivi frowned.

'Oh no, nothing of that sort,' Serene said. 'Wait, did you have another brain freeze?' Serene asked, seeing Vivi's expression and noticing that she had ordered iced tea, even though she didn't normally take iced drinks, something Margaret kept on reminding them to do since childhood. Margaret believed that cold drinks messed up the internal temperature of the body and could eventually lead to health issues.

'No, I'm fine. I was frowning because of your preamble,' Vivi smiled now.

'How much do you know about Mummy's childhood and teenage years? Does she talk to you about her younger days?'

'Why would you ask me that? Haven't you had this kind of conversation with her?' Vivi said, biting into a piece of macaron. 'Hmmm, this is delish, try it,' she said giving half of the salted caramel-flavoured piece to Serene.

'Hmmm, yummy indeed. This is the first time I'm having this,' Serene said, savouring the macaron in her mouth before swallowing. 'You know you're the only one among us who could really talk with Mummy. So does she tell you anything about that part of her life?'

'Not at all. What she always talks about is how difficult things were in her time. It was right after the war and how Akong and Ama were fresh off the boat and all that,' Vivi said, referring to their maternal grandparents.

'That, I've also heard from her,' Serene said.

'But sometimes I could sense her wistfulness. Now that you ask me, maybe I should investigate à la Nancy Drew, huh?' Vivi said with a mischievous look.

'Oh please don't. If she found out that it was my idea, it could trigger another row. I swear I simply want some peace from now on. No more family conflicts.'

A few days later, Vivi called Serene with what she described was a 'scoop'. The two met for lunch at a Greenhills restaurant for the 'low-down' on Margaret, as Vivi had put it. It wasn't Margaret, though, who had answered Vivi's questions, but one of their aunts. Vivi found out that indeed, Margaret did have a first love that she had had to break up with because her parents had already committed her to an arranged marriage. He had been her classmate at Chung Hua Institute. And though he was 100 per cent Chinese, his family had been struggling financially. And the only reason he had been able to attend the private Chinese school had been because of his generous uncle, who had helped him with his studies.

Somehow, Serene was saddened after learning this information about Margaret. This could be why she became so austere and reticent. But in all the years that Margaret had been with Henry, hadn't she come to love him, eventually? Serene wanted to know this, but this time she didn't want to burden Vivi with her question. She watched Vivi and was amused at how young her sister looked; although she was in her late twenties, at times, she still behaved like a child. Serene didn't want to sour her disposition or colour her lens with her questions. 'Now, let's talk about your love life. Hasn't Mummy started pairing you off yet, isn't it high time?' Serene said.

'Nope. Thanks to you, I think the parents have learned their lessons well. But I also have this feeling that they want to keep me single all my life so that they would have company and someone to take care of them in old age,' Vivi laughed.

'Is that something that you want for yourself?'

'Well, I wouldn't have to worry about rent. Or food. And perhaps even allowance. So why not?'

'No boyfriend?'

'You would be the first to know.'

'I don't want to be like the annoying *titas* of Manila, but don't you have any suitors? Come on, you're more than a pretty face. And this is objective, there's so much to like and love about you.'

'Achie, please. I'm not actively looking, okay?' She said, addressing Serene with the Hokkien word for older sister.

'You make it sound like a job.'

'But it is, especially if you want to go by everyone's wishes and expectations,' Vivi sounded irritated now.

'Sorry if the topic annoys you. I'm not going to ask you about this again,' Serene mentally stepped back. She should stop treating Vivi like a baby and remember that she belonged to a different generation; the millennial in her family.

'Thanks. I'm happy being single and unattached. Just because I'm not going out or not keen to do so doesn't mean I'm not complete. As it is, there's enough to do without having to factor in another person's wishes or quirks,' Vivi said. 'You're lucky that you found a good match in Lance, but not everyone has the same fortune.'

'Okay, I get the message. I wasn't trying to be smug. I'm just curious, like any other older sister.'

'I never said you're smug. You're passionate about your profession, so I guess even outside of home, you'd still be happy because you're doing something you love and something that's also worthwhile,' Vivi looked away for a second. 'Now that's something I have yet to figure out.'

'You have a great job. Very few people have your skill set.'

'Yes, but it's nothing compared to what you and Ahia have achieved. While I'm okay living with the parents, sometimes when they compare me to you or Ahia, I feel like I should just be independent, get a place of my own,' she said, using the Hokkien word to refer to their elder brother, Joseph.

'I should tell Daddy to stop nagging you like that. Joseph was fortunate to have found his job at a Chicago bank when he did. The same holds true for me. Luck had a role to play in my career,' Serene said. Having graduated before the technological revolution, she understood that things were different for young millennials. Breaking through was more challenging now, with all the noise and clutter out there.

'God knows how many times I've wished that I were technologically savvy so that I could ride the wave and be a successful professional like the two of you,' Vivi sighed wistfully. 'Unfortunately, I'm not your typical Chinese who's good with numbers and all. I'm an aberration.'

'Oh please. Your job is equally important. How many business opportunities would have been lost if it weren't for you translating for all those investors? Besides, you're still young. You'll have time to create greater impact,' Serene tried to reassure her.

'I hope so. The erratic schedule can be frustrating. Sometimes, I work for days non-stop, like when a delegation is in town. But in-between visits, I mostly just sit around. I feel like I'm wasting time,' Vivi said, sipping from her straw but realizing her glass was empty, she put it back on the table with a sigh.

'What do you feel happy doing? I've seen you doodling and completing all those therapeutic colouring books. By the way, Chrystal loves hers too, thanks for giving her a copy.'

'Is it weird if I say that I have this urge to sometimes just splash colours around and create something out of nothing? I've always been curious about painting, you know. Not calligraphy or one of those meticulous Chinese arts, but simply mixing colours together à la Jackson Pollock.' Vivi excitedly pulled out her phone and showed some images to Serene.

'What are these? They look interesting,' Serene said, looking at colourful pages, some of which even looked like Marimekko prints.

'Those are my tiny watercolours, my outlet whenever I'm stressed out. But now I want to experiment with real paint, with oil, though if I start doing all that, Mummy will become suspicious.'

'There's nothing wrong with having a hobby,' Serene said. 'Why don't you join an introductory art class?'

'Isn't it odd to start learning things only at this age, though?' Vivi expressed her doubts, even though earlier, while listening to Serene, her eyes had widened as though the possibility had never even occurred to her.

'It's never too late to start learning anything. "Late-bloomer" wouldn't have been part of our lexicon, otherwise. Do you know that J.K. Rowling started writing *Harry Potter* only when she was your age?' Serene paused to register Vivi's reaction.

'Really? Interesting,' Vivi was almost jumping in her seat.

'If painting is what you want to do, go for it. Life is short, as they say,' Serene smiled tenderly at Vivi. All these years, she had thought of her younger sister as carefree. It never occurred to her that Vivi might need guidance or some push to make her own dreams come true. Serene was fortunate that she had had the guts to pursue what she had wanted for herself. And though her path had been thorny at times, including almost failing her board examinations because of a bad flu, Serene had found contentment in the fact that she was now doing what she had always dreamt of doing since childhood. Whenever her father had asked her to pick a toy as a prize for getting good marks in school, Serene would choose medical paraphernalia like stethoscope, thermometer, injections, masks and so on, over traditional dolls. She also had a doctor's coat by the time she was seven. But now she felt guilty that she hadn't been paying sufficient attention to her sister.

After her tea with Vivi, Serene called one of her friends, who was a graduate of the University of the Philippines College of Fine Arts to find out about classes Vivi could take. She then connected her painter friend to Vivi, and hoped that it would lead to something worthwhile for her younger sister.

Chapter 8

2019

Because she believed that life is short, Serene wanted to learn about the past, as a way to understand the present. One afternoon, Henry arrived with Lance after a round of golf. 'How was your game, Daddy?' Serene cleared a seat for him in the drawing room and called their helper to serve Henry's favourite Pu Ehr tea.

'I could never beat Lance, if that's what you mean. I started playing golf late in life so I'll always have that handicap,' he laughed at his rare pun.

'Don't be too humble, Daddy. Lance updates me about your regular hole-in-ones.'

'Oh those, they were flukes. They're not the norm with me,' Henry smiled.

'Daddy, you know how I've always been honest with you and how I've always felt comfortable asking you even the most provocative of questions, right?' she asked while pouring out Henry's tea for him.

'Ah yes, nothing ever shocks me anymore if it's coming from you,' Henry said, taking in the aroma of the tea.

'Well, I wish that would still hold true after this question,' she joked, a joke that was partially true.

'Come on, ask away.'

'You know how I've always wanted to know more about you and Mummy. I know you've told me your story, and I've learned since then that Mummy had to break up with her then-boyfriend because she had to marry you.'

'You've been busy.' Henry adjusted his position on the chair so that he now faced Serene squarely.

'Uh-huh,' she nodded. 'And the only reason I'm going to ask you this question now is because I could never ask Mummy.'

'Okay, I wonder where this is leading to.' Henry looked amused.

'Daddy, do you think that Mummy ever regretted her decision of marrying you? Or did she come to love you genuinely and therefore doesn't regret anything at all?' Serene asked seriously.

'In our generation, parents didn't allow children to ask questions. So, this, you and me talking like this, is itself unconventional in many ways,' Henry said putting his empty cup on the tray.

'I know, Dad. I really appreciate your open-mindedness. I'm lucky we could talk openly like this.'

'Your mum had sacrificed a lot by setting her own feelings aside. She probably saw me as an antagonist, earlier. Yet, she did her best. She'd always prepare warm food for me. My clothes are always freshly ironed to this day. Our house is always in order,' Henry sighed. 'She took very good care of you all.'

'I sometimes complain about my struggles as a wife and mother, but I know they're nothing compared to what her generation went through.'

'Those times were unfair to women, in general.'

'Mummy is fortunate to have you, Dad. I feel that men don't recognize the sacrifices of women enough.'

'I'm aware of women's struggles. I have sisters. I've also witnessed how my mother quietly carried huge responsibilities by herself.'

'I'd say that you're more enlightened than others of your generation.'

'I've also worked in a corporate environment for decades. But going back to your mum, I'd like to believe that she has also learned to love me along the way,' Henry smiled gently at Serene now.

'Does she tell you how she feels, Dad? I can't imagine Mummy being lovey-dovey with you, you know,' Serene almost laughed at the thought.

'Oh please, don't be too harsh on your mummy. Obviously, she's not that expressive, and that's precisely why you're taking up all this with me.'

'I hope I'm not unnecessarily adding to your burden?' Serene asked, now concerned that Henry might start worrying.

'I'm retired now, so I can take all this,' Henry laughed. 'There are ways for a husband to know, and over the years, I could feel that your mother has come to love me, too. It would be a waste of life, not just of hers, but mine too, if it were otherwise,' Henry smiled that enlightened smile of his.

That night, Serene was somewhat pacified knowing that Henry had deemed his marriage worthwhile. Indeed, what a sad state of affairs it would have been if her parents were merely wearing the years away because of blind obedience to tradition. While Henry seemed confident that Margaret was content in their marriage, Serene couldn't help but wonder if she would ever have a chance to talk candidly with Margaret, the way she just had with Henry. What all had Serene lost due to her lack of ability to reach out to her mother and vice versa? This distance between her and Margaret needed to be bridged, but Serene didn't know how. One thing that she learned from this experience, though, was to ensure that history doesn't repeat itself when it came to her relationship with Chrystal. She wanted to be the person that Chrystal could run to whenever she had questions about the world out there. After all, even an adult found it hard to navigate this world, how much harder must it be for an adolescent?

Chapter 9

2019

Because she believed that life is short, Serene had to listen to her heart. It had now been more than sixteen years since that pivotal day that had defined Serene's destiny, when she had flouted tradition and chosen to follow her heart. All the sacrifices after that had been worth it. This, Serene knew, without any doubt, as she looked at Chrystal in her fluffy pink gown. Chrystal was now taller than Serene's petite self at five feet and two inches, but she was every bit a baby in the way she ran to greet Serene and how she cuddled so sweetly still, with her and Lance. Chrystal had requested for a pink costume party to celebrate her sixteenth birthday. Some teenagers might cringe at pink, but Chrystal unabashedly stuck with this colour that had been a favourite of hers since childhood. Tonight, the garden on one side of Serene's house was illuminated with candles and torches. Serene had commissioned a party planner and caterer to set up and decorate the area according to Chrystal's theme and specifications. They installed a couple of booths, one meant as a self-care/indulgence corner with fluffy couches and footrests. Inside, soft toys were scattered around, all in pink, and cotton candy and other sweet snacks were being served. A picture booth stood in another corner, supplied with several costumes and paraphernalia, all in pink. Chrystal decided to invite just sixteen close friends and cousins. She didn't want any adults at the party. After Serene had ensured that Chrystal was happy with the arrangement, she left the garden to Chrystal and her guests.

When the party was over at about midnight, Chrystal shrieked like a little kid, scooping some presents in her gown and running into the house. 'Daddy, Mummy, look at all my presents,' she said. One of the helpers followed with a trolley filled with more delicately wrapped boxes.

'Wow, they all look lovely. I'm amazed that your guests really followed your request,' Serene was truly impressed at the pile of boxes in different shades of pink.

'Are we going to open all the pink gifts now?' Lance paused his Netflix movie and rose from his recliner in the family room.

'Oh no, I'll open just one each day. Please help me choose the first one,' she said, jumping with excitement.

Lance inspected the pile and picked up the smallest box. 'What about this one?' he asked.

'Hmmm, let me see, it's from you and Mummy,' she said, jumping even more. By now, she had kicked her shoes off and started opening the present carefully. Underneath the pink wrapper was a blue box from Tiffany's. 'Oh Daddy, Mummy, you cheated. The box inside is blue,' she said with a huge grin.

Serene wanted to remember Chrystal's expression as she opened her gift, so she took videos and pictures using her mobile phone's camera. But after some time, she put the phone away and simply took in her daughter's excitement. Chrystal lifted the necklace out of the box and asked Lance and Serene to put it around her neck. She twirled around and skipped towards the framed mirror on one of the walls. Serene was silently thankful to have a cheerful daughter in Chrystal, who expressed her feelings honestly, regardless of where they lay on the happy/sad spectrum. Chrystal returned and hugged them both. 'I don't want to grow up,' she said with a pout.

'We also don't want you to grow up,' Lance said, hugging her tightly and kissing the top of her head.

'Stay sweet, my baby,' Serene kissed her cheeks.

Lance and Serene returned to the family room after Chrystal had gone upstairs to her room. He popped open a bottle of champagne. They had this ritual of celebrating Chrystal's birthday with a rare bottle of wine that they had picked up on their travels. It reminded them what they had overcome, sixteen years ago. It reminded them how truly precious the gift of life was.

Serene had had a difficult pregnancy, which she hadn't revealed to many people. Aside from having conflicts with her family, Serene had become more anxious when her Ob-Gyn had discovered that she had extremely low amniotic fluid index or AFI in her sixth month of pregnancy. A low AFI could cause premature delivery, which in turn could lead to the baby being monitored in the Neonatal Intensive Care Unit or NICU for however long necessary. Lance and Serene knew that they could never prepare sufficiently for a situation that was riddled with uncertainties. Throughout her last trimester of pregnancy, Serene had been burdened with an unknown threat. True to her Ob-Gyn's prediction, Serene had given birth prematurely and by emergency C-section. Chrystal had stayed in the NICU for two weeks. During those tumultuous weeks, Serene couldn't even cradle Chrystal during the first few days, all while being aware how critical this period was in creating a bond between the mother and child. When she had been discharged three days after her delivery, Serene had had to leave the hospital without her baby. It had felt even more strange that they could see Chrystal only for a few hours each day. Even as a doctor, Serene hadn't been allowed to stay in the NICU beyond the visiting hours. Every night, she had cried on Lance's shoulder in longing for the baby that they couldn't yet hold. Every night, they would go to the fully decorated nursery that stood empty and forlorn without its much-awaited resident. She was at her lowest. Sometimes, she still wondered how she pulled through. Then she remembered how Lance had been a tower of strength. And how the Room 216 girls had immediately come together for her. Tintin, who was still based in Manila, had visited every day. Sandy had flown in and spent the week with her. Issa had been prepared to do the same at a moment's notice.

Chrystal had been a cause of great worry as much as a blessing, from the outset. Her first year had been punctuated with visits to the emergency room. She had picked up all types of viruses, likely because she didn't have the antibodies that one developed after a natural birth—Serene knew that babies who were delivered through C-section risked having lower immunity. She couldn't be more grateful that those times were behind them now. She looked up from her introspection and was amused to find Lance looking at her intently, seeming to read her thoughts.

'Here's to surviving that rollercoaster of a month,' he raised his glass.

'And to all the happy months, afterwards,' Serene said as their glasses touched.

'Even my turns changing the diaper and feeding the baby at night,' Lance said.

'Don't you miss those?' Serene raised one eyebrow, but burst out laughing because she couldn't keep up the act for long.

'Nah, no more. But I did enjoy every day and every night at the time, except for those first weeks at NICU,' he smiled before sipping his champagne.

Chapter 10

Because she believed that life is short, Serene sometimes had to accept that some things aren't meant to last. 'But I thought you're happy doing what you're doing?' Serene asked Michelle after reading her resignation letter. To say that she was shocked, would be an understatement. 'And I thought you liked working with me,' she added.

'Yes po, Doctora. I've truly enjoyed working with you, that's why I've stayed on in this role since passing the board exam. I'm sorry that this has come as unpleasant news,' Michelle almost choked, out of nervousness. 'The thing is, Mark and I have broken up. For good,' Michelle said, the corners of her eyes starting to glisten.

'What does he have to do with your job? You were anyway in an on-off relationship for the longest time, maybe it's better for you to be off him for good,' Serene fumed at the thought of Mark.

'That's what I also thought. I'm tired of waiting,' Michelle said, her voice quavering. 'My friend has been asking me to apply for this job in Dubai for the longest time. I hadn't considered it earlier, in the hopes that Mark would come around.'

'When did you apply?'

'Three months ago. I'm sorry, Doctora. Up to the last minute, I was hoping it wouldn't come through. But then the approval came in, and Mark was still Mark. So I guess that decided it for me,' Michelle said, her tears flowing uncontrollably now.

'Oh, Michelle. I don't want you to go, you know that,' Serene went to hug her.

'I also don't want to go if it were just about you, Doctora. But I need to start anew or I'll be trapped in this situation with Mark forever,' she said, crying harder.

'When are you planning to fly out?' Serene asked, somewhat accepting Michelle's resignation now.

'I'm hoping that we could get and train a replacement within a month. Will that be too short notice?' Michelle asked.

'Well, it is too short, but it's more important for you to get a fresh start sooner. Do you have any friends who'd be interested in your position?' Serene asked.

'I might have a couple of referrals. Thank you po, Doctora. And I'm truly sorry,' Michelle said. They hugged each other until Michelle gradually stopped weeping.

'I'm sure things will work out fine for you, eventually. You're a good person and you've always been kind to others, this good karma will come back to you,' Serene said. 'I hate to see you go, but I care about you so much that I'm giving you my blessings,' she added before releasing Michelle from her embrace.

That evening, on her way home, Serene couldn't help but feel saddened at Michelle's imminent departure. It would be a great loss for her. It would be difficult to find someone as diligent and as dedicated as Michelle. Serene's professional life had gone smoothly largely due to Michelle's efficiency as an assistant. Over the years, Serene had also come to treat her not just as an employee but almost like a member of her family. She cared about what would happen to her and wanted her to be happy in life. She didn't believe that Michelle would find this with Mark. If after all these years, he still hadn't mustered the courage to make a single sacrifice for Michelle, then nothing would ever push him into that direction. She hated Mark. Serene was relieved that she didn't end up siding with Mark at any point. If she hadn't had the courage to elope with Lance, she wouldn't have had the greatest joy called Chrystal now. She knew several people in their social circle who were like Mark. Or even worse. Some went ahead and followed their parents' wishes when it came to the choice of spouse, but later on, they had inevitably got involved in secret affairs. It was unfair to the betrayed spouse as well as the other party; the 'other woman' or the mistress, or conversely, the 'boytoy'—as though the only reason a married woman would have an affair was for carnal pleasure.

On Michelle's last day at the office, Serene organized a lunch party and invited Michelle's close friends at the MAB and the hospital. Throughout the lunch at the Italian restaurant, everyone tried to entertain Michelle with a funny anecdote or two, and though it made her laugh, she was moved to tears towards the end, having to say goodbye to her colleagues of more than eight years.

When lunch was about to end and they had a moment to themselves, Serene led Michelle to a quiet corner and gave her a send-away gift. 'I wish you all the best in this new phase. But I want you to know that if ever Dubai doesn't work out for you, you'll always have your old job to come back to. Any day,' Serene said, hugging her.

Michelle became teary-eyed again, but then her colleagues came over and cheered her up with some popular songs. The team requested for a karaoke machine to be brought to the function room they had reserved for the party. Serene left them to enjoy themselves, ensuring that their snacks and drinks were paid for.

She stepped out into the bright summer sun as she waited for her driver to pick her up in the restaurant's driveway. She put on her sunglasses and looked at the leafy tamarind trees along

Tomas Morato Avenue. Quezon City could do with more trees; the few left standing along the avenue now glistened in the afternoon sun. She reflected on the life of trees. Some had short lives either because of human folly or natural disaster, though most of the time it was the former. Without man's intervention or nature's fury, trees could last thousands of years. Serene remembered the redwood trees of California or even the bonsai trees at the Meiji Shrine in Tokyo, that she and the Room 216 girls had visited during one of their reunions. Those trees had been witness not just to generations, but to several civilizations. Those trees had long lives. Unlike man, who only had a fraction of the life of trees. Or Darwin's tortoises.

The drive to her house was relatively quiet due to the off-peak hours, the rush-hour traffic still a couple of hours away. They passed by a leafy portion of New Manila. Serene gazed out at the old mansions and their famed Balete trees. Some of the old mansions were crumbling, but surprisingly, the trees in front of them remained sturdy. Serene smiled to herself. While human life might be shorter compared to other species, she didn't have any regrets about hers. She had loyal friends who would flock to her side at the shortest of notice. They had weathered many storms together, like those sturdy trees. Knowing this gave her so much courage.

Serene had also fought for love. She had suffered because of it and she was prepared to suffer even more, if required. She believed that living without true love wasn't living at all. It only reduced one's 'real life' span to meaninglessness. Marriage without love was a sentence worse than death. Serene was grateful that she had made some right decisions in life. She hoped that when the time came for Chrystal to live her own life, she would always have choices and maintain her zest for life. Life was short, and clinically, Serene knew this better than many people. And everyone deserved to live a full life here on earth, however short it may be.

Part IV

Issa

Chapter 1

Manila, 2009

It had been after more than ten years since their university graduation that the former roommates unanimously decided to celebrate this milestone in Manila, in support of Issa. Serene was hosting the reunion. She reviewed her task list and underlined the top priority: reserve the restaurant for their special dinner. From there, they could head to Conway's, where she enjoyed the pianist's repertoire; she knew that her roommates would at least enjoy the music, if not the drinks. Serene cherished the regular get-together with the three of them. Previous reunions were held in Hong Kong, Singapore and Tokyo. Their days together were typically filled with shopping, visits to the theatres and museums, a side-trip here and there, and in-between, talks about the 'boys they had loved before'. She knew, however, that while previous reunions had been light-hearted, this year was going to be more subdued. Just two weeks ago, Issa had found out that she had stage-III breast cancer.

When Serene had first learned about Issa's condition, she hadn't wanted to believe it. Issa was too young to get breast cancer. But when she had found out that it had likely been caused by a genetic mutation, she had begun to digest the information like a typical doctor, immediately thinking of the therapeutic options and calling an oncologist friend up for her opinion.

'The technology is much better these days. There's hope for stage-III and even more so for earlier stages. Of course, the success rate also depends largely on the patient's health. Some patients make it through better than others, that's no secret,' the oncologist had explained to her.

Serene had inhaled deeply and put on a cheerful tone. 'We're getting rid of those cancerous tumours immediately,' she had announced in her most confident voice during the multi-way calls with Issa, Tintin and Sandy.

After their group chat, Serene had received a call from Tintin, who had sobbed uncontrollably on the line. 'This is the first time someone particularly close to me has been diagnosed with cancer. While I've been joining breast cancer walks out of peer pressure, the disease had remained abstract to me until today. Now, it has a face, and sadly it's that of Issa's,' Tintin had said between sniffles.

Though she had live-in helpers, Serene had spent time choosing the bed sheets, picking a floral Laura Ashley for one bed and a burgundy Marimekko print for the other. She had ensured that her maids dusted all the surfaces and corners of the large guest room twice and sprayed a dark amber Zara home fragrance. There were two queen-size beds in the room and Serene planned to sleep there together with the three girls, just like old times.

Sandy arrived from Singapore a day before Issa and Tintin, to help Serene. Tall and dressed in all black, with her sleeveless blouse, cigarette pants and a long cardigan reaching just above the knee, she exuded confidence and straightforwardness. But people close to her knew that underneath her serious demeanour, Sandy had a great sense of humour that she tended to share only with those she knew would understand.

Issa arrived on a direct flight from Barcelona, the next day. 'Thank God for non-stop flights,' she hugged Sandy and

Serene as soon as she had taken off her mask, which the doctor had advised her to always wear in public places. Issa used to be a swimming athlete. She was slimmer now, but her muscles had remained toned. Despite being an athlete, though, Issa was the only one who smoked. The roommates had earlier wondered how she was never caught by the night guard at the dorm with a strict no-smoking policy.

Apparently, Issa used to hide in one corner of the view deck, where she would light one or two cigarettes just before the guard did his regular inspection. By then, Issa would be done with her ritual, and with the help of her personal ashtray that looked like a jewellery case, she took care to never leave a stub behind. She also used to carry a cheap perfume with her, which she used to mask any residual odour. Issa was known for her mantra, '*Que sera sera*', whenever she turned up unprepared for an examination, back at the university. But her inherent aptitude for languages had helped her graduate her Bachelor of Arts in European Languages course with high honours. After university, she had applied for and been granted a scholarship in Barcelona, where she had completed graduate school and subsequently stayed on to teach English as a second language to Spanish students.

Sandy and Serene fussed to the point of being solicitous, which made Issa start complaining. 'Oh please, ladies. I'm not totally frail or dying already that you want me to just sit in one corner or lie on the bed,' Issa said.

'Issa, I don't want you to unnecessarily strain yourself. You have had a long flight; even if you were healthier, you'd still need to rest after.' Serene helped her sit more comfortably on a recliner. 'You can adjust the settings with these buttons,' she said, handing the remote control to Issa.

'I can't take this, Serene. Please don't. Not yet, anyway.' Issa chose one of the ordinary armchairs to sit on instead.

'I hope you've been taking Vitamin C and other antioxidant supplements?' Sandy asked.

'I am. That's one thing I'm conscientious about,' Issa said.

Later that day, Serene went back to the airport for Tintin, who lived in New York. Her husband, Patrick, worked there at a global consulting firm. When Serene opened the door to usher Tintin into the house, Issa and Sandy practically jumped from the sofa in excitement. All three were reminded that Tintin was the life of the party—there would be no boredom in the room whenever Tintin was in it. She started regaling them about the people she met on her flight and the couple who suggested they should all join the New York City marathon together.

'That fast?' admired Serene, who squirmed at the thought of talking to strangers. She always wondered how Tintin had a knack for it, but maybe that was what one learned from a course in mass communication. 'You look good, you never seem to gain weight,' she added.

'No talking about weight, please,' Sandy laid down the first ground rule. She had gained the most weight among them, despite having been the frailest at university. She blamed it on job stress and her erratic work schedule due to frequent travel. She had resorted to 'comfort food' to cope with stress. She could not focus unless she was chewing something, especially the 'homemade' almond cookies that she bought regularly from the coffee shop near her office building.

As if by tacit agreement, the roommates didn't talk about Issa's condition on their first dinner together, a barbecue on Serene's patio. But the following day, while having a long brunch in a café at Ortigas Center, Serene started sharing her medical perspective, setting the tone for a more objective and less emotional discussion. They supported Issa's decision to undergo treatment in the Philippines, as Serene could help oversee it, along with Issa's cousin, Anton, who was a medical director at a large hospital in Quezon City. After all, the Philippines had a thriving medical tourism industry with several world-class facilities catering to patients from various parts of the world. However, it had not been easy for Issa to persuade her partner about this option. 'It's taken me a long time to convince Enrique,' Issa said.

'But given the lack of legal attachment, Enrique shouldn't have much say in the matter, I guess,' commented Tintin.

Both Serene and Sandy gave Tintin a sharp look that prevented her from saying anything more.

Issa had met Enrique at an exhibit at Fundacion Joan Miro. They struck up a conversation after Enrique overheard that she taught at the same university, though in another department. The rest, as they say, is history. While Enrique and Issa had been living together for five years, the roommates joked that he was so engrossed in his teaching that he had forgotten to propose to Issa.

'Oh, in fact, he proposed after we had found out about my condition. But of course, it isn't fair to accept such a proposal at this time,' Issa said.

'What's so unfair in that?' Sandy couldn't help but speak her mind, though she tried to sweeten her tone. 'You've spent many of your most productive years with him, anyway.'

'Yes, but I'm not one to pressure him into marriage, if that's what you mean. You know my view about marriage, Sands. You were there when Mum and Dad went through the annulment. In fact, that's what triggered my smoking.'

Issa was in her second year at university when her parents' marriage unravelled. Twenty-five years of union had disintegrated in a second, she used to say. Just like that. Issa never found out why. Both her parents insisted that their marriage had run its course through no fault of theirs. Sometimes things just happen, they said. Years later, Issa heard rumours about her father having had an affair with an assistant of his. Being an only child, Issa had felt torn at that time. While close to her mother, she had also bonded well with her father. She avoided taking sides and she didn't want to be forced into such situation. She had wished then that she had a sibling—she would have had someone to talk to and they could have comforted each other. Her roommates rallied behind her at the time, but having their own orderly lives to live, Issa doubted if they ever really understood what she was going through. She spent the most time with Sandy during this tumultuous period. Sandy was perceptive and expansive even then, despite her seeming detachment. She went out of her way to ensure Issa was never alone and invited her to her home province during holiday breaks.

'Issa, I know what you went through back then, but aren't you selling yourself too short by living with someone for this long and never expecting legal commitment?' Tintin knew her comments weren't appropriate, but she was too irritated by now.

'Tin, just because I'm in this condition, doesn't mean you can say anything you want,' Issa sighed, not having the energy to fight, but annoyed with Tintin.

'I'm sorry, but I don't want you to be taken advantage of,' Tintin said.

'I choose my battles. Now let's leave this topic alone, shall we?' Issa lit up a cigarette and excused herself to go to the smoking area.

All three glared at her. 'Yeah I know, I will have to quit this anyway once I start my treatment. Now let me enjoy my last few puffs, okay?' she yelled on her way out.

While smoking in a far corner of Serene's backyard, Issa recalled her earlier discussion with Enrique. 'Issa, you don't have a family in Manila, your mother has passed on and your father is not even in the Philippines,' he had said.

'Serene and Anton, both highly capable doctors, are there. The Room 216 girls will be with me.' Her roommates had promised that at least one of them would be there to assist her during the most critical radiation and chemotherapy sessions, with Serene starting off discharging this 'duty'. 'They're the closest thing I have to a family, honey. Closer than I ever was to my own father,' Issa had wept.

'Issa, don't cry. I know it's difficult, but you don't have to go all the way there for treatment. I can manage it here. I have some savings. And how would I feel, with you being there all alone, across the oceans from me?'

'Enrique, *por favor*. Think about it. You can't take leave from work just now, not when you're waiting for your promotion, which is long overdue.'

'But what's the point if I can't be with you?'

'Honey, I'll be fine. We'll chat every day. And you can even come pick me up after my treatment,' Issa had been hugging him by now. In all their years together, this had been the first time Enrique had looked uncertain and this had made Issa feel even more dejected. Ultimately, Enrique had agreed to Issa's plan, fervently promising that he would join her as soon as his promotion got confirmed.

On the second day of their reunion, the four roommates drove to Antipolo for a much-anticipated art session, followed by a blissed-out afternoon of massages at the Chi Spa in Shangri-La, where they were staying overnight. Later in the evening, they retreated to the balcony of their adjoining rooms and as if they were college kids again, played their version of Truth or Dare, with a tequila shot for each dare. After this, they went to the bar downstairs where a live band was performing, and a group of patrons jammed and danced around. Though they each had only four shots of tequila, Sandy felt like they were behaving sillier than their age, but she went with the flow anyway. Issa was soon pressured into leading the group in a choreographed rendition of '*Liberté*', by Gilbert Montagne. After all, she was the only one who could speak French among the four.

The next day, they lounged by the swimming pool, happily recalling last night's escapades. 'In fairness, your French singing was impeccable,' teased Tintin.

'Oh yeah, thanks to you. But never again,' Issa replied before jumping into the pool.

Serene and Sandy were sitting on the deck, having done their regimented swimming earlier. 'Okay guys, time for our mani and pedi,' Serene called out, sometime later. She then led them to the salon in the hotel's basement.

Over lunch, Issa shared details of her plans, which Serene supplemented with her own medical perspective and her discussions with Anton. 'Obviously, I'm taking a sabbatical next term to attend to these twins,' Issa made light of her situation. 'Serene and Anton helped map out the plan,' she nodded at Serene.

'Oh please, it's Anton mainly. He's far more experienced than me in this,' Serene said.

'Well, with two experts onboard, I'm confident that we have a strong plan. Now, that calls for a drink,' cheered Tintin as she ordered champagne.

When Tintin and Sandy were alone in the restroom, Tintin could not help but weep, 'Why does it have to be Issa?'

'Never show that you're crying. We have to be strong for her, you know that,' Sandy reminded Tintin.

'Yes, Your Frostiness, I won't show a single tear,' Tintin replied.

'Okay, let's go back before the two get suspicious,' Sandy pulled Tintin out of the powder room. She was used to this moniker by now, slapped on her for not being a touchy-feely person. She was never good at expressing her emotions. In fact, Sandy didn't cry at all when she first learned of Issa's condition, though she kept on misplacing her things, including her car keys and her phone. She expressed an emotion only when it was that of dissatisfaction, and one would know it well in advance, thanks to her deep frowns and sarcastic remarks.

On the short drive back to Serene's house, the four started singing songs from their youth, mostly from the tail-end of the New Wave era. They all loved The Smiths and The Cure. Who could forget 'Friday I'm in Love', their room's anthem that they sang dutifully on Friday afternoons—never mind if most of the time they sang it out of tune? Or 'Heaven Knows I'm Miserable Now' whenever the mid-terms or final exams were approaching.

The next day, the roommates shopped at the Rockwell Power Plant Mall in Makati City. Serene never missed checking her favourite French and Italian luxury brands for their latest season offerings. In fact, she had registered her shoe size in most of the stores there. The sales assistants would know to promptly show her the latest designs in her size whenever she dropped by. Understandably, Issa was in no mood to shop, so she sat at a café with a book she had grabbed from Fully Booked. Sandy or Tintin would alternately sit with her between their browsing at the shops.

On the last day of their reunion, the four wound down at Serene's house, reminiscing about the past with the help of Serene's faded photo albums. Issa took a picture of her favourite photo of the group, all four of them in a wacky pose in the corridor, with Room 216 in the background. They had arranged themselves by height, with Issa being the tallest and Serene the shortest. Both Issa and Serene still had the same build as before, while Sandy had developed into her 'womanly shape'. Tintin used to be frail, but was now more toned.

Chapter 2

Manila, 2009

If she could live her life all over again, what major life decisions would she change? Issa asked herself again, as though she hadn't been through this drill several times before. She was sitting on her Aunt Doreen's porch one morning, with Doreen's cat, Figaro, sitting quietly at her feet by the lawn chair. After the reunion at Serene's, Issa had shifted to this teacher's cottage at the state university where Doreen taught, at the College of Education. It was a tranquil neighbourhood of tree-lined streets, quite secluded from the bustle of the city, such that it was almost like an island of its own. Issa tried to read a book, but she couldn't move beyond page ten of the slim novel she had picked up from Doreen's library. She closed her book and turned to Figaro, who seemed to be sleeping, her furry white tummy rising and falling rhythmically. She thought about why she was back here at this juncture. As a foreign worker in Spain, she still didn't have full access to the healthcare system. Her healthcare plan from the university didn't cover specialized care. Treatment in Barcelona would cost a fortune, which she clearly didn't have. On the other hand, both Serene and Anton had offered to help her if the treatment was done in the Philippines, plus Issa still had the health insurance plan that her mother had purchased for her, years ago. Her mother had insisted on paying the premium for it even when Issa was already living overseas.

In a way, she had continued to watch over her long after her death.

At times, Issa blamed herself for not having been prepared for 'rainy days' like now. She was the least financially secure among her roommates. Teaching was among the least-paid white-collar professions. Issa's salary could barely cover her basic necessities, especially in a city like Barcelona, which had become extremely expensive to live in because of the regular influx of tourists. She and Enrique lived in a small, one-bedroom apartment, but their monthly rent ate up a good portion of their salaries because they lived in an area that had been gentrified over the past few years. More cafés and bars popped up just steps away from their building. Because they were now near the 'happening' places, they ended up eating out or drinking more often than they could truly afford. While this made their lives seem more interesting, Issa realized they had been paying such a high premium for the small convenience.

Why did Issa not take up a more lucrative job? By now, she could have become a diplomat at the Philippine embassy or a director at the Instituto de Cervantes. She had effortlessly passed the exam for the highly competitive Foreign Service Officer role in the Philippines, but then had decided to follow her passion for teaching, instead. It gave her no greater pleasure to see her students transform from awkward and hesitant English speakers into confident ones. She had empowered students to communicate better with anglophiles on the international stage. She knew this by the cards of appreciation from various English-speaking countries that arrived in her mail regularly. She smiled at the thought of having contributed to the opportunities they were enjoying now.

Issa repositioned her lawn chair to face the rising sun, careful not to wake Figaro up, who opened her eyes just for a split second but then promptly went back to sleep. Issa put on her sunglasses and offered her face to the sky. Financial wealth was not the only yardstick in this world. While she had made less palatable choices from a financial perspective, Issa took pride in her contribution to the world. Wasn't that a better and more lasting legacy? Hadn't she made more impact that way, instead of amassing wealth from a meaningless job? Issa didn't regret anything. She had made her peace with her past. She had accepted the consequences of her choices.

Chapter 3

What's the minimum requirement to be truly considered a human being? A car is still a car and can run even if it's missing one of its side-mirrors. Or if one of its windows is broken. But a car won't be serving its purpose if even just one of its wheels is deflated. Similarly, what parts of the human body are truly essential and which ones are merely accessories? Was Issa still a human being without some body parts? Thinking back to her surgery, Issa didn't find this to be the most painful part of her treatment, as she had been under the influence of anesthesia that had numbed her pain during the procedure. At the hospital where Anton worked, the medical team implemented Issa's treatment plan by starting with the total mastectomy to remove Issa's cancerous tumour, which had grown beyond five centimetres. Issa had been brave throughout the process, helped by the cheerful and caring disposition of the attending team and the reassuring presence of both Anton and Serene. Through it all, Issa remained convinced that she had done the right thing by coming back home, looking at all the extra care she received.

It was the aftermath of the surgery that almost broke Issa. On her first day back at Doreen's house, Issa saw her body in its post-surgery state for the first time. In the bathroom, she stood in front of the mirror and stared at her reflection.

Issa, who used to revel in her athletic physique, was now a few pounds lighter than she had been a month ago. A plaster was wrapped around her former 36B-size breast. She didn't have the courage to peek at the still-fresh wound. But even with the plaster bandeau around her chest, she already felt incomplete. A huge part of her had been taken out by the surgery. Before this, she didn't have any physical scar, not even a tiny one on her knee that some of her friends had, perhaps acquired from an injury during childhood. Issa, who used to turn heads in university even in her simplest outfits, white tees and faded jeans, was now a flat-chested woman. With the weight loss and mastectomy, she also noticed wrinkles around her armpits. She worried about what Enrique would think when he saw her in this condition.

Serene visited Issa that afternoon. 'The team did a very neat job, don't you think? They managed to remove the tumour and leave only the tiniest of scars,' she smiled.

'Yes, and they are a happy bunch, too. That, I really appreciate. But they also took out my twin assets along with the tumour,' Issa sighed.

'I'm sorry, but there was no other choice. That's the only way to stop the growth and spread of the tumour,' Serene held Issa's hand in an attempt to comfort her.

'So am I cancer-free now? Am I totally cured and can now go back to Barcelona?' Issa smiled at the mere thought of returning to Barcelona.

'I wish it were that easy. While the surgery was done with curative intention, no doctor worth his salt would tell you that you're totally cured of cancer,' Serene explained.

'What does that mean?' she asked.

'You still need to do the adjuvant chemotherapy to ensure that all the tiny cancerous cells are removed, to ensure nothing is left,' Serene said. 'It will be uncomfortable. I'm already warning you. But it's for the better. It's to help you live a healthier life for the many years to come.'

'I don't know if anything can be more uncomfortable than my current state. I feel too light, without any substance to hold me up. I've lost an integral part of me. It's the one thing that defined my womanhood, and now it's gone.'

'Oh, Issa,' Serene hugged her but was mindful not to squeeze her around the chest. 'Have you considered reconstructive surgery? It can be done after the chemotherapy.'

'I'm not sure about that. I don't have any fake parts in my body and I hope it stays that way. I used to love my body,' Issa finally bawled.

'You're still beautiful, Issa, you know that, don't you? You're as stunning as before, if a bit frailer.' Tears also pooled in Serene's eyes. Indeed, Issa's beauty was undiminished, though now she had the air of fragility, which made Serene want to protect her even more.

'I don't know. I've always stood tall with my chest out because I've always been proud of every inch of my body,' she mumbled as she dabbed at her tears with the tissue that Serene handed her.

'I believe in you, Issa. You've got inner strength that will pull you through this episode. This too, shall pass. And we're all here for you,' Serene reassured her.

When the chemotherapy sessions started a few days after her surgery, Issa began to lose a good portion of her lustrous hair. She decided then to shave the remaining hair off, like many cancer patients do. She also suffered from nausea and threw up on some days, but Doreen stayed home to comfort her on such days. Doreen also hired a nursing assistant who came to help Issa out in the morning.

Throughout the week, Issa's daily calls with Enrique were fraught with tears and emotions. 'Issa, be strong, I'll soon be there for you,' Enrique reminded her, as he had done in previous calls.

'This is the most terrible time of my life. I feel doubly incomplete with integral parts of me removed from my body and you being away as well. I'm not sure I can get through another week of this,' Issa couldn't control her tears from falling.

'I'll come as soon as I get the news from the dean. His secretary said the decision will be announced this Friday. The wait is almost over, honey,' Enrique said, wiping off his tears.

'Call me as soon as you get the news. I can't wait for you to finally be recognized for all your hard work. It will definitely cheer me up,' she said, crossing her fingers as she did so.

It was Sandy's turn to be with Issa the following week. 'Issa, I'm glad that you're down to your last session. I should have been with you sooner, but I got caught up in our annual planning,' Sandy explained.

'Oh, Sands, thank God you're here now. I feel better knowing that you'll be with me at the next session,' Issa said, still holding on to Sandy. 'The sessions are physically draining. But I tend to feel better after that meal replacement you sent.'

'That's one product I'm immensely proud of. We earn more from our vitamin supplements and milk products, but it's therapeutic products like those that make a vast difference to society. The science behind it is quite impressive.'

'I've been drinking it regularly. I don't have any appetite for real food, so it really helps.'

'How do you feel, otherwise? I mean, emotionally,' Sandy asked while helping Issa put her dress on.

'I feel raw and incomplete. Is this still me, Sands? Is this still your friend, Issa?' she pointed at herself.

'Issa, the body is just a shell. Your true essence can't be destroyed by a mere thing like cancer. You are stunning as ever, perhaps even more so now that I can see the perfect shape of your head. I'm not saying this just to flatter you,' she reassured her.

'Oh, Sands, you and Serene never fail to make me feel good about my appearance,' she hugged Sandy tightly.

'It's true though, Issa. None of us would ever consider competing with you in the beauty department. Remember how many flower bouquets you used to receive on Valentine's Day? How we all got spoiled by the overflowing supply of chocolates for you? I can assure you, Issa, if you were still available today, you would still receive as many chocolates or even more, with your new look,' Sandy lifted Issa's chin so that Issa could look at her reflection in the mirror.

'Oh God, those chocolates. Why did you have to remind me?' she tore her eyes from the mirror to look at Sandy.

'Because I almost tripped over a delivery downstairs,' Sandy replied.

'Really, another one? Enrique has been sending them regularly, along with the flowers, even when I told him there's too much of them already and I don't even have an appetite at all. He said to have a feast when I'm better,' Issa smiled.

Chapter 4

Manila, 2009

Enrique arrived in Manila the following week. It was the most emotional reunion for him and Issa, who ran into his arms and immediately cried uncontrollably as soon as he entered the drawing room. Enrique, too, couldn't stop his tears, almost oblivious to Anton, who picked him up from the airport, and to Doreen, who was waiting to welcome him. Anton excused himself and went to the adjacent room to make a call. Once their tears stopped, Doreen led the couple to the dining room, where coffee and some refreshments were waiting for them. Anton joined them after a few minutes and they tried to talk of happier times, like the holidays they had been on together, once to Boracay and another time to Barcelona, when both Doreen and Anton had visited them.

When Issa and Enrique settled for the night in their room, he helped Issa change into her night dress. He undressed her carefully, as though she was a delicate and fragile gem. Issa watched Enrique's expression as he looked at her naked body for the first time since the surgery. She didn't want to see pity in his eyes. Although she still wore a bandage around her chest, her wound had started drying and didn't require as much gauze and cotton as earlier. 'Issa, darling, if anything, I love you even more,' he said, kissing her bandaged chest. Yet, Issa dreaded the time when Enrique would see her ghastly wound.

Issa also let him open her paisley bandana, a gift from Doreen. She had a tuft of hair now, less than an inch, so she wasn't exactly bald or a skinhead, but she felt naked without the protection of her long hair. Enrique leaned over and kissed her head, gently and slowly. 'You're more beautiful than I remember, darling,' he whispered.

'You're not just saying this because I'm unwell, are you?' she asked, holding back the tears that threatened to cascade any moment now. She could see the sadness in his eyes, but she was quietly glad that there was no sign of pity in them.

'No, darling. You know me better than that. I don't want to be away from you. Ever again. The past couple of months were sheer hell. Filled with such agony,' Enrique squeezed his eyes shut as though trying to shake off a bad memory. He mustered a smile before opening his eyes again. 'Though I got my promotion in the end, I don't think it was worth the sacrifice of being away from you. But then, you wanted the treatment to be done here,' he started kissing her on the lips. Then he cradled her face in his hands, and implored her to wipe away whatever tears were left. 'I don't want you to cry like this again. Things will be better from hereon. I promise.'

The following morning, Enrique enlisted Doreen's help to decorate the garden. He ordered bouquets of red roses and spread them strategically around a koi pond. Enrique then fetched Issa from her room for breakfast, and after that, led her out to the patio and to the koi pond with its clear water. There, he kneeled on the petals of roses and begged her to marry him.

'Enrique, *te amo con todo mi corazon, mi querido*,' Issa wept bittersweet tears, a combination of her frustration over her health condition and her elation over Enrique's proposal.

'You're my life, Issa. I don't ever want to be apart from you again.' He kissed her fingers after putting on the ring. 'It's a bit looser than I expected, but we'll have it fixed back home,' he said.

That evening in the drawing room, Issa mindlessly watched the news while Enrique was upstairs, freshening up. Doreen soon joined her on the sofa and congratulated her once more. 'I'm so happy for you, hija. I'm still a romantic at heart, despite my age, as you probably can tell,' Doreen hugged her tightly.

'Oh, Tita, thank you. And thank you so much for taking care of me like I was your own child,' she held Doreen's hands as she solemnly expressed her gratitude.

'I promised your Mum, Issa. I promised her that I'll take care of you the way she took care of me back then. I owe Ate Myrna so much,' Doreen said. When their parents had died prematurely in a boating accident, Myrna worked double jobs to put Doreen through college. 'Ate Myrna ensured I always had whatever I needed, even if it meant yet another sacrifice for her. I still miss her after all these years,' Doreen looked at Issa wistfully.

'I miss Mum too. A lot,' Issa's eyes glistened at the mere thought of her mother.

'You and Anton are my only family, Issa. I can never forsake him or you. This is your home as much as mine or Anton's,' she assured her. 'Though I doubt he would want to live here again, now that he has a grander place,' she smiled with pride at Anton's accomplishment.

'I can never thank you enough, Tita. I wouldn't have considered having my treatment here if it weren't for you and Anton,' Issa added.

'We're always here for you, Issa. Never ever hesitate to ask me for anything,' Doreen hugged her once again. 'This might not be the best time to ask you this, but don't you think you should talk to your dad now? He might want to be part of the wedding,' Doreen suggested.

'I don't know, Tita,' Issa took time to answer this. 'I've never quite understood Daddy. I would have forgiven him for his infidelity if he had shown any remorse,' Issa replied. 'I haven't told him about my condition, but he might know because one of my cousins visited me at the hospital.'

'Which cousin?' Doreen asked.

'Do you remember Trina? She's about the same age as Anton. When Trina visited me after the surgery, I told her my tumour was benign and that I'm on the mend. I can't handle any fuss from that side of the family. They will just keep on pressuring me to reconcile with Daddy,' Issa said.

'It's been a long time. This grudge between you and your dad . . .' Doreen said, her eyes almost imploring Issa to start making peace.

'I haven't spoken to him for a long time now. I don't want to speak to him at this point. I have enough on my plate as it is,' Issa said, looking away into the distance.

A few weeks after Issa completed her chemotherapy sessions, she and Enrique stood in front of an officiating minister for their marriage ceremony at a private beach at Punta Fuego in Batangas province. Issa looked regal in her high-necked gown that she had managed to find in a boutique in Glorietta, and subsequently altered with the help of Serene's seamstress. Sandy, Serene and Tintin were all matrons of honour, marching proudly in their old rosewood gowns matching Issa's colour motif. After the ceremonies, they took fun shots acting as though they were still teens at university. Doreen, Anton and family were there, too. From Issa's paternal side, Trina and her parents, who represented the only branch of the clan still in the country, also attended. Most of Issa's immediate relatives, including her father and his second wife, now lived in California. Given the short notice, Issa doubted that they could come anyway. Only a select list of friends and relatives outside of her inner circle joined the wedding party. Enrique invited a couple of his friends: a former classmate whom he met at the Spanish embassy in Manila, and an acquaintance from Instituto de Cervantes.

'You've made me the happiest man today, darling,' Enrique kissed Issa's hands and then her lips after the marriage ceremony.

'And I, the happiest woman,' Issa kissed him back.

At the reception, the roommates took turns toasting to the bride and the groom, to the amusement of the audience. Enrique's former classmate also came forward and made an impromptu speech. After that, Enrique and Issa were surprised when Enrique's parents and elder brother's faces were projected on a screen. Then someone played the recorded video messages from Spain.

In the evening, some of the guests, including the Room 216 girls, Anton and Doreen, stayed back for the bonfire. They gathered around the fire by the beach, champagne and conversations flowing easily among all. Issa leaned on the big cushions, resting her head on Enrique's shoulder. She soaked in the evening breeze and the laughter that drifted in and out with it. This moment, that started to glow in pink from both the glorious sunset that the Philippines was known for, and the gentle flames of the bonfire, was truly a precious one. Issa wished she could freeze time and stay in this moment forever.

Life assumed a new rhythm for Enrique and Issa upon their return to Barcelona. Enrique was now less anxious and more settled after getting his promotion, assured of his tenure at the university. Issa resumed her teaching as well. She had become more mindful in her interaction with her colleagues and her students, savouring each moment with them, rather than merely breezing through meetings and classes, such that each occasion felt more meaningful. Each day was a bonus for her.

Issa and Enrique took the cancer episode as a chance to relook and change around a few things in their lives. They moved into a slightly larger house that afforded them greater space and had a small yard that Issa used to its full potential. She found joy in her morning ritual of tending to her plants, her roses and bluebells, begonias and gladioli, that now filled the tiny backyard. Issa had realized how fragile life is and how existing order can easily disintegrate in a single second, when fate intervenes. She was grateful that she and Enrique had got this second chance to better appreciate the preciousness of life.

In time, Issa had gotten used to her flat chest and ultimately forgotten how things were before her mastectomy. She had forgotten the ghastly wounds she didn't dare look at after her surgery. Her fears that her mastectomy would end the physical side of her relationship with Enrique, were clearly unfounded. It was awkward at the beginning, but in time, a new muscle memory developed, and Enrique and Issa learned to navigate the new terrain. While their lovemaking had become less playful, it had gained a new level of intensity, as though each time was the last time, making it more fulfilling than ever.

Chapter 5

Milestones became more special with the awareness of life's fragility and having been on the brink of losing it. Enrique and Issa marked their fifth wedding anniversary with a trip to Paris. He booked their stay in Castille Hotel on Rue Cambon, and Issa found out only later that it sat next to the former apartment and atelier of Coco Chanel. But knowing how pricey items were at the boutique, Issa contented herself by merely gazing at the mannequins behind the glass windows. There were other pleasures to be had that didn't require her to pawn whatever jewellery she owned, as that was the only way she could afford any items from Chanel. The hotel was within walking distance of the Jardin Tuileries, which offered greater pleasure than the dazzling items at the shop. And so, Enrique and Issa found themselves sitting on a bench under a freshly trimmed tree, with the garden's huge fountain to their left and a view of the Eiffel Tower to their right. They sipped their coffee quietly as they watched the pigeons gathering nearby and the kids running around the fountain, playing with the water.

Issa looked at Enrique, who for some time, wore a wistful expression on his face. When he realized she was looking at her, he smiled and squeezed her hand. Issa wasn't sure if Enrique's wistful look should be a cause for concern, but for now, she didn't want to alter the mood they were in. After a few more minutes of simply watching passers-by, they rose from their chairs and headed leisurely toward the Saint Germain district, stopping now and then to admire the ornate lamp posts along the Seine. Along the way, they checked out the stalls and browsed through old books and artworks. At midday, they reached the storied cafés in the district and decided on Café de Fleur, with the intention to visit its equally popular competitor across the street the next day. Issa ordered the chef-recommended salade flore. Enrique, meanwhile, went all-out French and ordered the 'must-have' escargot.

After lunch, they strolled further down until they stumbled upon the iconic Shakespeare & Company bookshop at Paris's Kilometer 0. They stood in the queue patiently waiting their turn as the shop manager limited the number of people inside. When they were eventually allowed in, Enrique darted straight away to the old books section, while Issa picked up one about the secrets of Paris from the featured section and brought it to the third floor room that looked out to the boulevard outside and the Seine beyond. She browsed through the book while waiting for Enrique, glancing now and then at the picturesque view from the cozy corner of the bookshop. Enrique soon joined her excitedly, showing off some rare finds, including works from the bookshops' early visitors, like Julio Cortazar and James Baldwin, to name a few.

Enrique and Issa crossed Rue de la Bûcherie on their way to their next stop, the Cathedral of Notre Dame. There was another queue, a much longer one, starting from the cathedral's entrance and winding all the way to a bridge over the Seine. Their friends back in Spain had warned them about the long wait, but Issa had felt compelled to visit the church by the grand stories she had read about it. Enrique pulled out one of the books he had just purchased and started reading while waiting for their turn. At some point, Issa sauntered towards the bridge and watched the day cruisers in the river. Tourist-packed boats floated by, which wasn't the best way to enjoy this historical city. After seeing two more boats full of tourists, Issa returned to the queue and decided to simply soak up the magnificence of the cathedral from the outside. She fixed her sunglasses as she gazed at the edifice's tall spires and ornate Gothic designs.

A few minutes later, the queue moved along and soon they were at the entrance. They headed directly to the south shoulder, where it was less crowded. Issa picked several tealight candles and placed them on the round candle stand. She lit the candles and prayed quietly as Enrique stood by her side. When she looked up, the pillar in front was shining in the light of the hundreds of glowing candles. She found solace in this sight, the soft illumination helping her find some clarity. The moment right after she had said her prayers, was devoid of fears and doubts. She felt much lighter now than at any other time. She looked at Enrique and motioned for them to move closer to the altar. She chose a vacant pew and sat for a few minutes of silence as Enrique excused himself to check out an exhibit of the cathedral miniatures in an adjacent wing. Issa had read countless citations about Notre Dame in reference books. To be there right now where she could touch for herself the historic pillars that she had only read about all these years, overwhelmed her. From her station, the gold cross gleamed like the sun. What a privilege it was to be there in peacetime, to have the opportunity to take in the splendour that had been standing for hundreds of years!

On their second day in Paris, Issa and Enrique explored the quaint shops at Marais, nondescript from the outside but full of unique trinkets inside. Though Issa barely bought anything, she found contentment from the mere sight of the *objets-d'art*: they represented the endless possibilities that creativity could spawn. By lunchtime, Enrique and Issa found themselves queueing up, yet again, but this time for 'the best falafel in the city'. When they were finally led to a table and subsequently served their orders, the two tucked into the food on their plates and lost themselves in savouring the distinct taste of the Mediterranean dish, a mix of ground chickpea, herbs and spices. After lunch, they moved on to a dessert place, where Issa truly enjoyed the crêpes; unusual, as she didn't normally take dessert. Soon, they set out for Saint Chappelle, another destination that was highly recommended by Enrique's colleague. Entering this chapel was less daunting than the other attractions they had visited so far, as the queue was much shorter. They quickly toured the ground floor so that they had more time at the main attraction on the next floor. Once again, on this visit, Issa was awestruck by another historic place—this time a royal chapel with the grandest stained glass windows that she had ever seen; all fifteen of them. When the late afternoon light filtered through the mosaic and reflected the colours on the floor, Issa stopped in her tracks and simply basked in the dazzling and glorious sight. Enrique pulled her closer to him and she rested her head on his shoulder as they followed the colours shimmering across the chapel.

On their last day in the city, Enrique and Issa spent the first part of the day at Musée d'Orsay, where they challenged each other to lose themselves in the museum, deciding to meet up only at noon by the giant clock on the fifth floor of the north-east-facing corner. The museum was not as huge as the Louvre, which they had only had a brief glimpse of, but both Issa and Enrique instantly preferred the ambience here, as visitors had more time to view the exhibits, and there was minimal intrusion from security guards. Issa took her time to view the permanent exhibits of modern artists from Monet to Renoir and Van Gogh. But while touring the section by herself, she absentmindedly reached out and took the hand of the person next to her, thinking it was Enrique's. Fortunately, the woman saw the humour in the situation and laughed it off with her. Issa checked her watch. It was still fifteen minutes before noon, but she anyway made her way up to the meeting place in front of the clock. When the lift door to the fourth floor opened, she turned right and followed the arrows leading to the clock. Upon reaching, the first person she saw was Enrique, standing there, waiting for her. With a wide grin. Holding a bouquet of roses. Issa couldn't help but hug him tight and forget everything else around her. Later, she looked around and was relieved that there were only three other people in the room who were oblivious to her and Enrique. They remained at the same spot until after noon, just looking out at the sprawling city from under the gigantic clock. Enrique pointed at the more recognizable buildings, but what captured her attention more were the eye-catching graffiti along the banks of the Seine. Indeed, art was everywhere in this city, whether in the cloistered walls of museums and churches, or outside of the walls, amid gardens and the flowing waters.

On their last night in Paris, they dined at a restaurant that Enrique had chosen partly for its vantage point, offering an unblocked view of the Eiffel Tower. 'Happy anniversary, my dearest Issa,' Enrique raised his glass of wine.

'To more happy years ahead,' Issa clinked her glass before taking a sip of the champagne.

'I hope the wine is to your liking, madame?' Enrique joked.

'Not our good ol' Rioja, but this will do, monsieur,' she laughed.

Their six-course meal was meant to be consumed without rush, each course to be savoured and appreciated in itself. Issa shook her head when dessert came, as she didn't have room for anything anymore, but Enrique begged her to have one bite for taste. He would finish the rest, he said, as what always happened whenever they dined out. Then he leaned over and held her hands, 'How do you feel about trying for a baby now?' he asked in all seriousness.

'But, why all of a sudden and why now?' She hadn't expected the question as she had assumed they had firmly closed the door on becoming parents in their life.

'I'm better established in my position. We both earn enough and can very well afford to have a baby now,' Enrique explained.

'I didn't know that you were still considering that, given my health condition,' Issa slumped on her chair.

'Only if you want. But maybe it's possible?' Enrique prodded.

'I'll think about it,' she looked out of the window to avoid Enrique's gaze. Just then, the Eiffel Tower lights flooded the city in brightness. She pointed this out to Enrique and both of them turned in the direction of the tower to get a better view. For some time, they sat there looking in one direction, absorbed by the play of lights.

In their hotel, Issa kept on thinking well into the night about the implications of having a baby. Enrique was now sleeping soundly beside her, but she couldn't bring herself to follow suit. She had reservations about conceiving now, because of her health condition and age. Was it right to have a baby at this point? Wasn't it irresponsible? But setting aside her health and age issues, did she even want to have a child at all? She had never contemplated being a mother before because she felt she wasn't maternal enough. But having conquered her battle with cancer, had her desire changed?

Back in Barcelona, Issa started researching the possibilities of conceiving. She instantly thought of checking with Serene. 'I've just read this article that says it's possible for cancer survivors to conceive and have a baby. How reliable is that?' she asked.

'That's well-proven. It's absolutely possible for a breast cancer survivor to conceive and become a mother,' Serene replied. 'Have you changed your mind about motherhood?'

'I don't know, but our financial situation has improved and Enrique would love for us to have a baby,' Issa shared.

'I'm glad to hear that it's a consideration now. It's a privilege to be a mother and I'm sure you'll love being one. You're great with kids, I've seen you with Chrystal, Alex and even Jamie,' Serene rattled off the names of the Room 216 girls' offspring. 'They enjoy their time with you, too. You'll definitely be a wonderful mum,' Serene replied excitedly.

'I'm also worried about my age. I'm in my late thirties now,' Issa's voice trailed off.

'Why don't you visit an Ob-Gyn? Maybe they can do some fertility tests and advise you about the viability. Otherwise, there are many ways now to become a mother. IVF, surrogacy and so on. And if all else fails, there's always adoption,' Serene suggested.

'Okay, let me think about this more thoroughly. And you're right, I should look for an Ob-Gyn and get an assessment,' Issa absentmindedly nodded to herself.

'Will you call me after your visit? I want to know straightaway. I'm getting excited on your behalf,' Serene sounded truly thrilled.

After her call with Serene, Issa stepped out for a walk in a nearby park. Walking helped clear her head; it was her preferred way of meditation. Along the way, she noticed that the trees looked more robust, their leaves glinting in the afternoon sun. The cherry trees in particular were in full bloom and some of the orange trees were also now bearing fruit. It was quite tempting to reach out for the lowest hanging one but picking fruits in public parks was prohibited, so Issa contented herself by merely looking at the bounty of the trees. She walked farther, aiming for her usual spot near the fountain at the centre of the park. A wild mix of yellow from jasmines and Spanish brooms lined the footpath leading to the centre. A huge oval-shaped flower bed blooming with carnations, lantanas and gazanias filled the space across from the fountain. But before reaching the fountain, Issa turned right, toward a quieter area of the park that had a row of benches. She chose one under a cherry tree and sat for a while, watching the pigeons as they came and went in their search for breadcrumbs.

How did one know if she was meant to be a mother in the real sense of the word? How did one know if she was generous enough to subordinate her needs to a tiny person's? How did one know that she would have this generous spirit constantly and not just when it was convenient? After all, motherhood required dedication and constancy. Earlier, Issa found it easier to reject the idea of motherhood because of a practical reason: economics. But once that barrier was broken, Issa couldn't think of any other compelling reasons not to be a mother. Perhaps, motherhood was one of those things that she simply had to do. She didn't need to analyse and rationalize endlessly. Issa got up from her bench and decided to visit a nearby library. Once there, she walked straight to the non-fiction section and picked up references about reproduction, checked them out, and headed back home.

Along the way, Issa went into further introspection. She wanted to see categorical signs that she indeed was meant to be a mother and would make a good one. She loved attending to plants and seeing them bloom. She liked to bake and cook. She enjoyed other activities that tend to nurture. And indeed as Serene pointed out, she loved her time with children. After all, she was a teacher, a job that required her to nurture the minds of her students. When she reached home, Issa deposited her books on the coffee table and scrutinized their drawing room. It was cozy. A place of warmth; a hearth. She even had a miniature statue of Hera the Greek goddess of marriage and motherhood on a corner stand. On the other hand, she also had one of Hestia, the virgin goddess of the hearth, right beside

Hera. She had picked up the souvenirs from one of her and Enrique's earlier trips to Greece.

Issa went into their bedroom. She undressed slowly, first taking off her flower-printed skirt, then her soft white cardigan, and her pastel pink tank top underneath. She entered the shower room, turned her face up to the water spray. She took a leisurely shower and was in deep thought as she slathered the body wash on her skin, lingering on her womb. After a few more minutes, she finally turned off the shower knob and reached out for the towel that she had hung earlier by the glass door. She stepped onto the fluffy bathroom mat and turned to face the mirror. She untucked the towel and dried herself gently. Then she looked at her body. Was this vessel, this battle-scarred body of hers, capable of and ready to spawn another life? Issa took out a long dress from her closet, put it on, sprayed a lavender-scented perfume, before heading to the nook that was their home office. She switched on her laptop and started her search for women's health clinics. She didn't want to ask any of her colleagues or friends in Barcelona for reference. She wasn't comfortable sharing the plan with them this early on. Eventually, Issa found a potential Ob-Gyn who had good reviews from several sources. She booked an appointment, scheduling it for the end of the week.

Chapter 6

What lengths must one go to, to affirm life? While still ambivalent about her capacity and capability for motherhood, Issa didn't want to break the chain, and more importantly, she didn't want to deprive Enrique of his right to parenthood. 'Though it's uncommon, I've seen women older than you who have successfully conceived and given birth to their first child. It's not easy. Very complicated, I must tell you. Now, this is rarer, but I've seen breast cancer survivors who, likewise, succeeded in becoming mothers. It's even more complicated, I must tell you,' the Spanish Ob-Gyn explained to her in a mix of English and Spanish. 'But the combination of the two, I must be honest with you, I haven't seen yet,' the elderly female doctor looked at Issa steadily but with a trace of concern.

'I understand. That's why we came to you. We'd like to hear an expert's opinion on whether it's possible or not, given my health condition and age,' Issa replied, also defaulting to a mix of English and Spanish.

Enrique sat by her side, filling in and adding on to Issa's explanation.

'You are my first patient who has both conditions. So while I'm not saying it's impossible, it's just that it's rare,' the doctor said. 'Do you want to go ahead?' she asked.

'*Si,*' Enrique answered first. The doctor waited for Issa's response.

'Yes, we'd like to go ahead,' Issa confirmed.

'*Entonces*, these are the things you have to do,' she said, taking out a brochure about reproduction and advising them on how to maximize their chances. She also prescribed supplements for both Enrique and Issa to 'improve their fertility'.

From that visit on, Enrique and Issa did their best to conceive, up to a point that their efforts almost became comical. Lovemaking started turning into a chore that was now dictated by the calendar, a task that they had to tick off, especially when Issa was at the height of ovulation. They also started checking both their temperatures regularly to ensure they didn't miss an important opportunity. Issa took folic acid and other supplements daily, as per doctor's instructions. She and Enrique also embarked on a healthier diet, reducing their trips to the tapas bar. These days, they went out for walks, runs and generally exercised more. Whenever the weather permitted, they would go to a nearby beach or the community pool, so that Issa could swim. In all this, Issa realized that lovemaking stopped being an expression of their passion for each other, and had turned into a task that needed to be accomplished at the appointed time, not too different from the homework and assignments that they gave to their students.

Every month they returned to the doctor, who advised them to keep trying. It had only been the second month, third month . . . the doctor would say every time. In the sixth month, however, the doctor prescribed additional tests, not just for Issa, but also for Enrique. The doctor needed a sperm analysis. They returned the following week for the results. 'I'm sorry to let you know, but aside from señora's problem with age and health, it looks like you also have a low sperm count and some issues with quality,' the doctor's eyebrows practically formed a unibrow as she conveyed the results to Enrique.

'What, this is not possible. How could that be?' Enrique's eyes widened in absolute disbelief.

'It happens, it could be hormonal. I can give you some medicine and perhaps, we can try again for the next six months?' The doctor suggested.

Enrique and Issa looked at each other. He hesitated, but Issa squeezed his hand to let him know that she would like to try. They had come this far. In the end, they took on the doctor's prescription. But with the passing of each month, both grew depressed, not only because of the negative results on each pregnancy kit, but because of the loss of precious time. They returned once again to the doctor after six months and further analysis.

'Given the situation, we might need to try other solutions. How open are you to IVF?' she asked.

'Do we have to resort to that?' Enrique sounded almost caustic.

'At this point, it's the most viable option, yes,' the doctor replied.

Enrique and Issa looked at each other. They both knew that IVF would cost them an arm and a leg. Issa shook her head. Her throat constricted but she did her best to quell any tears. Over the past few months, as she threw away one pregnancy test kit after another, her hope had gradually dimmed. Even Enrique commented that they had lost their ability to enjoy precious moments. Any lovemaking became merely a race to plant that sperm. And despite all their efforts and sacrifices, they had failed.

Issa could hear her stomach grumbling on the ride back to their house. She bit her lip not knowing how to comfort Enrique, who himself was uncharacteristically quiet. At their house, Enrique went in only to pick up his bag for his classes, his shoulders hunched and his steps heavier as he moved toward the door. He merely gave her an absentminded wave as he closed the door behind him. Issa, likewise, had a heavy heart throughout the day, forgetting one thing or another, and having to return home to pick up the keys to her desk at the college.

When she reached home in the evening, she hesitantly inserted the key into their door. She somehow didn't feel like entering yet, though she couldn't think of what else to do. She rested her forehead on the door while debating whether to go in or not. But then she heard some movement inside. She straightened and turned the doorknob. Enrique was already home, unexpectedly early. He was there waiting for her with a bouquet of flowers. 'I have some good news,' he beamed at her.

'What is it? And these are lovely flowers, the loveliest I've seen in a long time,' she took the bouquet from him and burrowed her face into it, smelling the fragrance of the mix of roses, baby's breath and a couple of other blooms.

'Do you remember last month, when I said I'll submit my application for a fellowship programme in Oxford?' he asked.

'Of course, I remember. How could I forget, you were so tense when the internet wasn't working and you only had less than an hour left to upload your documents. What about it?'

'And do you remember how we both thought it was crazy but I should try anyway despite the very low probability, right?'

'Yes, yes, yes, I remember all of it, now tell me, what's the latest?'

'Guess what?'

'What? Say it, say it.'

'I've been shortlisted.'

'Oh my God, are you serious? Oh my, this is such marvellous news!' Issa placed the bouquet on the table and dumped her bags on the nearest chair. She was dancing in excitement by now.

'It is. Even I still can't believe it,' he picked up Issa and started twirling her around.

'So what's the next step?' she asked when Enrique finally put her down and she found her balance.

'There's a panel interview. They want me to talk about one of my papers, they're especially keen on that paper about how culture impacts language and vice versa,' Enrique said.

'I love that paper. It's very practical and helpful.'

'Thanks to you.' Enrique kissed her forehead, then her nose, and was now aiming for her lips.

Later in the evening, while Issa had her herbal tea by the window, she felt her disappointment starting to dissipate. Perhaps Enrique's good news had helped to blow the dark clouds away. She was more hopeful now. The days ahead wouldn't be as dreadful as they had seemed.

Chapter 7

United Kingdom, 2016

Can time and distance reduce the weight of disappointment? Enrique and Issa left Barcelona for the United Kingdom, the following summer. Their failed attempt to conceive felt like a million years away now, the memory buried in the blur of the whirlwind relocation and related activities. First, they had to pack away years of belongings and accumulations, all their knick-knacks and their gifts to each other during their anniversaries, birthdays, and other special occasions. Together, they had accumulated boxes of mementoes, each marking an important milestone in their relationship or growth as individuals. These alone took at least a week to sort out. Then they had to cancel subscriptions, update their banking transactions and attend the send-off parties that their friends organized for them. Even the Room 216 girls threw a virtual party and looked more excited than Issa herself about London. They promptly started researching where to go, what to do and all that when in the city.

After the ceremonies and welcome parties in the UK, a long list of chores awaited Enrique and Issa. They had to look for permanent housing as the university only sponsored one month of temporary living in a cottage near the campus. Visiting close to twenty rental houses took a fair amount of time. Then they had to open bank and credit accounts. When

they found their own cottage, it took over a month to unpack
the boxes that arrived from Spain, busying themselves in tasks
that felt banal, but if avoided, could spell an inordinate amount
of chaos that could seep into their daily lives for many weeks
or months to come. One afternoon, while taking a break from
the round of unpacking, Enrique and Issa carried their wine
into their backyard, where they had set up two lounge chairs on
their porch. It was the first time they were enjoying the mild
English summer in their backyard. Issa couldn't help but link
their relocation to their failed attempt at conceiving. 'It must be
God's way. Maybe this is why we couldn't conceive. This option
was waiting for us,' Issa said.

'Could be. Although if you ask me, if we'd successfully
conceived, all three of us would be here, and it would have been
more fun, wouldn't it?' he asked. 'Look at all this space, there's
so much room for a playhouse, a swing and even an inflatable
pool.' Enrique pointed at the space before them.

'Oh, let's savour what we have right now. After all, this
opportunity is rare,' she reminded him.

'I'm excited to be both a lecturer and a fellow, for sure. But
what about you? What will you do in the meantime?' he asked,
holding her chin and turning her face to look at him.

'I'll look for a translation job. But for now, I'll soak in the
laidback vibe. And if I ever get bored of this sight, which I doubt
I will, then I can hop onto a bus and spend the afternoon in
London,' she replied.

'Sounds like a good idea,' he said, kissing her cheeks, then
her lips. Without the pressure of conceiving, they had reverted
to their normal lovemaking, which was inspired more by the
moment, rather than the calendar or temperature. They reverted
to their natural way of expressing their love for each other.

Chapter 8

United Kingdom, 2018

When does time stop to matter? Time advances inexorably. After shedding their leaves, the trees inevitably grow them back. The twigs that were the lonely caricatures of winter soon sprout buds that bloom into flowers. Life blooms on, as they say, which is especially true in springtime. Movement is integral to life in this universe. For some, the movement is forward, while for others, it could be backward, a regression. In Enrique's case, it was clearly a progression. He woke up every day excited for his lecture series and returned in the evening full of anecdotes about his international colleagues and students. Conversely, for Issa, the relocation was both a forward and backward move, the drag backward cancelling out the forward motion, practically resulting in stasis. Her career was suspended. She had left her full-time job in Barcelona without any clear prospects in the UK. Though this employment gap wouldn't look good on her resumé, she was prepared to be a stay-at-home spouse. A few months into their stay, though, Issa met a former dormmate, who now worked at the Oxford University Press. She referred Issa to some freelance opportunities, tutoring Spanish students who needed help, especially with their literature classes. And whenever a prospect came up, Issa translated for academic publications.

It had become Issa and Enrique's ritual to sit on their porch in the evenings as they watched the sun go down behind the trees across their backyard. Issa would listen to Enrique's stories while savouring a glass of Rioja, a wine that they realized they couldn't do without. Occasionally, they would join acquaintances at nearby pubs, but on their own, they would much rather pick up a bottle of Rioja to drink at leisure on their porch. Going to the pub, a quintessentially English tradition, was something that they had yet to adapt to. Meanwhile, Rioja was one habit from Spain that they couldn't discard.

Every now and then, Issa would go on a day trip to London. Sometimes, she would explore the city on her own, while at other times, she would arrange to meet acquaintances based in the city. She enjoyed both such excursions. On some days, she would simply sit by the café at the British Museum and stare at the dome for minutes on end. She loved having her tea and scone at the café in the lobby. Then she would head out to Bloomsbury and lose herself in one of the bookshops, including the London Review of Books Shop. After that, she would check out the blue heritage buildings in the area. At other times, she would walk aimlessly along Oxford Street and pop into whatever store caught her interest. She would invariably end at Fortnum and Mason, simply browsing around, or occasionally picking up a can of tea or a bag of coffee. Sometimes, she would walk along the quieter streets without entering any shop; she simply wanted to soak up the city. People on the streets would be rushing to or from work, while others would be rushing to or from a tourist bus. They had limited time. She would smile to herself thinking that though she couldn't afford all the shopping, at least she had the luxury of time. And what a great satisfaction it was to know that she didn't have to rush. She relished walking around town without the pressure of having to accomplish a specific mission, even though technically, she could only be this aimless until four o'clock, when she would head to the Victoria Station and board the bus that would take her back to their house in the Oxford suburb.

Over time, Issa and Enrique came to enjoy the quiet rhythm of their academic lives. They got up early and had coffee while reading the daily papers in their pajamas. After an hour of leisure, they would get on with their day, Enrique heading to his classes and Issa to her gardening, before heading out to either her tutorials or some errands. In the afternoon, she would do her translations or visit the nearby library and would be home before Enrique arrived from college. This rhythm was only broken a few times, when one of the Room 216 girls visited: Issa met Sandy in London during one of her business trips and they promptly spent her free afternoon looking for the best high tea they could find. When it was Serene's turn, she went with her to Bond Street and Sloane Street. It was West End with Tintin.

On Christmas, they travelled back to Spain to be with Enrique's family, and during other holidays, they explored other cities in the UK. Enrique still favoured old cities and civilizations, but now that they were financially secure, they could travel comfortably to choice destinations, too.

Ahead of their tenth anniversary, Enrique booked a trip to India, where they travelled to the golden triangle and its nearby provinces. Visiting the Taj Mahal was a trip of a lifetime, not just for Issa, but more so for Enrique, who was fascinated with old civilizations and their remnants. He spent the entire day touring the edifice, marvelling at the perfect architecture, staring at each corner of the mausoleum for hours. He was in awe at what had inspired the Mughal emperor Shah Jahan to have built this temple of love for his wife, Mumtaz Mahal. Love indeed knows no bounds, as this 400-year-old edifice attested. Enrique held Issa tightly as it dawned on him just how much his love for her had bloomed in their ten years together as a married couple. Issa, in turn, was elated and in perpetual bliss. She couldn't ask for anything more. She didn't need a mausoleum like the Mumtaz's. She simply wanted to savour every moment of their togetherness, like when they discovered new things together and were awed by similar things. When they could stand together like this in front of the most enduring monument to love—what else could she ask for?

Two weeks after their return from India, Issa was distraught when she discovered blood spots on her panty shield. She had assumed it was all part of the hormonal changes; after all, she was not young anymore. But when the spotting persisted, she told Enrique about it, and together they checked with a doctor, who in turn recommended a series of tests. In the days that followed, Issa couldn't sleep while she waited for the result of the test. 'You've been extremely conscious of your diet, sticking to organic food, you've become vegan, and you exercise regularly. You'll be fine,' Enrique reassured her.

'I hope so too,' Issa's shoulders sagged. She had this terrible feeling of heaviness. It took so much effort for her to even just hold her spine straight.

'Are you having other pains, honey?' Enrique was overcome by concern.

'I'm losing weight again. I thought it was because we had been walking a lot during the trip. But now we're back and despite my healthy appetite, I keep on losing weight,' she said with a lump in her throat.

On their next visit to the doctor, Issa was devastated to learn that she had a second cancer. This time, in her ovary.

'I can't go through that process again,' Issa wept on Enrique's shoulder.

'And I can't bear seeing you go through all that again. I thought we were doing fine. All along, we'd only been given a few years of reprieve,' Enrique whispered, between sobs.

When their sobbing subsided, the doctor informed them that the cancer was at an advanced stage. He recommended palliative care more than any other treatment. Issa still needed chemotherapy to help her manage the pain, but its intention wouldn't be curative, even if she was willing to have another surgery to remove the tumour at this point.

It was a difficult pill to swallow. Enrique and Issa couldn't sleep that night and yet, couldn't come up with a clear plan to tackle their situation. In the end, they sought a second opinion from another oncologist. But the second doctor concurred with the recommendation of the first one.

In the next three months, Issa went through rounds of chemotherapy. Enrique took emergency leave from his work to attend to Issa. True to his word, he was never apart from her, not even for a single night. As painful as this time was, Issa couldn't be more grateful for their togetherness.

In the end, Issa decided not to tell anyone about her condition. Not even her roommates, the Room 216 girls. When Sandy, Serene and Tintin received a call from Enrique, the line went silent for a while. Overcome first by disbelief then distress, none of them knew what to say.

Epilogue

Quezon City, 2019

Where do birds go when they're about to die? They go to a safe and quiet place like a nest, a home. 'She wanted to be buried in the Philippines,' Enrique told Issa's three roommates over the phone. 'But I couldn't bring her back by myself,' he said. 'I'm sorry to ask this from any of you. *Pero, por favor*, could one of you come with me?' Enrique asked.

'I'll come with you,' Sandy offered instantly.

'But Sandy, I'm closer to Barcelona, I'll do it,' Tintin said.

Both Sandy and Serene wore black dresses and huge eyeglasses when they went to pick up Enrique and Tintin from the Manila Airport. Enrique was stone-faced as he carried the vessel containing Issa's ashes. Tintin released her pent-up tears upon seeing Sandy and Serene. All of them, including Enrique, cried uncontrollably, causing an airport security guard to come and lead them to a private room in the VIP lounge.

'Enrique, I'm deeply sorry for your immense loss,' Sandy said in between sobs, offering to hold the urn on his behalf.

'It's as much your loss as mine, I know that,' Enrique said haltingly. He placed the urn gently on Sandy's lap. Soon, Sandy's tears flowed freely, a few droplets falling on top of the urn. Serene and Tintin placed their hands gently on top of Sandy's.

It took a while before they could talk without crying, and when everyone had calmed down, Serene called her driver to pick them up. They proceeded to Our Lady of Mount Carmel Parish in New Manila. Doreen and Anton were waiting at the chapel, where they had organized the wake and a series of *novena* prayers for Issa. By the end of the week, once Issa's father had arrived from San Francisco, Issa was interred at Manila Heritage Park, beside her mother's grave.

Sandy, Serene and Tintin felt that sending Enrique off at the airport was as excruciating as picking him up had been, only five days earlier. He kept staring into space and was often biting his nails. 'I don't know how to live without her,' he said to the three who kept him company at a restaurant near the departure gate, before his boarding. 'This isn't fair. Why her? Why us?' he asked.

'I wish I was beside her during her waning days,' Sandy said.

'I also wish you three were there beside me, to comfort her. It hurt so much to see her fade away like that. She kept losing weight. I'd look at her every single morning and quietly say goodbye to the part of her that waned away. At night, I would hold her tight knowing that I would have to hold her even tighter the next day, if I didn't want her to slip away,' Enrique said. 'But Issa didn't want to worry you. She knew what you had gone through the first time.'

'She had always prided herself for being physically strong. For her athletic build. Losing all that and becoming too weak without any muscle in the end would be too much for anyone, most especially for my Issa,' he added.

'I should have sensed something was amiss when she stopped doing Facetime and resorted to voice calls when we talked. It was so unlike her,' Serene said.

'I could have visited her in her last few days, at least. I'm closer to Barcelona than either of you,' Tintin said.

'Please, ladies. Don't start the blame game now. Issa wouldn't be happy if she saw you in this mood. Try to cheer up for her sake,' Enrique said.

'The same can be said for you,' Sandy said.

'But you know I can't. I've seen her in her last days. I have all the images here and here,' he said pointing to his head, followed by his heart. 'It's all too fresh.'

'Enrique, please call us if you need anything and please call us regularly,' Sandy said. 'You are our only bridge to Issa.'

'I promise to be in touch with you all regularly,' he said, drying his eyes before he picked up his carry-on luggage.

'Be strong, for Issa's sake,' Tintin said as she released him from her hug.

'I'll do my best,' Enrique said.

'Try to take that melatonin I gave you as soon as you reach home. It's important to get back to a natural pattern of sleep, especially during this trying time,' Serene said.

Enrique nodded and started heading toward the departure gate. He waved once more to the three women before entering. Then he vanished from their view.

Sandy and Tintin decided to stay over at Serene's house that weekend.

'Things will never be the same again,' Serene said.

'How fragile life is. How short,' Tintin said. 'Why did it have to be Issa? She was the gentlest person I know. She couldn't even bring herself to kill an ant.'

'You know what they say, the kind ones are always the first to go,' Sandy said.

'Still, it shouldn't have been her,' Tintin said.

'Drinks, anyone? Shouldn't we have Rioja in her honour?' Serene asked.

'I need one badly,' Tintin said.

'Same here,' Sandy rejoined.

Friday night turned into an all-night cryfest, and the ladies fell asleep on the sofa in Serene's family room. It was nearly five o'clock when one of the helpers came to wake Serene up, and she led Sandy and Tintin to their room.

That Sunday, before Sandy and Tintin left for the airport, they all had brunch on Serene's patio. The sun shone gently, casting shadows of swaying palms on the breakfast spread. While having coffee, Sandy noticed a yellow and white butterfly fluttering over a hedge of roses nearby.

'That must be Issa,' Tintin said.

Sandy showed her goosebumps to Serene. 'She'll always be a part of us,' Serene said.

'For sure,' Tintin said.

'We should make our reunion more regular and time it around this week, in her honour,' Sandy suggested.

'Shouldn't we set up a foundation in her memory? Clarissa R. Vasquez Foundation for Cancer Research?' Tintin said.

'That's a brilliant idea!' Sandy and Serene replied at the same time. 'Let's talk to Enrique about this,' Sandy said.

As a final activity, the three drove to their university campus in Quezon City. As they drew closer to their former dormitory, Serene told the driver to turn right and park the car. Tintin and Sandy were surprised, but followed Serene's lead anyway. 'Come, I spoke to the administrator when she had come to the wake. She told me that we could come and visit anytime,' she said. 'Wait, I need to get the basket from the trunk,' she added.

They all alighted and entered the dormitory. Serene spoke to the lady at the reception as Tintin and Sandy looked around. The lobby hadn't changed that much but for the fresh coat of paint, the newer sofa and the flat-screen TV. But the dividers were still the dark wood slats from decades ago, and the floor remained the same as Sandy remembered it, rectangular off-white tile interspersed with brown ones, every few feet. Soon,

Serene beckoned to them and the receptionist led them inside, taking them past the cafeteria, through the first-floor corridor and up to the second floor. They turned left after the stairs, past the view deck, where Issa used to hide her smoking from the night guard. They stopped in front of Room 216.

The receptionist asked if they would like her to knock and request the current residents to show them the room. But the three unanimously shook their heads. They didn't want the next Room 216 girls to see what they would be like in twenty years. Yes, they all had come a long way. Yes, they were all pictures of success in their respective endeavours. Yes, they hadn't disappointed their alma mater. But they were without their Issa. The three ladies couldn't bear for the young girls behind the door, whose carefree laughter rang in the hallway, to see a future version of themselves in them. Without their Issa.

Instead, Serene asked for a few minutes on the view deck. The receptionist showed them the way, and left them there, as she had to return to her desk.

The three started sobbing once the receptionist was out of view. Sandy tried to reassure Tintin and Serene that Issa was now in a happier place, no longer suffering from the pain of cancer and the emotional hurt that came with it. Tintin and Serene nodded quietly.

Serene opened the basket that she had brought with her. She took out a bottle of champagne and three disposable flutes. Sandy uncorked the champagne and passed it on to Tintin, who poured it out into the three flutes.

'To Room 216 girls,' Serene raised her glass. 'That we may continue to be strong, while Issa watches over us from up above,' she said.

Sandy tilted her glass, the rim meeting that of Serene's and Tintin's. She looked around. She wanted to see something ineffable. At that moment, she looked up, saw the sky clearing up and realized how bright the day was, without any clouds to mar the blue Diliman sky. It was just like Issa. Optimistic. Always looking at the bright side of things, even when she was in so much pain. Sandy silently thanked Issa for all the great times they had had together, and the life lessons she had inspired in her. She glanced at the trees bordering their dormitory. Branches of a leafy acacia tree stretched out onto the deck, shading them from the sun. Soon, a cool breeze blew their way. Sandy watched as a flower fell from its twig and swayed gently in the breeze before finally landing on the grass below. 'She's with us,' she said.

'Always,' said both Tintin and Serene.

THE END

Acknowledgements

Writing a book takes a village. I've realised this when I published my debut novel, *The Rosales House*. Writing a second book is not any easier than the first. And so I'm grateful for having a family and community that continue to support me in my creative writing pursuits—*Room 216* wouldn't have been possible without their help. Thanks especially to:

My cover designer, the multi-talented Carol Sidney Bravo, who's wise beyond her years.

My wonderful editor, Amberdawn Manaois, for her thoroughness and dedication.

The Editorial and Marketing teams at Penguin Random House, for making me feel I'm not alone in this pursuit.

My publisher, Nora, for betting on this book in particular, and for nurturing us, PRH SEA authors, and for working tirelessly to bring contemporary and classic Southeast Asian writings to a broader audience.

My friends, near and far, who motivate me to keep going.

My alma mater, the University of the Philippines, for planting the seeds of creativity.

My family for understanding what it takes to be a writer, and for giving me the space and time to create.

Mama and my brothers for all their support, past and present.

Taatu for being an inspiration in her own way.

Bubba for always believing.